The Boyfriend Contract

The Boyfriend Contract

VICTORIA JAMES

Entangled Publishing, LLC
2614 South Timberline Road
Suite 105, PMB 159
Fort Collins, CO 80525
rights@entangledpublishing.com

Amara is an imprint of Entangled Publishing, LLC.

Edited by Liz Pelletier
Cover design by Bree Archer
Cover photography by PeopleImages and AndrewSoundarajan/Getty Images

Manufactured in the United States of America

First Edition September 2019

Chapter One

After six months of driving aimlessly across the country, Emily Birmingham had finally decided she was ready to claim her new life—in middle-of-nowhere Maple Hill. She'd written her three-point plan on the back of a Starbucks napkin at two o'clock this morning. She'd even signed it to make it like a binding contract:

1) Break addiction to Diet Coke and Cheetos
2) Turn crappy old house into fabulous country inn
3) Get a life and make real friends

She peered through her filthy windshield as she eased her foot off the gas and slowed her SUV, trying to find a coffee shop on Main Street. Panic filled her at the thought of there not even being one in a place this small. There had to be. Towns without coffee shops couldn't exist. That would be impossible. Maybe.

Maple Hill was situated on the shores of Lake Erie and was where her father had grown up before he ditched it to start his hotel empire.

As soon as she'd pulled off the main highway and onto the quiet country roads, wide open land and fresh air had greeted her. Horses, cows, and farmland were the view now instead of skyscrapers and taillights. Driving through the winding, tree-lined streets of Maple Hill, she'd gathered that it was a picturesque little place. It was a far cry from the city she'd grown up in. But maybe this was good. Maybe this tiny rural town, hours from Toronto, was exactly what she needed.

Twenty-six was far too old to be taking six months off to "find herself." She'd never had that need; she'd always known who she was…until her parents died and all her illusions about them and her role in their family business had been shattered.

First things first, she needed coffee, and lots of it. Relief flooded her as she spotted a sign—THE SLEEPLESS GOAT COFFEE HOUSE—and she pulled into one of the empty spots outside the storefront. She hadn't passed a Starbucks in the last three hours; she was pretty sure withdrawal symptoms were imminent. She absently dropped her keys into her purse—or what she'd thought was her purse, but the sound of crumpling plastic forced her to check. Emily groaned as she spotted her keys in the middle of her almost empty bag of Cheetos. She tugged them out of the bag, the orange crumbs hopelessly sprinkled across her hand and keys in a way that seemed to highlight the current state of her life.

Empty Diet Coke bottles and bags of Cheetos spilled out the door, onto the road, and she cringed, hoping no one was witnessing this. *Not* the way to make new, lifelong friends. She quickly scrambled out of her SUV to round up the garbage as it blew around in the wind. Her legs protested any kind of movement after being stuck in her SUV for the night. She dumped her pile of garbage into a nearby trash bin.

Squinting against the sun, she made her way onto the

sidewalk of what seemed like a very charming Main Street. There was no parking meter in sight, which she took as a sign this was the right town for her—she was notorious for getting parking tickets. She threw her purse over her shoulder and headed toward the coffee shop, brushing errant crumbs from her shirt as she walked.

An A-frame chalkboard sign on the sidewalk promised all-natural pumpkin spice lattes and pumpkin scones, and she picked up her pace. Pumpkin spice was exactly what she needed. It was another message—she was in the right town. She loved the fall and everything that went with it. Her Diet Coke and Cheetos addiction would be *so* easy to kick if she had access to pumpkin spice.

The red-brick building had large windows with black awnings, and the massive front doors had glass panes with "The Sleepless Goat" stenciled on them in blocky, old-school, gold-foil lettering. Reaching for one of the oversize tarnished brass door handles, she paused as she caught a glimpse of her reflection in the glass. Who the heck was she? Her hair looked as though she'd been finger-combing for the past week—which she had, but still. There was not a hint of makeup or any kind of grooming skill. She didn't even dare glance down at the rest of her because she already knew her T-shirt was rumpled, her jeans were stained orange from Cheetos dust, and her bare toes in flip-flops weren't showing off a cute pedicure. Hopefully seven a.m. was too early for anyone else to be here.

She pulled open the heavy door, and the aroma, and the sound of coffee being ground, and the vibe of the place made it seem a refuge. The black-and-white hexagon-tiled floor spread across the space, and dark, weathered counters housed a variety of silver stands with glass dome covers. Vintage schoolhouse pendant lamps hung in a neat row and cast a warm glow over the freshly baked goods. Small, round, marble-topped bistro tables filled the shop, and a few people were seated at the tables by the floor-to-ceiling front windows. She avoided eye contact with anyone and tried surreptitiously smoothing her rat's-nest hairstyle as she walked forward to place an order.

A young woman, maybe around her age, was behind the counter, laughing with a man in front of it who had his back to the door. Judging by the way they were leaning toward each other and their easy smiles, it was clear they knew each other well. Or maybe that's just how people in small towns were. His face was turned away from Emily, and neither of them had noticed she was even there. The woman was very pretty. Her dark brown hair was up in a messy topknot that actually looked like she hadn't spent loads of time perfecting it like the carefully arranged topknots she was used to seeing at Starbucks in Toronto. An oversize apron with the Sleepless Goat logo—showcasing a wide-eyed goat jumping over a cloud—enveloped her small form.

It was all really cute—except for the fact that no one had noticed Emily and she was dying for a coffee. She checked her watch, worried that she was running late for her appointment with the contractor. Of course, there was no one asking if they could get a drink started for her while she waited. She shifted from one foot to the other and cleared her throat, hoping that would move things along.

The man in front of her turned around, and she *really* wished she'd never walked into this place looking like she lived out of her SUV. He was a man who made her wish she was still the polished—if tightly wound—former version of herself. He was a man who made her regret not combing her hair prior to being seen in public.

He was tall, definitely. But he was much more than that. He could have been the cover model for some kind of country-boy magazine. Something filled with ads for sports and power tools. His T-shirt highlighted large, broad shoulders and hugged impressive biceps, hanging loosely over his flat stomach. His jeans were well-worn, the legs slightly bunched up where they met the tops of his work boots. He definitely wasn't the kind of man she was used to. He stirred something deep inside her, awoke something she'd never experienced. He had strong, lean features, and stubble—again, not the carefully groomed stubble she'd see on men in the city, picking up their soy lattes between the gym and the office. His blue eyes were vibrant, and he watched her curiously… the sort of look one might give a friendly alien, should the alien walk into a coffee shop.

"Good morning! I'm so sorry, I hope you weren't waiting long!" the woman behind the counter said in a bubbly voice, and Emily read the name tag pinned to her apron. *Callie.*

Emily swept a clump of hair away from the side of her face in a pathetic, futile attempt to resemble a somewhat put-together person. She forced herself to smile back at the chipper woman. "Hi, no, not at all." She approached the counter. The man moved to the side, and she swallowed hard as their eyes met. He gave her a slight nod with, perhaps, a slightly amused twitch of his lips. And he didn't leave; he just stood there with his coffee.

"Great," Callie said, oblivious to their exchange. "What can I get you?"

"Um, do you sell anything by the gallon here?"

Callie laughed. "Rough morning?"

Rough life was more like it. She nodded and scanned the blackboard menus lining the back wall. So many temptations to choose from. "Oh, I'll try your pumpkin spice latte with a double shot of espresso."

"Good choice," Callie said. "My brother over here refuses to try one, but they're one of our bestsellers. Clearly he has terrible taste."

Emily glanced at the silent man, but he was just leaning

against the counter, looking unenthused by life in general and like he was used to his sister's commentary. "Well, it sounds delicious," she said.

"Can I get you anything to go with that?"

She focused her attention on the mouth-watering display and the little folded cards with neatly printed labels in front of each stand. The maple-glazed pumpkin scones were calling her name this morning. They would *any* morning. A wave of self-consciousness engulfed her as she spotted her reflection again, this time in one of the mirrored trays. *Oh no.* She became hyperaware of what she was wearing, her disheveled appearance, and her desire to order scones in front of one of the most attractive men she'd ever seen. She thought of the other men in her life and the brother she'd grown up with, the one who didn't stand across from his sister with ease like the man at the counter. His sister actually seemed happy and comfortable around him.

Heat infused her face, but she had to do this. She opened her mouth to order half a dozen scones—some for now and some for later—when an old memory, an old voice, hijacked her own. *You're so ugly. You're so fat. Look at your ugly fat face. Men don't like women who shove food down their throat.*

She frowned as the wave of childhood and adolescent memories flowed through her; she hated that they still came up without warning and could still make her pause. Or maybe she was just vulnerable; maybe it was that final betrayal from her family that allowed these insecurities to plague her.

Her gaze darted back and forth between the scones and Callie behind the counter, who stared at her expectantly. What was wrong with her? *Just order the damn scones, Emily.* She had always hidden when she'd eaten something sweet at home, because if she didn't, she'd be ridiculed. Eating treats had always been something to be ashamed of.

Those days were over. She was a new woman—a

successful woman who ate scones whenever she darn well pleased. Tilting her chin up, she made eye contact with Callie. "I'll take half a dozen pumpkin scones."

There. She'd said it. But the man didn't smirk. He didn't stare her up and down, judging whether or not she made a habit of eating six scones for breakfast and whether or not there was evidence of it on her hips. Callie plucked six scones out with tongs and placed them into a white box. "These are my favorite," she said. "You've got great taste." She rolled her eyes toward her brother. "Unlike some people."

Emily smiled at her, her shoulders relaxing. She liked the woman. If she had female friends, she imagined they'd be like her. Callie seemed the type to hang out and drink wine and talk about real-life things: goals, problems, dreams. Maybe she could be friends with her.

Emily fished through her purse for some cash while Callie finished packing up her order.

"Coop, don't you have to get to work or something?" Callie joked.

Emily glanced at him from the corner of her eye, pretending to be occupied with something inside her purse. "You know I'm here getting my coffee and going to work." His voice was deep and rich, but it was the warmth in it directed toward his sister that made her heart squeeze.

"Right. Here you go," his sister said, sliding him a fresh to-go cup of coffee. "See you at Mom and Dad's later."

He snapped the plastic lid down and then shot Callie a smile before heading out. He did have the manners to give Emily a brief nod before walking—*striding*—out of the coffee shop. Her heart rate returned to normal as the door shut behind him, and she made a mental note to start taking more care with her appearance when she went out in public. Clearly, there was a whole different breed of men out here in middle-of-nowhere Maple Hill, and so far they beat the ones from the city. Not that she was searching for a man or anything. All the men in her life had betrayed her. If she ever allowed another man to get close, she would make him sign a contract first.

"Okay, finally done. Sorry about the delay. Are you in a rush?" Callie asked.

Emily glanced at her watch. "I'm okay. I have a few minutes," she said.

"Oh good. My brothers are always wasting my time. Always around to bother me," Callie said with a laugh as she placed Emily's latte beside the box of scones.

"You have more than one brother?" Emily asked, trying to make conversation.

She winced. "He's one of three brothers, I'm afraid. They take turns coming in throughout the day for coffee." Her eyes sparkled, and she appeared completely relaxed, like it didn't actually bother her that her brothers came in to see her. In fact, her voice was laced with fondness as she spoke of them.

Emily smiled awkwardly and handed her the cash. "That sounds fun. Thanks. This looks great," she said, picking up her items.

Callie returned the smile. "Anytime. Are you here to stay or just passing through?"

She took a deep breath. "I think I'm staying. Well, I mean, I know I'm staying. I just arrived today." She wanted to tell her that she'd be back tomorrow, and she was looking forward to...she didn't know what. She wasn't a child anymore, and she couldn't go around advertising that she needed new friends and a new life, and that Callie seemed to have it all together.

The bells on the door chimed, and a group of elderly ladies walked in, their chatter loud and boisterous.

"Well, welcome to Maple Hill," Callie said, her eyes darting to the group of women barrelling toward her.

Emily nodded and smiled as she walked out. Main Street greeted her with a sense of longing that hit her in the chest. Making her way back to her car, she took in the quaintness that surrounded her. The old brick Victorian buildings had been beautifully maintained, the trim painted rich navy or creamy white on each of the shops. The lampposts were black iron, and beneath each was a pot of bright-orange mums. Shop owners were just starting to open their doors and put signs out on the sidewalk. She climbed into her SUV and took a sip of the best pumpkin spice latte she'd ever had. Not too sweet, not chemical-y, and very pumpkin-y.

She pressed the navigation button and pulled out onto Main Street, following directions to her new home. She sipped her coffee and tried to enjoy the easy drive out of town. The rundown house should be somewhat liveable because her father paid for a maintenance company to keep her grandmother's place from falling into complete disrepair, but Emily's expectations weren't too high. No one had lived in the house for twenty years. Her parents had referred to it as "that ridiculous house in the country" that Nanna Julia refused to sell.

Emily had very little memory of her father's mother.

From what she knew, her father and grandmother had argued and then severed their relationship. They'd visited the house one Christmas when she was small, and Emily could remember yelling and then the drive back to the city, during which her parents spoke in hushed, angry tones. She remembered the house had seemed like something straight out of *Anne of Green Gables*, and she'd been fascinated by how old it was.

Emily took the last turn onto Maple Lane; the tree-lined street was filled with old homes deeply inset and hidden behind massive trees. As she drove, the houses became farther and farther apart, until she slowed at the last house on the street. Her navigation aid stated she'd reached her destination, and she pulled into the driveway flanked by two brick posts with large round lights on top.

Her breath caught as she slowly entered the property. Her tires crunched over crushed gravel on the circular driveway. There was a faded yellow barn with a navy roof on the one side and an old red-brick house on the other. Woods framed the property, and weeds and shrubs obstructed her view of what she knew, thanks to Google Maps, was a river at the bottom of the steep hill.

She parked her SUV, leaving her empty coffee cup and scones, and slowly stepped outside. The smell of fresh air filled her body, and goose bumps pricked her skin as the cool morning breeze from the river floated over her. She took in the enormous porch with its large pillars and wood planks. The house was Gothic revival style, but she only knew that because of her research. She would have assumed the style was Victorian based on the ornate gingerbread trim and detailed porch.

As she stood in the middle of the driveway, that sense of belonging—or maybe of longing to belong—hit her, just as it had in town. She had never really felt as though she belonged anywhere before. At home, she'd never truly been herself. At her father's company it was the same, though slightly better than home because she'd established herself as a respected leader.

But here, *this*, something about it felt so right. It *was* her. It spoke to her. This house, in its imperfection, spoke to her. It was real—all of its flaws were real and visible. She could make this into her own little empire. It would one day be a beautiful, five-star country inn. She slowly walked toward the barn, something she had never imagined owning, but completely suited the property.

Staring at the narrow river at the bottom of the grassy hill, she imagined skating on it in the winter. She could already imagine the marketing for the winter season—she could offer picnic baskets with slices of cranberry bread, a thermos of hot chocolate, and a charming red-and-green plaid blanket. She'd hang twinkling white lights in the trees. She could smell the fresh cedar boughs she'd hang on the porch. The brochures would create themselves out here. In the summer she would have hanging baskets of ferns on the porch. She could see flower baskets under the two barn windows, once the barn was restored and looked less like it might fall with one good gust of wind.

Did she want this place? Oh, yes. It was a ten-minute walk to town, yet because it was a three-acre property, it was as though she was way out in the country.

This one boutique country inn would lead to another, and then soon she'd have a dozen. Then she'd be on the cover of Toronto's most prestigious business magazine…maybe featuring entrepreneurs under thirty. This time next year, her nightmare of a family would be a distant memory…

She needed to put her years of hard work on a family business behind her. She needed to stop replaying that last day when the company she had slaved over had been ripped from her hands and given to her undeserving brother. She needed to forget the humiliation of being told her inheritance would only come when she got married. She shut her eyes and took a deep breath…and then the sound of an approaching truck reminded her where she was.

The truck parked. It had a Merrick & Sons Construction decal on the side, and a thrill of excitement zinged through her as she waited to meet the people who were going to help her build a new life.

She shielded her eyes against the sun as the driver got out and circled around the truck. As he came into view, her stomach dropped, and she inhaled sharply. He was the one man she "knew" in this town. Coop.

Chapter Two

"Hi again," Cooper said as he walked toward her.

"Hi," she said, forcing a small laugh and trying to appear casual, even though she was dying of humiliation. She was still as much a disaster now as she was at the coffee shop. Maybe even worse, because she was pretty sure she had dribbled some of her latte down her shirt, and she wasn't sure she'd dusted off all the crumbs from the scones. She felt like she should toss her hair over her shoulder or something, but considering its current state, she'd probably get her hand caught in the tangled mess.

"I guess we haven't formally introduced ourselves. Cooper Merrick," he said, extending his hand.

"Emily Birmingham," she said, shaking his hand. His grip was solid and sent a warmth through her body before he withdrew it, placing it in the front pocket of his jeans. He stood beside her, and she became very aware of his height, his large size. He was a man's man—that much was obvious. She glanced at his truck parked beside her SUV. Hm. It suited him. Cooper Merrick.

"I was thinking we could do a walk around before we start tomorrow. My dad went over everything with me and my brothers. I'll be heading up the construction on this site, so I'd like to assess it myself."

"Of course," she said, trying to appear nonchalant. There was something about him that made her kind of flustered, like she couldn't quite catch her breath. Maybe it was the sheer masculinity of him. The strong forearms, the wide shoulders. *Those jeans*. The hard lines of his face, the stubble. His eyes were like the ocean on a bright summer day. If she were to imagine what he was really like, since she didn't know him, she'd imagine he was loyal and strong and hardworking. He was also nice to his sister—that beat out everything else in her book.

She wasn't so pathetic as to let her reaction to him show, though. So the fact that he was standing there looking at her, waiting for her to say something, was a good clue that she might be playing out her fantasy about him a little too long. "Right. Yes, your father mentioned you and your brothers run the day-to-day."

His father had been charming. An older, more cheerful version of Cooper, he'd been chatty and friendly with her on the phone. He'd exuded almost a fatherly presence. Cooper didn't give off a fatherly vibe.

He gave her a nod and stuck his chin out in the direction of the porch. "Yeah, there's quite a few of us. Let's go through the house?"

She nodded, and they began walking together across the property.

"Nice piece of land you got here."

"Thanks."

"Nice piece of land" was how country people talked, she assumed. Where she was from, there was no land. Sure, she'd lived in a sprawling penthouse with a wrap-around terrace, but there was no land.

"One of my favorite places in Maple Hill," he said.

She smiled at him. "Really? I wish I knew more about the history. I only visited my grandmother here once, and my father rarely spoke of this place. I'm going to do some digging around. I hear the historical society is great for researching the local stuff."

He gave her a half smile. "You should speak to old Mrs. Snyder."

"Who?"

"She lived next door forever. She's still alive. In her nineties I think."

"Oh, wow. How do I find her?"

"I think she's on Facebook. In the Maple Hill Residents Group."

"Oh. Are you on Facebook?"

"No."

Of course, he wasn't on Facebook. He didn't seem the type to be posting memes or what he ate for breakfast.

"Or you can ask almost anyone in town," he said. "She lives with her daughter now."

They were standing on the front porch, and he ran his hands down the columns then walked over and poked at the shutters. Several of them were missing slats, the paint had been chipped off, and most of the windows had broken glass.

"I'd hate to just barge on over there and intrude," she said.

He shoved his hand into one of the bases of the columns and dragged out a clump of rotting wood. He brushed his hands together, flinging off some of the straggling pieces onto the grass. "Oh, don't worry about that around here. People welcome it, expect it even. By the end of your first week living here, your neighbors are going to know what day you buy your groceries, whether or not you go to church on Sundays, and if you get your garbage to the curb on time."

This made her uncomfortable. She was a very private person. Sure, she'd heard the rumors about small towns and their gossip, but she didn't really think it would be that bad. She had no idea what the reaction would be when they heard she'd be turning this into an inn. "You're teasing, right?"

He glanced up from the broken step he was now examining. "Nah, I don't really tease."

Oh.

"Plus there's the fact that you're Julia's granddaughter. She was well-known and well-liked. People are curious about her granddaughter coming to town."

She looked at the ground. How quickly news traveled. Would these people hate her? She had no idea what her grandmother had said about her father. In retrospect, she wished she'd made more of an effort to keep in touch with Nanna Julia. But everyone in the family had called her crazy and eccentric, and since Emily had only met her a few times, the bond wasn't strong enough to make her question her parents or even miss her grandmother. She shot Cooper a quick smile. "I'm not that interesting. Hopefully they'll lose their fascination quickly."

He shrugged, his eyes sparkling, and then ripped off one of the rotted floorboards from the steps and tossed it onto the lawn. "I wouldn't count on it. Especially with the construction going on over here. Don't be surprised if you find some neighbors poking around when the doors are open. Let's go inside," he said. "Don't use the front steps. We can use the back door until the porch is restored."

She unlocked the front door, he held the door open for her, and she stepped into the vestibule. A wash of familiarity swept over her, and that strange sense of being in the right place enveloped her again.

Cooper looked down at the small white tiles, slightly

kicking the floor with his boot. "We're keeping these, right?"

She nodded, not even having to think about it. "I love them."

He gave her a nod, like he approved of her reply. "They're from the thirties. You don't see too many of these left. Just needs a good cleaning and we can touch up the grout."

She agreed. The hexagon-shaped tiles with the Greek Key border in black screamed vintage charm. The ceilings in the vestibule were super high and the large interior French door, transom, and sidelights allowed sunlight to filter into the hallway. She could picture a small antique desk with a brass bell, vintage telephone, and oversize paper ledger with guest bookings just outside the vestibule.

"Will the wallpaper be damaged when the knob and tube wiring get pulled out?" she asked. Unfortunately for her budget, the electrical tab alone was going to be in the tens of thousands to bring it up to code. The pale-yellow wallpaper with tone-on-tone damask was something she totally wanted to preserve.

"We'll try. Old Norm Newell is the best electrician in the county."

Old Norm Newell. She tried not to let her amusement show, but this kind of small-town stuff made her giddy. She hadn't had much to be giddy about lately. She could get used to this kind of thing. It was straight out of a Hallmark Christmas movie.

She followed Cooper into the hallway, and her gaze immediately went to the staircase. It was spectacular; for sure it would be a talking point among the guests. The dark mahogany handrail was so thick her hand couldn't grip its entire width, while the ornate spindles were painted white. The yellow damask wallpaper extended all the way into the upstairs hall, and sunlight streamed in from the vestibule. She desperately tried to envision her grandmother there but couldn't. She could barely remember the layout of the house. Cooper's father had sent her pictures after he walked through with the maintenance company.

The hardwood floors were wide-planked with some gaps in them, and they creaked loudly—not that she minded. Guests would love this, especially when she topped the floors with antique Persian runners and hung carefully selected artwork on the walls.

They walked through the rest of the house, and room by room, he efficiently pointed out the areas that were fine and the areas that were going to need work. The dining room was large and could easily accommodate a dozen or so tables for two. The two parlors could serve as a sitting area and perhaps a room with a small bar.

When they arrived at the kitchen, she stood in the doorway, surveying the large space. It would do in terms of size. There would be enough room for multiple sinks, an island, refrigerators, ovens, and stoves. The eating area was massive, and since she wouldn't need it for guests, it would make for a fine working kitchen.

Cooper sighed roughly, and she wasn't sure if she'd heard a muffled swear as he crouched and ran his hands across the floorboards.

Still hunched on the ground, he turned his head toward her. "So, my dad mentioned he thought we're going to take up this entire floor and reinforce the joists. Are you planning on keeping the hardwood in here?"

"No, because this will be a commercial kitchen, I think tile will be much more practical and durable."

"Agreed. We'll get going on permits, too. I know my father gave you a ballpark figure, but we can get solid numbers by the end of the week. There will be some big expenses on this place, though. I haven't looked at the roof yet, but it might be the original slate, and if that's the case, you should be prepared to replace it. I'll look for signs of water damage as we do our walk-through."

She was prepared for the expenses of renovating. Her condo value back in Toronto was astronomical, and she'd sold it in a day to the highest bidder, thanks to a healthy seller's market. She'd inherited this house and the land, so really she could afford to put all her eggs in this basket and make it a five-star worthy inn. Of course there were risks, but there was no way she would fail. While on the road and in different hotel rooms, she'd prepared her business plan and was ready if she needed to secure more financing. This wasn't her first rodeo. She'd opened inns under her family's business and knew exactly what she was doing. Sure this would be a bit different because it also entailed the renovation of a century-old home and it would be marketed as a country inn, but the basics were the same.

"I'm prepared for that," she said. "Actually, that's something I wanted to ask you about. Timeline—I need this place finished, like, yesterday. Also, I need to live here during the renovation."

His eyebrows rose slightly, and she didn't know if it was because she was coming across as demanding or simply because of what she said. He rubbed one of those large, tanned hands across his jaw and sighed. "I wouldn't recommend living here. As far as timeline goes, we'll do our best. We already have kitchen people ready with drawings for you to review tomorrow, since my father took all the measurements."

"That's great about the kitchen...but is there a way we can organize the renovations in a way that would make sense and you could just...work around me?"

He stood and rocked back on his heels. "Honestly? It's not ideal. It's going to be loud and dusty. You might not have power for a couple nights, definitely not in all areas of the house. You might have to move from room to room to avoid the mess. We'll have to tarp off some areas and..."

"I won't be any problem at all. If we could pick one room that requires the least amount of work, I'll sleep in there. I can also set up a desk and my laptop. Oh, maybe a coffeemaker. Probably a mini fridge... It can be my one-room apartment until this is done."

He gave her a nod. "Okay. We'll start on that tomorrow. Let's uh, go upstairs and see the rest of this place. You can choose your room, and we'll take it from there," he said, pausing at the bottom of the stairs so she could walk up first.

She led the way up the staircase and resisted the urge to cover her butt, because it occurred to her that during her drive she may have sat on errant Cheetos. She walked up the stairs as quickly as possible and then stopped at the upstairs landing. A breathtaking Gothic window let in a stream of light in the upper hall, and she counted five doors. "This is gorgeous," she whispered, walking toward the window. The river below flowed freely, with hundreds of trees draped over it and swaying in the wind. This would make an excellent upstairs common area. Maybe a chess table, built-in floor-to-ceiling bookshelves. Soft music playing...

"It is," he agreed. "Mind if I go through these rooms?"

She shook her head, happy to have him lead the way. If there were mice or rodents of any kind, at least he'd be the first to find them. They toured the upstairs efficiently, and she was pleased by the condition and size of the bedrooms as well as how clean everything was. "These floors are in great shape," she said, noting the details in the wood.

"They are. I think a light sanding and buffing will make it seem like new."

"How hard will it be to get a bathroom attached to every bedroom?"

His eyes widened. "In every room? You have ten

bedrooms here and only two bathrooms. I'm betting that's all galvanized plumbing, so…"

"Well, that would mean we'd have to redo the plumbing, anyway, so that would be perfect for the bathrooms, right?" she asked, lifting her brows and smiling.

One corner of his mouth turned up, and he almost smiled. "I guess. It'll add to the timeline. The thing about an old house is sometimes you don't know what you're dealing with until you start ripping things apart. Sure, we can do it, but it's not easy putting plumbing in a house that was originally built when indoor plumbing wasn't common. These bathrooms look like they're from the thirties, which means this is all concrete under here. We can do it; I just want to make sure you're aware of how big a job it'll be."

She shrugged. She had no choice. She didn't want to run a B&B; she wanted to run an inn. A five-star inn. That meant full luxury bathrooms for each and every guest room. "I have to have one in each. Some could have just a glass shower, toilet, and sink. But the others will require a full bath."

He nodded. "Okay. I'll have the plumbers here tomorrow, so you can go over plans with them and me. We can set your pricing and move forward if you still want an en suite after you get the quote."

No one here would understand what was at stake for her. Maybe they'd think she was being picky, but she had to be. If this inn wasn't successful, all her inheritance, all her life savings would be gone. But more than that, her family would have won. "I appreciate the warning, but for what I'm trying to accomplish here, it's a must."

He braced one arm on the door jamb, and despite the fact that he made her slightly jittery, he also made her comfortable. Cooper asked her things and seemed genuinely interested in her reply and enthusiastic about the house. Working alongside her brother for years had made her defensive. "So, is this a company you work for?"

She wasn't sure how much she should reveal about her plans or her history. She should get in touch with her lawyer and see how the zoning and permit applications were going. Then again, the contractor would have to know, and they would also be taking out their own permits. "Uh, no, this is my company. And I have experience running inns."

He held her stare for a second, probably thinking she was way too young and in over her head—but he never said it. "Okay. Well, we'll get moving on permits for you. We work with the guys at county all the time, so they're usually pretty quick for us."

She nodded. That was another good thing about small towns. Everybody had connections to one another. "I'm fairly familiar with that, so just tell me what you need."

They started walking down the stairs together. "Right, so our full crew will be here by seven a.m. tomorrow morning. Do you have a place to go tonight?"

She shrugged. "I'm just going to stay here."

He didn't say anything for a second and then ran his hand over his jaw in a gesture she was beginning to find familiar. His jaw was pretty great, too. He was great. But not very warm and fuzzy. "You're staying here?"

She nodded.

"Okay…"

She followed him to the door, trying not to let her own trepidation over staying here show. "Is there a Walmart or anything around here? I should probably get…a blanket or something."

"About twenty minutes from here. The next town over is about a fifteen-minute drive, but it's bigger and has a few big-box stores."

"Perfect," she said. She could pick up a sleeping bag and pillows and maybe some dinner. Maybe Cheetos. Maybe

Diet Coke. It was way too ambitious to try and tackle both addictions while moving to a new town and tackling a renovation. What had she been thinking? How bad would it be to have some Cheetos tonight? She'd knock off Diet Coke. "Oh, and what about internet and all that?"

His eyes twinkled. "There's one company in town but don't expect miracles…or anything remotely comparable to what you'd find in the city."

Her stomach dropped. "You're kidding."

"It's bad, I can't lie."

"Wifi?"

He winced. "Dicey at best. A lot of these walls in here are triple-bricked. You might have to consider hard-wiring for fast, reliable connections. Call Maple Cable tomorrow—it's a family business. Brenda and Barbara run the office. Charlie, their brother, will come out and hook you up. Just don't get him chatting because he has a tendency to never stop, and soon you'll be looking at pictures of his fifteen grandkids. If he pulls out his wallet, cut the conversation and run."

She laughed, and he smiled for a moment before glancing away. He was gorgeous when he didn't smile, but when he did, his blue eyes sparkled, and his smile made her heart race. "Wonderful," she said.

The people she was relying on to wire her inn had one technician, they were all related, and the place was called Maple Cable? It was all fine. She would not reveal the fact that she had never gone more than an hour without checking her phone or lived in a place without a solid-four-bars of service. "Okay. Great. So, I'll see you tomorrow."

He nodded. "Good luck."

Three hours later, Emily had pretty much confirmed her

own naïveté. How had she actually thought she'd be able to get any sleep in this house? What had been a grand old home during daylight hours had basically become a haunted mansion. She huddled inside her new sleeping bag, trying to find a comfortable position. But the hard floor made it impossible—as did the numerous loud, strange noises inside the house. There were no sirens or horns outside. There were, however, owls and crickets; they were fine. But then the howling of what she assumed were wolves startled her into an upright position.

Were there wolves out there? She grabbed her phone to google what parts of Ontario wolves lived in, only to find it at one bar. Dammit. Maple Cable better fix this situation for her tomorrow.

Relax, Emily. It's not like she needed to go outside or anything. Those wolves were probably really far away. She took a deep breath and settled back down on the floor. She could do this.

Staring up at the ceiling, she tried not to think of her condo back in the city. It had been perfect. Her bed was big and soft and had lots of fluffy pillows. She had a security system. She had wifi. She had a fridge and an oversize glass shower and a separate deep soaker tub with a ledge just large enough to hold her wineglass and phone.

She closed her eyes, and then a second later, some kind of scratching noises in the wall had her wide awake again. She scrambled up, her heart pounding. She was on the floor. Not smart if you didn't like spiders or mice. Why was it so dark in this place? No streetlights to break up the darkness. She stood inside her sleeping bag and hobbled to the light switch. There was no shame in a grown woman sleeping with the lights on. She'd already mopped the floor and it was gleaming. *Still.* Her gaze went to the bag of Cheetos—which she hadn't opened. Well, if there was ever a time to go back on a major life change, an imminent infestation of rodents would be it. What if something crawled on her while she slept? Maybe she should sleep in her SUV. After another scan of the room, she hobbled over to the Cheetos and water bottles and sat back down.

Her phone vibrated and she read the new text. At least there was reception again.

Her stomach dropped. It was from her brother.

When are you going to stop acting like a spoiled brat and come back to work?

She ripped open her bag of Cheetos and angrily chomped while trying to think of a reply that would end this text stream quickly. She dusted off her index finger and typed furiously. *I'm not working for you. Ever.*

Don't be petty. You owe Mom and Dad. Don't be selfish.

If Dad wanted me to run the business, it would have been split between us. I'm moving on. Starting my own life. I'm allowed to do that. Good luck with Dad's company.

She did the unthinkable and turned her phone to airplane mode. She was done. She was also mad at herself for eating Cheetos. She folded the bag and drank water, trying to wash away the flavor. She should have added wine to her shopping list. She wasn't going to let her brother send her spiralling into an abyss of misery; she'd already done that. The first month after she'd left the city, after her parents' death, she'd been a shell of her former self. It had taken her six months to get here, to a place where she could focus on her future and put her past behind her. But then her brother would text or call out of the blue. Some days just communicating with him, even through her phone, was too much.

She could barely stand to make eye contact at the end, that last day. All she saw and heard were the words he'd hurt her with her entire life. No more.

But as she sat there in the dark room, wind whistling

through the old windows, tree branches swaying against the old roof, and wolves howling in the distance, doubt about her ability to pull this off crept in. She held her head in her hands, not knowing what she was doing anymore, helplessness engulfing her. She'd come here almost out of spite, to prove that she could build a company from the ground up, to make her brother suffer, but now she was the one suffering. She was risking everything, putting her entire life savings into this project, into this giant old house that no one wanted. There was no exit plan. If her business flopped, she wouldn't even be able to cash out and sell this house, because the real estate market here wasn't like the one in the city. The value of this home would be too high to sell for a profit. It might take five years to find the right buyer for a house like this.

She had loved talking about real estate acquisitions with her father. She had grown up by his side, at their offices, in their different inns, seeking out potential new properties. She had thought she'd be running that company one day. She'd lived and breathed it. It was a part of her. She had been his right-hand woman. Her brother had *never* loved it. He'd argued with their father constantly, mocking all of them.

And he'd tormented, ridiculed, and belittled her when they were growing up. Twelve years her senior, he had used his position of authority to demean her, and she had always vowed that one day she'd have her own life—at her father's company. She had thought her father was a kindred spirit.

She was done with her old life. She was done playing the good girl, the one everyone in the family could dump on and treat like garbage. She'd done her soul-searching in the first month after she'd left Toronto. She knew it was her own fault she'd let all of them treat her that way. She wasn't her brother's puppet to manipulate anymore. She was a grown woman who had a life to build. She needed to shed all her old inhibitions, all the limitations that others had put on her. She needed to not care anymore what people thought of her. She needed to live. She needed a social life, she needed friends.

She needed to prove she could be successful on her own.

The biggest betrayal had been her father leaving the company to her brother. The two closest men in her life had hurt her horribly, each in different ways, but both powerfully. She refused to be the victim any longer. She was here to build her own life, without a man to interfere. She took a deep breath and scanned the room one last time, looking for scurrying rodents. After seeing none, she lay back down again, slowly. Neither man nor mouse would stop her.

Chapter Three

Cooper Merrick sat across from his two brothers at the Sunshine Diner. He'd always thought it was an ironic name, considering the place was like a hole in the ground and the windows were so grimy that sunlight barely got through. They made the best damn breakfast, though, so it was usually packed every morning. And because it was on one of the rural highways just outside of town, truckers often stopped in, as well as early-morning blue-collar folk. It was a bit of a rough crowd, but the food was fresh, the coffee strong, and the service was efficient, with the same waitresses for at least a decade.

His older brother, Brody, set down his mug of coffee. "So rumor has it that the woman moving into Julia Birmingham's old house is widowed with three kids."

Cooper snorted and shifted in his seat. "Uh, no. Not quite. More like twentysomething from the city, planning on turning her grandmother's heritage home into a profitable luxury inn."

His younger brother, Austin, leaned forward. "Hot?"

Hot… *Hot* wasn't exactly the adjective he'd use to describe Emily Birmingham. She was more beautiful than hot. *Maybe slightly in over her head*, he thought as he remembered the slight orange tinge to her fingertips and the stains on her shirt when she'd walked into his sister Callie's coffee shop. And now he was thinking about the woman under the disheveled clothes. Curvy, beautiful. He didn't like thinking that way anymore. Those days were long gone. These were the solitary Cooper days, and he'd decided precisely five years ago that he preferred solitude. Solitude didn't kick you in the ass when you were down, couldn't lay a finger on you. Solitude didn't force a grown man to his knees with only a bottle of whiskey to comfort him at night.

He took a sip of coffee and answered his brother. "She's attractive."

"What, are you eighty?" Austin asked with an irritating smirk.

Brody laughed, the sound as irritating as Austin's smirk.

He frowned at both of them. "No. It doesn't matter if she is or isn't hot. She's a client. We're the contractors. Oh, and here's some actual relevant information to make our lives hell—she's going to be living there during the renovation."

Brody swore under his breath. "Seriously? That place isn't going to be liveable."

Cooper shrugged and sat back in the orange vinyl booth. He had been surprised when she'd sprung that piece of info on him, but he'd also felt bad for her. She seemed very alone. "None of our business. The home has been maintained; it's not like it's falling apart. But this reno is going to be on a massive scale. And she wants it done fast. We're installing eight new bathrooms as well as removing the two existing ones. Every damn window and shutter in the house needs to be restored. New boiler. New kitchen, new electrical… The scope of this project goes on and on. I made up some preliminary notes last night. We're going to be there for months."

Austin set his coffee down, looking serious for once. "Does she have zoning approval to turn that place into an inn?"

Cooper shrugged. "I don't know, though I doubt it, or we would have heard about it by now. We'll have to find out. I'm sure there will be a lot of protest over that. Even though she's not looking to change anything that's already protected, she is changing it from a family home to an inn. Wait till the historical society gets wind of it." It was well known the Maple Hill Historical Society was…overzealous in their mandate to ensure strict adherence to whatever parts of the home were protected under the heritage code.

Brody leaned forward, giving him his classic worried frown. Out of the three of them, he'd say Brody was the most serious and a classic Type A personality. "What's she like? Is this going to be a lot of high-maintenance stuff?"

What was she like…? He thought about that for a moment. He wouldn't say she was high maintenance in the usual sense, because despite the luxury Mercedes SUV sitting in the drive, she seemed very down-to-earth and casual. But she did seem complicated. Definitely not a pushover. She'd also looked like she was going to pass out when he mentioned the possibility of crappy wifi. She *was* from the city, though. The last couple of years there seemed to be more and more city folk relocating when they got wind of the cheap real estate out here. They sold their homes in Toronto for well over a million bucks and then bought the best properties around here, thinking they were getting bargains. He finally said, "She seems normal."

"Great description. So glad we met for breakfast. At least now we'll know exactly what to expect," Austin said, bunching up his napkin and chucking it at him.

He caught it and was about to throw it back when

their waitress appeared. They kept their mouths shut as Penny delivered their breakfast. It was common knowledge whatever Penny overheard would be broadcast to the whole town by dinner.

After she left, Cooper started with the bacon and turned his attention to his younger brother. "Fine. What are you dying to know?"

Austin shrugged. "Nothing."

"Good." It was good, because that's all he would say about the matter. He certainly wouldn't let them in on the fact he'd found himself thinking about her last night while he was making his notes.

"Is she going to do anything with the barn?"

"Didn't ask yet. She doesn't strike me as the type to have use for a barn. It's designated historical, though, so the barn stays. We'll just repair it enough so it's not a hazard."

"Why the hell would anyone want to turn that old place into an inn?" Austin said.

Austin had always hated historical houses and had built himself a home that was modern in every way. Cooper loved heritage buildings. He liked working on them, restoring them to their former glory. He was actually excited to be working on the old house, and he was relieved Emily didn't want to make it completely new or strip any of its character. He was under the distinct impression it was a restoration, not a renovation, and he liked that. He stuffed food into his mouth so his brothers wouldn't expect him to answer the question. But then someone else did.

"Because it's a beautiful piece of property. And it's our job to make sure we do her vision justice."

They all looked up to see their dad standing there. Cooper slid over in the booth so he could sit. "Didn't think you were meeting us this morning," Cooper said as his dad settled in.

"Well, I thought I'd tag along for a bit, make sure you

boys are nice to Ms. Birmingham."

Penny came over with her famous carafe coffee, poured a fresh cup for their dad, and gave the rest of them refills. "The usual, Mac?"

"Just the coffee today, Penny." She nodded and then walked off.

"We're always nice," Austin said, wiping his mouth now that he'd polished off his Hungry Man plate of three eggs, Texas toast, bacon, sausage, and ham.

"Well, she's a special case. Her grandmother, Julia, was a well-respected member of this community, and we're going to treat her granddaughter the same."

"You don't need to make us sound like animals you're trying to tame. We have excellent reputations," Austin said.

Their father gave Austin a pointed stare. "Excellent business reputations, yes."

Brody snorted in agreement.

"But I'll leave that conversation for another day. So, you boys ready to head over to the house?"

Cooper nodded. "Yeah. I'll meet you over there."

Their dad put his coffee down. "Great. Now, let's all do our best and treat her like family. Your mother's already talking about inviting her to Sunday night dinner. I'll stop by Callie's and pick us all up some muffins on my way."

They watched their father leave in silence. Cooper shrugged off the discomfort that came with the mention of inviting Emily to dinner and treating her like family. Their dad always stopped in to visit Callie at her coffee shop—they all did, every day at different times. Their father was still pretty fit, aside from the small paunch he'd put on in the last five years. He still had a full head of hair; it was all gray now, but it was there. He was active in the business, not doing much work, more just giving running commentary critiques of their work and then meeting with prospective clients.

Every night he'd go home to their mother. Their parents had been married forty years and were still very much in love.

Cooper stood, wanting to leave before he was forced to answer more questions about Emily Birmingham. "I'm outta here, too. See you two slackers at the house," he said, not bothering to wait for a retort.

He walked into the fresh air, the heat of the early fall day searing him before he got into his even hotter truck. He pulled out of his parking spot, tires crunching on the gravel.

His thoughts went back to Emily. Truth was he didn't think she was cut out for this kind of town. People from the city thought it was charming, but it was a different kind of life, and after a while, he bet she'd be packing. People here were all friendly to visitors and tourists, but it was hard to actually break into social circles and be accepted. But it also wasn't his business. He had enough experience with women to know you didn't tell them what to do. Or, if you did, you'd never get lucky again.

His late wife, Catherine, could hold a grudge for days. Luckily for him, she'd found him irresistible. Whenever she'd frozen him out after a disagreement, by the end of day one, he'd upped his charm, done all the usual things like flowers and extra smiles and compliments. By day two, he'd see some glimpses of her smile. On day three, he'd get a full-on smile, followed by a hug from him, followed by a kiss, followed by the evening in bed.

Some days he woke up dreaming about her, forgetting she was gone, that she wasn't still within reach. Those were the days he'd stay in bed a few minutes longer, thinking about their life together, and snapshots would flicker through his mind like slides from old family vacations his parents would make them sit through as kids. Just like the end of his parents' crappy slide show, the last picture would be glaringly blank.

• • •

"As soon as all you guys clear out of here, I'm going to take a hot shower, order a giant pizza, pour a glass of wine, and watch *Call the Midwife* on Netflix," Emily said from the hallway where she and Austin were standing while he finished up work in the bathroom. Cooper heard his brother's stupid laugh and rolled his eyes.

He was trying not to think about Emily in the shower, and knowing Austin, his brother was doing the same. Cooper also found himself smiling. Week one of the project had proven to be an exercise in patience and avoidance. Emily knew exactly what she wanted, and she had no trouble making clear and smart decisions. The only problem was that her timeline was driving everyone crazy.

But she was charming. Every tradesman loved her and was willing to rush her order. His brothers were infatuated with her, and that fact shouldn't bother him, but it did.

"I don't even know what that show is, but you deserve a break and the house to yourself."

Cooper rolled his eyes again at his brother's response then finished adjusting the old faucets in the bathroom Emily was planning on using for her impromptu apartment.

"So, do you think this bathroom will be working by tonight?" she asked, poking her head through the doorway.

He tried not to notice how cute she was with her hair up high in a ponytail and paint streaks down the front of her jeans. She had no problem helping out here and there if it meant getting the job done faster. He admired that. He'd spent the whole week trying not to notice how attractive she was, and it was getting tiresome. In the last five years, there had been plenty of beautiful women he'd had to work with, and he'd never had issues with trying to focus. "It's working now," he said, turning the faucet on and off to demo his handiwork.

"Yay! Thank you so much," she said, giving a little clap and a gorgeous smile. He glanced at his brother, who had joined her in the doorway, and frowned because Austin was smiling at him.

"It's not a problem," Cooper said. He hadn't wanted to like Emily—but he did. She was always complimenting their work and thanking them when they did something extra. The week had gone smoothly, and so far there hadn't been any big surprises. "I wouldn't drink this water, but it's fine for showering. Once the new pipes are in, you won't have to worry about that. We'll start the other bathrooms as planned and keep this one going until the end."

She kept smiling. "Perfect. Thank you."

He shrugged and said again, "No problem."

"Great, so um, I guess I'll see everyone on Monday?" she said, glancing back and forth between him and Austin. His brother glanced back and forth between him and Emily, and Cooper caught the gleam in his eye. Austin looked like he wanted to say something stupid, but thankfully Emily's phone rang. The Darth Vader theme ringtone echoed loudly in the large bathroom, stopping all conversation. Her face turned bright red, and her smile fell faster than the plaster wall in the parlor had.

"We're done here, so if you need to answer that…" he said, raising his voice to be heard over the loud, never-ending music when she made no motion to answer the call.

"No, that's okay," she said, standing there as though it was perfectly normal to have Darth Vader theme music programmed for someone and not answer it.

Austin laughed. "That's a great ringtone."

Cooper didn't think there was anything funny about it, but Emily gave him a strained smile, relieved, maybe, that he was making light of it.

"Thanks. It's for a special individual. So um, I wanted to ask you guys about that barn before you leave," she said when the music finally stopped.

"Sure. You have something in mind?" Cooper asked.

Her eyes sparkled. "Yes. I have some images I can send you. I think it would be a great place to rent out for weddings or personal or corporate functions. I have a ton of pictures I can show you. It would be great for the inn, I think. Maybe we'll say the house is Phase One and then the barn is Phase Two?"

He glanced out the window at the barn she was describing and could easily visualize what she was proposing. "Sounds good. The barn is protected under heritage, same as the house, but restoring it shouldn't be a problem. Did you hear back from zoning?" Cooper asked.

She nodded. "It goes to council in four weeks. I hope no one objects. I don't really think I'll get too much opposition. This land here is pretty isolated, and it's not like I'm turning it into a large hotel or anything. We aren't touching any of the designated historical parts of the house except to restore them."

He didn't want to burst her bubble or deflate her optimism, but the old people in this town hated change, and they'd probably oppose an inn just because it was new. Her phone rang again, the Darth Vader theme echoing through the bathroom, and she shut her eyes briefly. It was the first time he'd ever seen anger flash across her face.

"Sounds like Darth really needs to get a hold of you," Austin said.

Her face took on a greenish hue. "Worse." She slowly pulled her phone out of her pocket and shook her head. "I guess I should answer this," she said, shooting Cooper and Austin a wobbly, sorry attempt at a smile.

Cooper tried to appear disinterested. It wasn't his

business to find out who had earned the dreaded Darth ring. It wasn't his business that she had someone in her life she deemed worthy of that ringtone, someone who could completely destroy her light. He pretended to be absorbed in the faucet again as she walked out of the room, slightly concerned because the voice he was getting used to hearing—the one that was soft and polite and sometimes held a note of laughter—seemed almost monotone now.

"You ready to leave?" Austin asked, leaning against the doorjamb. "Or did you want to stay and make sure she's okay? Maybe you could keep pretending that faucet needs more work."

Cooper wanted to tell him to shut up. He also wanted to do exactly what his brother was suggesting, but they barely knew her. Emily was a client and nothing more. He closed the cabinet and walked out of the room, ready to leave. "It's none of our business," he said.

Emily's voice was getting louder and more agitated, so much so that it was impossible not to hear what she was saying. Austin didn't look bothered at all by the fact that they could hear everything, and they both walked slowly down the hallway.

"...I don't answer to you," she said. "Your opinion means nothing to me anymore. You can't control me, what I do, where I live, or anything. You got what you wanted, so enjoy running it. I'm just the stupid girl who doesn't know anything, right? You're the smart man who knows how to run the company? Maybe I should just concentrate on doing my hair and nails and not getting fat."

"That doesn't sound good," Austin said in a low voice.

"Obviously," Cooper muttered. "Let's go." But he slowed down further as they walked the long hallway that led to the main staircase. It didn't sound like she was still speaking, and he wondered if she was crying or something.

"Oh, wait!" Emily shouted when they reached the bottom of the stairs.

"Everything okay?" Cooper asked. It was pretty damn hard to look at a woman who was clearly upset after talking to some asshole and not ask if she was all right.

She waved a hand. "Oh I'm fine," she said, the red splotches on her face turning even redder.

They waited, but she didn't say anything else. "Did you need something?" Austin asked, using his nice voice.

"Right, yes. So…I hear a lot of noises at night." Her hands were tightly clenched together and her eyes were wide. It was a pretty damn big house for one woman to be in by herself.

His muscles tightened. "What kind of noises?"

She folded her arms across her chest. "I don't know. Like, maybe…scurrying noises…in walls."

He relaxed his shoulders. At least there wasn't someone creeping around outside or in the house. "Probably just mice."

"Mice?" she whispered, all the splotches on her face now gone, replaced by ghostly white.

"An old place like this is probably filled with them," Austin added.

Her eyes went wider. "Filled? Like it might not be just one or two?"

"Oh hell, no. Where there's one there're probably dozens. We can set out some traps," Cooper said, hoping that would ease her worry. "But then again, it could be bats."

She inhaled sharply. "Shut. Up."

Maybe he shouldn't have mentioned the bats. "They'll leave you alone."

Austin coughed. "Unless they have rabies. Watch out for those ones."

He glared at his brother. "It's not like they'll be carrying a sign or something that says, 'I have rabies.'" He turned back to Emily. "Stay away from all bats."

She rubbed her temples. "I don't think I can deal with this right now."

"It's not too big of a deal to take care of," Cooper said, wanting to reassure her. "Do you have a fishing net? All you have to do if you see one flying by is catch it in the net and release it outside."

She threw her arms in the air. "There are so many things wrong with what you just said that I don't even know where to begin."

He glanced at Austin, whose face was red with strangled laughter.

She held up her thumb. "First off, why would I own a fishing net? Why on earth would I have a fishing net?"

He nudged his chin in the direction of the river. "There's freshwater trout in that river."

She shut her eyes briefly and then held up her index finger. "Second, if I see a bat, I'm not going to go chasing it with a net; I'm going to dial 911."

This time Austin burst out laughing, and Cooper almost smiled.

"Do you guys have a wildlife company or rodent company you'd recommend?"

He nodded, sensing she was taking this hard. "Sure. No problem. We see Leo all the time at the Sunshine Diner. I'll have him call you to arrange a time to come over."

She had rolled her lips inward. "Great. But it might not be mice or bats, right? Like, maybe it was nothing."

He shook his head. "Nah, pretty sure it was something. You might have squirrels in those old chimneys. I'll see if we can get the chimney guys out here sooner rather than later. They can clean those out and then cap the old things with mesh so no pests get in. We'll get the bat possibility checked out, too. Have you been in the basement?"

She winced. "I try to avoid it at all costs."

Austin let out a muffled laugh. "It's not that bad, considering the age of the house."

She waved a hand. "The holes in places aren't really my thing."

"Holes?" Cooper repeated.

"You know, in the walls?"

Cooper nodded, trying to follow her description. "Oh. The crawl spaces with the dirt floors?"

"Yup. I would think if I were some kind of rodent, I'd like that to be my home."

He and Austin looked at each other. "Okay, well, we'll get moving on the wildlife and rodent situation," he finally said.

They started walking to the front door, and she followed them. "I see a lot of cats near the barn. That's probably a good thing for mice control, right?"

Cooper nodded. "Sure is. You could always get a cat for the house, too."

She paused and he could tell she was actually thinking about it. "Is there a shelter around here?"

"Not close by, but there are always people trying to get rid of kittens. A lot of people have barn cats and need to find new homes for some of them. Have a look on the Facebook page," Cooper said at the door.

She took a deep breath and smiled. "Okay, great. Thanks. I guess I'll see you guys on Monday?"

Cooper nodded, a wave of guilt catching him by surprise. It wasn't guilt. Maybe it was pity. She was standing there in the grand entrance of this amazing old house, and she was all by herself. She obviously wasn't even thirty yet, and she was trying to take on a monster of a project. She had upsetting people whom she was trying to get away from. But she was all alone. That was one thing he never was. With three siblings and two doting parents, he was always surrounded by family.

Even after Catherine died, he was never by himself, despite pleading to be left alone; no one in his family had listened to him. "If, uh, you need anything over the weekend, you have my number."

A hint of pink lined her cheekbones, and she nodded but didn't smile. "Okay. Thanks for everything."

He and Austin walked out onto the porch, the last of the sun disappearing behind the barn as they walked to their trucks. "Uh, I think I forgot something. I'll be right back," Cooper said.

"What'd you forget?" Austin asked, his voice laced with humor.

"You don't need to wait for me," he said over his shoulder.

"I'll be right here," his brother said.

Cooper gave him the finger and walked up the porch steps, trying not to let Austin's laughter irritate him. He knocked on the door and waited.

Emily opened it a second later. "Oh, hi. Forget something?"

He held onto the screen door handle and searched for the words that had been on the tip of his tongue just a minute ago. Wisps of hair fell gently around her face, and not for the first time today he found himself taken by how pretty she was. "Right. No, I just wanted to mention that you should be careful about leaving any food or crumbs around until we figure out the mouse situation."

She waved a hand. "I barely eat here since I don't have a kitchen."

He tried to put it delicately. "Well, I saw an open bag of Cheetos, and it being cheese and stuff…"

Her face turned a few more shades of pink. "Oh. The Cheetos. Right. They will now be burned and forever stripped from any food craving I ever have."

He laughed and backed up a step. "Well, that's good. Uh,

have a good weekend again."

A flicker of something passed over her eyes, and he cursed himself for his abrupt ending and for even coming back here in the first place. "You, too," she said as he walked back down the porch. His reward was seeing his brother still leaning against his truck and texting.

"If you need anything over the weekend, you have my number?" Austin said, doing a poor job of mimicking his voice as he put his phone in his pocket.

Cooper scowled at him. "What? We are her contractors. If something goes wrong, I wanted to remind her she can contact us, even though it's the weekend."

Austin grinned. "That's not what it sounded like to me."

He put his hand on the door handle when they reached his truck. "Well, you're a moron. Clearly you have difficulty understanding basic English."

Austin leaned against his truck, folding his arms across his chest. "What was it that you forgot?"

"To tell her something."

"I think you just wanted to go back to talk to her because you like our new client."

"I'm not in the seventh grade. And she's nice and pleasant."

Austin scoffed. "Hot."

"I hadn't noticed."

"Anyone with eyes noticed."

"I know where this is going, so I'll save you the trouble. I'm not interested." He opened the door, and Austin shut it.

"Get your hands off my truck, Tinhead," he said, using their childhood nickname for him because he knew his brother hated it.

Austin ignored him. "I think you need to get a damn life. She's perfect for you, especially since she's not from around here."

He shoved Austin away from his truck. "What does that have to do with anything?"

The minute he asked the question he knew exactly what his brother had meant. And now it was stamped across his dumb face—pity.

"Never mind. Don't answer. You mean she wouldn't know about Catherine. That doesn't even make a difference, anyway. You going to baseball practice tomorrow night?" he asked, hoping to change the subject.

He hated talking about Catherine with his family because they remembered her and they remembered him. They remembered him at his best, and they remembered him at his worst. They had saved him from his misery, but it made him uncomfortable to think about a time in his life when he hadn't even been able to get out of bed in the morning. He didn't like thinking about the tears he'd cried in front of them. He didn't like thinking about the sleepless nights with one if not both of his brothers in the house he'd shared with his wife. But they'd been there for him on his darkest nights, passing whiskey and drinking and crying with him, always making sure he wouldn't go over the edge.

His parents and little sister would take the day shift. His mother would make sure he ate enough to at least stay alive, as she'd say. She'd tidy his house, they would make him coffee, they would putter around, and he was pretty sure they were making sure he didn't kill himself.

That was five years ago. Sometimes he felt like it was just yesterday, and at other times it felt like a lifetime ago, almost like a dream. He'd been a different man, a child maybe, up to that point. He hadn't known the meaning of real pain. Or that the death of the person you adored more than anyone in the world could rob you of everything, could hollow out your insides until there was nothing left of you. He hadn't known a damn thing about life until he'd been faced with death. He didn't like thinking about those days, but he would never forget what his family had done for him.

"Yeah, I'll be there," Austin said, bringing Cooper's thoughts back to the present. Baseball. Right. His one outlet. He and his siblings had been obsessed with playing ball since they were kids. At one time, he'd even thought he had a shot at the major leagues, but a recurring elbow injury had him turn down a baseball scholarship to the U.S. But then he and Catherine had gotten serious and later married, and he rarely thought about it.

He was happy to work alongside his father and brothers every day. He'd been happy. He'd known what it meant to be happy. And now he knew what it meant to lose it all. The stupidest thing he could do in life would be to fall for another woman.

He had no need for anything more than this state of mediocrity.

Chapter Four

Emily stared at her laptop screen and took a sip of hot coffee. She was sitting in The Sleepless Goat on Saturday morning after deciding she really needed to get out of her house for a bit. Cooper had texted a little while ago, asking if he could access the house for an hour or so this morning, and she'd agreed. She'd left the key for him under the back doormat. She was relieved not to see him after her show of… vulnerability yesterday.

After almost having a breakdown in front of Cooper and Austin, she had decided she needed to get herself together. All Cheetos, their crumbs, and anything remotely resembling a crumb had been removed from the house. The hot shower, followed by peach-flavored Perrier and a pizza binge (and prompt removal of the cardboard box into the coach house recycling bin because she wasn't taking any chances) and Netflix had helped tremendously. The Perrier had taken some getting used to, but she was making strides in appreciating her new replacement for Diet Coke.

She was currently placing online orders for linens and

decor she knew she wouldn't be able to source in Maple Hill. Time wasn't a luxury she had, so a trip into the city for a day of shopping wasn't going to happen. She still had all her old contacts and names of suppliers and by the end of this session, she'd have almost everything essential purchased. The shopping would also help her keep her mind off her brother's phone call and all the memories it triggered.

It had reminded her of all the reasons why she shouldn't let people close to her without protecting herself first. Sometimes you became friends with someone and they seemed normal at the beginning, and then you realized they were actually toxic. She didn't need to invite people like that into her life, when her own sibling was one of them. No, this was her new life, and she was carefully choosing whom she allowed into it.

The coffee shop had been bustling all morning, and Callie had told her that as soon as it died down, she'd sit with her for a bit. Emily had been pleasantly surprised by the gesture. She was almost giddy with the prospect of having a new friend.

She had found a table right in front of one of the large floor-to-ceiling windows. The trim was painted black, a stunning complement to all the exposed red brick inside the shop. And outside, the view of Main Street beat the view of the city any day, with endless pots of mums and vibrant storefronts with their Victorian charm... She hadn't been this relaxed or at peace in a long time. Most of the tables were full, but the line had died down, and there was another woman working behind the counter now as Callie approached the table with her own cup of coffee.

"Ready for a break?" Callie asked.

Emily nodded, shutting her laptop and moving it aside as Callie sat across from her. "Absolutely. I'm not getting anything done anymore, anyway, between people-watching outside and inside. I think I'll call it a day in a little while."

Callie laughed. "I know. This is the best seat, but you have to be disciplined to focus. I like to sit here when it's not busy, but I end up daydreaming."

Emily smiled. "It's easy to do. This is such a pretty town."

"It is. I love it here. So how's the reno going? I hope my brothers aren't driving you insane."

Emily wrapped her hands around her coffee mug and lifted it to her lips. Callie's brothers. They were all amazing. Maybe one in particular was extra amazing, but she wasn't about to say a thing about that to his sister. "They have all been so great. I already have my room done. They are friendly and moving so fast. I'm so lucky to have them."

Callie beamed. "They do know what they're doing, I'll give them that. Have you met many people in town so far?"

She shook her head. "I haven't had any time to. Between all the house stuff and my business-planning for the inn, you're the only person besides your brothers or the tradesmen I've spoken to."

"For what it's worth, I think it's a great idea to turn that old house into an inn. I mean it's a huge place, way too big for the average family."

Emily nodded. "Thanks. I don't even know what I'd do with that place by myself, and I certainly don't think anyone would buy it if I put it up for sale."

"Yeah. Houses like that don't exactly sell fast around here. So…it was your grandmother's?" Callie asked, then took a sip of coffee.

"Yes. We… There was kind of a rift between my dad and my grandmother, and they never made up. She left the house to him, though, when she died. He hired a property maintenance company to keep an eye on it and prevent it from getting too run down. My parents died a year ago. It was a car accident, very sudden." She paused because that still sounded strange to her ears. Her father had survived the car accident and had been conscious and recovering in the hospital for a week when he'd died of a massive heart attack. She had mourned their loss this year, but it had left her unsettled; she'd never had closure.

Even though her father had betrayed her in the end, even though he wasn't the man she thought he was, she missed him. She wanted to see his weathered smile, to see the smile from her youth. She wished she could go back in time and recapture those years with him. She was here now as an adult, lost and alone. More than anything, she wanted to ask him why. Was the only reason he left everything to her brother simply because she was a girl?

"I'm sorry," Callie said gently, her voice drawing Emily back. She stared into her new friend's blue eyes, noticing they were the same as Cooper's, and forced a smile. No one liked a downer, especially in a new friend.

"Thank you. I'm doing better. Being in a new place helps. We had…*have* a family business, and my father left that to my brother. I inherited the house." Even just saying that made her want to choke. It wasn't about money; it was about what it meant. She was supposed to be domestic, and her brother was supposed to be the CEO.

She hoped her voice sounded neutral and not biting when she mentioned her brother. She didn't need to get into her stupid family history, because there was no way she could discuss what had happened and still appear like a normal person. Not exactly the way to gain a new friend. Callie was easy to talk to, and Emily really needed someone. People like Callie were all part of the new life she wanted so desperately. She was normal and down-to-earth and sweet—all the things Emily had wanted in a friend.

"Well, it's a pretty awesome house to inherit," Callie said.

Emily stared into her cup. She had to be careful about what she said. She didn't want to come across as a rich snob, but the truth was that getting the house was like a slap in the face. She sat a little straighter. It didn't matter. One day she'd get over her father's betrayal. She had mourned the relationship she'd thought she had with him. It had all been a lie. She would never be the daughter he wanted, because she wasn't a son. So he chose his son, whom he'd never had a good relationship with, who had never had the love for their family business, who had never had the passion for it…

"Sorry, I don't mean to pry and ask all these nosy questions," Callie said, pushing her chair back.

"No! It's me. I'm so tired, and I'm acting spacey. You didn't ask nosy questions at all. Really, I'm happy you came over here and sat with me," she said, taking a gamble and being honest.

Callie lifted her mug and leaned forward. "Good. This is a small town and you're going to need some allies."

"Uh-oh. That doesn't sound too good."

Callie crossed her legs and waved her hand. "Mostly harmless people, but very opinionated. I'm sure my brothers have warned you that there might be a lot of pushback on you converting the house to an inn?"

Emily nodded. "I've been warned. I'm waiting to hear back about zoning."

"People around here hate change. They are so resistant to it, even if it's for good. They are just stuck on the way things used to be and hate progress and would love to put this town in a little bubble. So, I'm going to ask another nosy question, I'm afraid," she said with a laugh.

Emily smiled. "Go for it."

"Do you have any experience with this kind of thing?"

Emily nodded and finished the rest of her coffee. "My family has a small chain of boutique inns across the country, and I've grown up in this industry."

Callie's mouth dropped open. "Oh my gosh, that's

amazing. What a cool business. So...you're not planning on going back to help them run it?"

Emily shook her head. "It's...a long story, but no, I decided it was time to venture out on my own. Permanently."

Callie gave her a smile that she could tell was filled with empathy. She obviously knew there was more to the story. Who left a successful family business to start an inn in a tiny town? "Well, good for you. I admire that."

"Thanks. This place is amazing, too. You didn't follow in the family business, either, I take it?"

Callie laughed. "I'd rather poke my eyes out with a plastic fork than work with my brothers every day."

Emily laughed with her. "Well, they seem great."

Callie nodded. "I'm joking, of course. My family is awesome. All of them. They are the typical overprotective older brothers, but they mean well. I just had no interest in construction at all. In high school, this used to be more of a diner-type place, and I worked here part-time. I always knew that under that fifties decor it could be something really great. There were some incentives from the county for new businesses starting up. The owner was retiring, and I swooped in. Obviously my costs were low because of the nature of the family business—they made this into my dream coffee shop."

"Wow. And now it's this amazing space. It's always busy, and you have this vintage, eclectic vibe."

"Thanks. I do love it. So...I'd better get back to work, but I was wondering if you had plans for tonight? My brothers and I are part of a community baseball league, and after practice tonight we're heading out to the Maple Tavern for wings and drinks. Do you want to meet us?"

Her first response was total elation, but then awkwardness set in. "I'm not sure I should intrude. I mean, if your brothers are there and it's a family thing..."

Callie scowled. "Them? They love you. They wouldn't

mind if you joined us. Meet us there at eight. Let's exchange numbers." After doing so, Callie went back to work and Emily opened her laptop again. She stared at the dark screen, realizing for the first time in months that she didn't feel completely alone.

• • •

Emily walked into the Maple Tavern later that night and tried to ignore her surprise. She'd been expecting something a little more…charming, like the rest of the town. Not that it was bad. It just didn't live up the allure of the building on the outside.

Inside, it was gloomier than she'd anticipated. It was… rougher. Or maybe it was just that the crowd seemed rougher. There were large bikers hanging out by the bar. Most of the tables were filled with loud and boisterous people, and she hoped her friend was already here because she was pretty sure she stood out like a sore thumb.

She let out a sigh of relief as she spotted Callie waving frantically from the upstairs balcony. She waved back and walked toward the staircase.

When Emily reached the top, Callie said, "Don't judge this place by the way it looks. They have the best wings in the entire county."

"No judgement," she said, even though she'd probably just judged the place. Callie led her to a long table filled with men and women.

"So this is our baseball team and some friends. Everyone, this is Emily, she's new in town." Callie ushered Emily to the other end of the table, where all the Merricks were hanging out, as people shouted greetings to her. Callie's brothers all greeted Emily by name.

Callie pointed to the empty chair beside Cooper, which

was so not the spot where she wanted to be seated. The man was far too good-looking to not be smiling like the rest of his brothers. He was wearing a worn-in Toronto Blue Jays baseball cap and a navy T-shirt that clung to his very fit body. She'd seen him hauling materials around her house and knew far too much about what those muscles could do. So far, he'd been pretty difficult to figure out. Most of the time, his blue eyes were guarded, with a hands-off message she received loud and clear. But then, he'd act completely opposite to that vibe—like when he came back to politely tell her to stop leaving Cheetos dust around the house. Very kind. Also, very humiliating.

"Hi," she said, because it seemed weird to sit right beside him and not say anything.

"Hey."

She really needed to get a life and stop acting so awkward around Cooper. It's wasn't as if something could or would ever happen between them. He was not her typical guy—not that she had a typical kind of guy, or any kind of guy, for that matter. But he wasn't it. Maybe one of his nice brothers. They were an exceptionally attractive family. But there was something about Cooper that made her very aware of all her nerve endings.

"Perfect timing, because we haven't ordered our food yet," Callie said as a server approached their table.

Emily listened to everyone's orders and then placed hers last, taking cues from what they chose and what sounded good.

"You have to try the blueberry beer," Callie said, leaning toward Emily. "It's from a new local brewer, and it's amazing."

"Great! Sounds good. I'll have the same wings and fries order as Callie," Emily said, smiling at the waitress and handing over her menu. She'd never ordered wings and beer before. She wasn't going to let the old Emily ruin this moment for her...even though she still heard that voice, the one that told her how gross it was to eat greasy wings and fries, especially in front of guys. She blinked a few times, trying to push those thoughts aside, trying to get back into the conversation.

"Cooper, you should try this beer, too," Callie said.

Cooper tilted his chair back, and Emily had the absurd instinct to reach out and steady it in case he fell over. But, he seemed perfectly confident, leaning back as he spoke. "Why would I want blueberries in my beer? If I want blueberries, I'll eat blueberries. If I want a beer, I'll drink a beer."

Emily turned to watch Cooper's expression because the humor in his deep voice and the affection he showed toward his sister made him even more fascinating to watch.

"You need to step out of your comfort zone," Callie replied with a pointed stare.

He pulled his chair upright. "Why would I want to do that? Comfort is the ideal zone to be in."

"So, how you holding up in that old house, Emily?" Brody asked with a smile.

She snapped her head to look at Cooper's brother, even though she wanted to keep listening to the conversation between Cooper and Callie. She liked Brody. He worked at the site, as well, but divided his time between some of their other projects, so she didn't run into him as often as the others.

"I'm hanging in there," she said, grateful when her beer arrived. It might help ease some of her self-consciousness. The loud music from the live band filled the room, and she had to speak loudly to be heard. She picked up her beer mug and took a sip. The ice-cold drink was infused with hints of blueberry. "This is delicious, Callie."

Callie gave her brothers a pointed stare. "I'm glad you like it."

"Oh, Emily, I have a cat for you if you want one," Austin said.

Emily put down her beer. "Really? Yes. For sure. I keep hearing those noises in the walls, and I'm thinking maybe a cat will be a good companion." That sounded sad. She needed a cat as a companion?

"Okay. It's one of my parents' friends. I'll text you her number."

"That's perfect. I'll pick up supplies this weekend. How old is the cat?"

"Two. She's well cared after, but her owner is elderly and has had some health problems. She just can't care for her anymore."

Emily nodded. "Okay. If…she ever wants to come and visit her, she's welcome to," she said.

Callie smiled at her. "That's very nice of you, Emily," she said, enunciating her words a little too loudly and staring across the table at Cooper.

Emily glanced at Cooper and caught him glaring at his sister.

"That *is* very nice," Brody said.

The awkward exchange paused as their plates of wings, veggies, and blue cheese dip arrived. Emily looked down at the heaping portion of fries and heavily sauced wings with a mix of dread and hunger. Everyone dug right in, and after a few seconds, she forced herself to let go of the irrational insecurities she was holding onto and picked up a wing. She had rejoined the land of people who knew how to live life. The world didn't stop as she finished one wing and moved on to the next.

"Are you having mice issues?" Callie said. "You should ask my brothers to deal with them for you. They have loads of spare time."

"We already talked to pest control. They're coming out

Monday," Cooper said, then took a drink of beer.

"I hate mice. I know it sounds stupid," Callie said, picking up a carrot. "But they are disgusting, and I refuse to deal with them myself."

Cooper let out a muffled laugh. Callie glared and he held up his hands. He appeared younger now, his smile and laugh changing his features. He had straight white teeth and a beautiful laugh, rich and deep and masculine, and it sent a tingle down her spine. "Too bad the mice didn't get your memo," Cooper said. Seeing him smile almost made her smile.

Callie rolled her eyes. "Coop, you're not funny."

Emily leaned forward, relieved. "I'm so glad it's not just me who hates mice. But I'm torn because I keep trying to decide if mice are worse than bats."

Callie glared at her brothers. "Are you guys kidding me? She might have bats in her house and you're sitting here gorging yourselves on wings and beer?"

"That's okay, they told me to buy a fishing net," Emily said.

Callie swatted Austin and Brody, who were seated on either side of her, and then frowned at Cooper again.

"Relax, Callie. There are no bats," Cooper said.

Everyone turned their attention toward him.

"Seriously?" Emily asked. "How do you know?"

He glanced at her quickly and then at his family. "I checked this morning. Went into the attic through the two different access points, so I've seen everything. No evidence of bats."

"You didn't tell us you were going," Brody said, his eyes narrowed at Cooper.

Cooper shrugged. "It was morning, and I assumed you were still slothing around in bed."

"I don't sloth in bed."

"Sorry to interrupt," Emily said, tapping on Cooper's shoulder. When he turned to her, her mouth went dry, because up close, with his full attention on her, he was even more beautiful. Like, so much so that for a moment she forgot what she was going to say, because his eyes had an intensity like he was really listening. "How sure are you?" she said.

"Very sure. We'll still have the wildlife guy out, but at least you don't have to worry about bats over the weekend."

"That's so nice of you, Coop," Callie said, leaning forward. "Anyway, enough about rodents. Emily, what are you doing Sunday night?"

"Um, nothing, I think."

"Great. You should come to Sunday night dinner."

She felt the heat of Cooper's stare and shifted in her seat. "Oh, thanks, but I don't want to intrude on a family dinner."

"It's not intruding," Brody said. "Our mother loves company. Besides, she'd hate to think you were all by yourself in that big old house on a Sunday night. Isn't that right, Coop?"

Cooper turned to his brother, and his jaw ticked. "Yes. That's right, Brody," he said.

"Um, okay. Thanks. A Sunday night family dinner sounds really nice." She took a sip of beer and then winced at the bitter flavor as she put it back down. She looked at the glass and then the one on the table, and heat flooded her face as panic set in. She'd picked up the wrong glass and drunk out of Cooper's. She turned to him, whispering so no one else would hear. "I'm so sorry, Cooper, I drank out of your glass by accident."

"Don't worry, Emily. He's not harboring any major germs. Despite Cooper's reputation as a ladies' man, he's as clean as a whistle," Austin said.

Emily thought she was going to die of humiliation.

"You did not just say that," Cooper said in a low voice,

leaning toward his brother and putting his elbows on the table.

"Oh, I know you're just joking about the ladies' man thing," Emily said with a wave of her hand, desperate to ease the tension. Except Cooper turned to her and his brothers and Callie burst out laughing. Only after a second did Emily realize what she implied.

Cooper had a way of looking intimidating without actually being intimidating. He wasn't smiling. It was the intensity, maybe. "Joking?"

She winced, wishing so badly that she'd just put the beer down without mentioning that she'd taken a sip out of it. She cleared her throat and shifted in her chair, hating that everyone was now staring at them like they were the stars of the latest blockbuster movie. "I mean…you just, um, don't really strike me as a ladies' man, that's all."

"I see."

She clutched the side of the chair, desperate to explain herself, trying to ignore the enraptured audience hanging on their every word. "Not…that you couldn't *be* a ladies' man if you tried. Because you have all the…um, right assets. It's more your um, bedside manner…not, like, bedside, because I wouldn't know, um, I just mean that you don't talk very much and, um, you have this silent stare and…"

"Holy crap, Cooper, bail her out! Emily, don't worry about him," Callie said, leaning across the table to shove her brother.

Cooper's eyes were actually filled with laughter and a corner of his mouth had turned up. "Well, thanks for that enlightening analysis on areas to improve in order to become a 'ladies' man,'" he said.

Relief flooded her, even though her face was still burning.

"I can give you a few pointers," Austin said, picking up his own beer and clanking it against Cooper's glass.

Cooper snatched his glass. “I don’t need help,” he snapped.

His brothers laughed, and Emily tried not to appear as though she was waiting intently to see if he’d drink his beer. What had she been thinking? She needed to learn not to just blurt things out in a panic. It was him. It was Cooper’s fault. This weird vibe he gave off.

“So, do you have a name for the inn you’re opening?” Brody asked.

Emily nodded, relieved to be talking about something else. “I was thinking of keeping it simple. Something like the Maple Hill Inn. I’m sure you guys are all used to the name of the town, but for people not from around here, especially from the city, it sounds very charming.”

“I can’t wait to get a tour of this place,” Callie said.

“Come over tomorrow! Maybe we can get the cat together?” she asked.

Callie beamed. “Perfect.”

“Let us know if you need any help preparing for the town council meeting,” Brody said.

“Thanks, but I think I’ll be fine. It’s just a zoning application.”

They all exchanged looks.

“What? Am I missing something?”

Cooper turned to her. “People are starting to talk. Notice of the meeting was in the paper today.”

“So? It’s not like I’m doing something crazy or even adding an addition that would affect any part of the building protected by heritage.”

“Doesn’t matter. People here have opinions on *everything*,” Cooper said. “So, just make sure you’re ready for people coming up with depositions and all sorts of stupid reasons you shouldn’t be allowed to convert your grandmother’s house into an inn.”

"Don't worry about that now," Callie said. "Coop will help you." She shot her brother a sweet smile.

They continued to chat about local gossip for the next hour or so, until Cooper stood to leave, and everyone joined him. They made their way outside, everyone going in different directions except her and Callie. "Okay, how about I swing by around eleven tomorrow morning and we'll go pick up the cat together?" Callie asked.

"That sounds perfect. I'm kind of excited. I never had a pet before," she said, fishing through her purse to get her keys once they stopped at her car.

A loud, angry man's voice made her pause and turn toward it, the way Callie was facing already. "Oh no, Moose," Callie said under her breath.

"What? Who? Did you say Moose?"

Callie nodded. "He's bad news. The town asshole. He's talking to his daughter."

Except it was more like yelling.

"I'm not going home with you," the girl yelled, yanking her arm from her father's grip. "You're a crap father, and I'm old enough to live on my own."

He grabbed her upper arm again, and judging by the way she writhed, he did so too tightly. Emily's heart thumped rapidly, and panic swelled inside her. "Do we need to step in?" she whispered.

Callie nodded. "Maybe."

"You're coming home with me, you ungrateful little bitch," he said, yanking her harshly.

"We have to do something," Emily whispered, walking forward, having no idea what to do in a situation like this. Callie walked beside her.

"Okay, he's a total asshole, but there's two of us. Also, he went to high school with Austin, Brody, and Cooper, and even though he was a total jackass, he wouldn't hurt us.

He's only been to jail a few times, and it wasn't for anything violent," Callie said casually.

"Oh, great," Emily said under her breath.

"Seriously. He wouldn't lay a hand on us; he knows who I am, and he knows my brothers would kill him if he did."

"Right," she whispered. "We should try to look tough or something."

Callie straightened her shoulders. "Good idea."

"I don't know how to look tough," she said as her heels almost got stuck in the gravel.

Callie shook her head. "I know what I'm doing, don't worry."

Emily took a deep breath and walked alongside the woman she knew she wanted to be her best friend.

Chapter Five

Cooper was about to start his truck when he spotted his sister and Emily walking toward Moose and his daughter. Hell. He knew trouble when he saw it. He climbed out of his truck, and Moose yelled in their faces about minding their own damn business.

He walked over there, telling himself to keep his temper in check and play things cool. "You can't drag her home if she doesn't want to go home. How old are you, sweetie?" Emily said.

Moose's daughter's lip wobbled. "Seventeen."

Moose stepped up way too close to Emily, his massive frame looming over her petite one, but she didn't back down. "Mind your own damn business, bitch," Moose growled.

"Back off," Cooper said, trying to keep his voice calm.

Moose backed up a step but glared at him. "Tell your sister and her friend to stay out of my family business."

"We are helping his daughter," Callie said. "He was calling her names and hurting her."

The last thing he needed was to get involved in Moose's

problems. But when he looked over at the daughter, who had tears rolling down her cheeks and her arms crossed in front of herself, he knew why Callie and Emily had gotten involved.

"I'm okay," the girl whispered.

"See?" he said.

Cooper glanced uneasily between father and daughter. He knew the home situation wasn't great, but he assumed Moose was just a deadbeat and nothing more.

"If you ever need a place to stay," Emily started, "I have more than enough room—"

"Who the fuck do you think you are, bitch?" Moose yelled in her face.

"Back the hell away from her. Now," Cooper said, bracing himself in case he was going to be on the receiving end of a punch. He needed to defuse this situation before it got out of hand. He stepped in front of Emily to block her from him. "There's no need to be insulting. She's offering your daughter support because you're yelling at her and manhandling her. We just want to make sure she's safe and that you haven't been drinking."

"I haven't had a fucking chance to even go into the bar yet," he growled. Cooper was standing close enough to him to detect there wasn't any alcohol on his breath.

He ignored Emily tapping on his shoulder.

Moose didn't say anything for a long, tense moment, and Cooper hoped to hell neither his sister nor Emily decided to throw him an insult. "You three mind your own damn business. My daughter can do whatever the hell she wants. I couldn't give a shit," Moose said, walking toward his truck.

The girl stared at them and then back at her father, who was almost at his truck.

"I live in the big old house on Maple Hill," Emily whispered to the girl. "I have lots of room, and it's a safe place. You come anytime, sweetie. Even now."

Cooper pinched the bridge of his nose and looked down, trying his best to keep his mouth shut. He tried to tell himself it was really commendable of Emily to open her door to a virtual stranger, but he was worried about her jumping headfirst into what could be a very dangerous situation.

"It's fine; I'll go home with my dad," she said, turning to run after Moose's truck, which was kicking up dirt. They stood there in silence, watching as Moose sped to the end of the parking lot and then slammed on his brakes, taunting his daughter by pretending to drive away. He finally stopped, and she jumped in, not sparing them a second glance.

Cooper turned to face Emily and his sister. Neither of them seemed to be paying him any attention. Their eyes were on the truck as it sped down the road. "Why the hell, of all people, would you two approach Moose?"

"Oh, because we wanted to ask him to tea," Callie said. "Obviously because we were afraid for his daughter, Coop!"

He loved that his sister had such a big heart; he just hated seeing her in any kind of danger.

"His name should be Beast," Emily said.

Callie laughed. "Agreed."

"Okay, I don't care what his stupid nickname is. You just started something with one of the worst people in town. And you told his daughter where you live," he said to Emily, trying not to sound angry. He wasn't mad at her, just at the situation.

She tucked a piece of hair behind her ear and crossed her arms over her chest. "It doesn't really matter; everyone knows everything in this town anyway."

He ran his hands down his face. "Still. Maybe he didn't know who you were. Now he knows where you live and you're in that giant old house all by yourself."

He caught the fear that flashed across her eyes, but she lifted her chin. "I couldn't stand here and watch him call her names and manhandle her. I was worried for her safety."

"I get it. I just… You two should have called for help," he said, not knowing what else to say because if he'd heard and seen what they had, he would have stepped in, too.

"Sure. How long do you think it would take the cops to get out here for some kind of domestic scuffle?" Callie asked.

"Well, at least don't go approaching people like Moose in a dark parking lot," he said, trying to make a point.

"Oh, so then you suggest next time we ask him to move onto the lit sidewalk first?" Emily said.

His sister burst out laughing. He shook his head and rubbed the back of his neck.

"So anyway," he said, shooting them each a look that hopefully indicated how he didn't find their brand of humor particularly funny, "I'm going. See that you can avoid trouble, please."

"Sure, thing, Sarge," his sister said, patting him on the shoulder and then saluting. "Oh. Wait. Don't forget Mom and Dad's on Sunday night."

"I'll see if I can make it. I might be busy practicing my ladies' man skills." He turned around so he didn't actually witness their outburst of laughter. But he did smile all the way back to his truck.

He sat in the front seat, deciding to wait and make sure they were both safely in their cars. The last thing he wanted was Moose making a reappearance. His smile lingered as he thought about Emily tonight and her analysis of what he was lacking. It bothered him that she perceived him as someone who didn't talk or… Basically she insinuated he wasn't fun. He hadn't realized that had stopped, that other people noticed. Emily's opinion of him shouldn't bother him…but it did.

Glancing over at Emily and Callie, he found himself smiling again as they laughed and continued to talk…for another half hour.

Their laughter actually made him smile, and he was happy to see Callie at ease with Emily. When Catherine died, it had affected all of them. Even though Catherine was older than Callie, they had been very close, and he knew his sister had hesitated to make new friends or get into relationships. Hell, he couldn't blame her, because he hadn't let anyone in again, either.

Emily seemed to be roping them all in. Something like longing or warmth filled him as he watched her hug his sister and then get into her car. Callie pulled out of her parking spot first, and he knew she'd be fine, because she was going home to their parents' house. That was why he followed Emily home. He just wanted to make sure she'd be okay going back to that old house by herself. She wasn't a woman who should be alone and yet there were no signs of anyone from her life—well, except whatever loser she'd been talking to on the phone. But no one visited her, no one had called her, except Darth Vader. He followed at a distance then parked on the other side of the road and waited until she'd unlocked the door and walked in safely.

She had fit in with his family perfectly tonight. She was easygoing and charming, and he could tell everyone loved her. He knew Callie had put her beside him on purpose, and he'd hated that his attraction to her only increased. When she walked in the bar, she'd stood out. She'd been wearing a deep-red sweater that clung to her curves in a way that made it impossible for him not to notice them, dark skinny jeans, and black leather boots that stopped just below her knees. He leaned his head back. He hated all of this.

He sat there for a moment longer, wondering why this one woman, who had been a stranger to him just a week ago, was now on his mind all the time.

• • •

"We're screwed," Austin said. "With Brendon not playing on Saturday, we might as well forfeit the game right now."

Cooper and Brody nodded in agreement. In truth, he was ready for baseball season to end; he had too much going on. But he hated losing—they all did. He and his siblings were sitting in the family room at their parents' house on Sunday night, trying to stay out of their mother's way while she buzzed around them, getting everything ready for dinner. None of them were permitted to help until clean-up duty. He didn't want to acknowledge that her extra attention to detail might have something to do with the fact that Emily was coming over. She had even sent their father outside to sweep their already clean porch.

Callie leaned forward, her eyes sparkling with excitement. He held his breath because he knew that look. You didn't grow up with Callie in the house and not recognize that smile—it was the smile that inevitably landed one of them in trouble. "I have the perfect replacement," she said.

He swallowed the curse words already bubbling in his throat with their mother still in the kitchen, which was open to the family room. Clearly he wasn't alone in his worry, because his brothers were already shifting nervously.

"Out with it, before you give us nightmares, please," Brody said, passing around beers.

Callie gave them her infamous shit-disturber smile and then proceeded to crack open her beer and take a long drink. "Okay," she said, finally, many long, tense minutes later. "How about Emily?"

No one said anything. Emily was the person he was trying not to think about. Now he was beginning to suspect that all these extra Emily meetings were a setup by his well-intentioned but very irritating family members. Like today, of course, attending Sunday night dinner. Now Callie wanted her playing in their championship baseball weekend?

"Emily doesn't strike me as a baseball player," Austin said, walking to the kitchen and then plucking a grape from a cluster on the fruit platter. He threw it in the air and caught it in his mouth. He was rewarded by a swat from their mother as she prepared the salad and pretended not to be listening to their conversation.

He knew she was allied with Callie in their plan to insert Emily around him wherever possible. He told himself he was indifferent to it. They'd been trying this kind of thing since about two years after Catherine had passed. At first he'd been angry, but as time wore on, he knew they were just trying to help. They wanted him happy again, and they assumed he needed to be married to be happy—that couldn't be further from the truth. Beer and a baseball game on TV made him happy, as did whiskey. Well, never as happy as a woman could make him, but he didn't want that anymore. He saw Catherine as a different time in his life, almost like a different *life*. He had tried to explain that to his family on a few occasions, after a few drinks, but his message didn't seem to take.

They were a bit overzealous in their infatuation with Emily, but he refused to give them the satisfaction of falling for their plans. Or Emily. The slight problem he was having was that he could see himself falling for Emily. Of course, hooking up with anyone in Maple Hill for the night wouldn't be the wisest thing, with how easily gossip spread. Then there was the fact that he'd never been one for the casual hookup, and going home with a stranger—or not so much a stranger—didn't appeal to him.

His mind immediately went to Emily and the fact that he'd thought about her. A lot. When she wasn't around. When he was alone at home. At night. There were other things he'd noticed… There was a strange kind of anticipation to start his day, one that he couldn't remember having in…a very long time. He was always the first one at her door, and he had a craving, almost an addiction, like wanting his morning coffee. He wanted to see her smile. He wouldn't admit that to anyone in this room, because they would pounce on that like a cat on a mouse.

"Well, why don't you ask her when she gets here, Cooper?" their mom said, not waiting for his answer before darting into the dining room.

He felt the blood drain from his face. Why was that question directed toward him? He glared at Callie, who held her hands in the air and tried to run past him. He blocked her and crossed his arms over his chest, doing his best to appear intimidating. It was futile because his sister wasn't intimidated by any one of them and had often been the one to kick or deck one of them, growing up, knowing they weren't allowed, nor would they ever be allowed, to lay a hand on her. "Cal, I think I made it very clear, I'm not interested."

He ignored the snickers from his brothers.

"I didn't say you were. We're being good friends."

"Well, I'm her contractor, not her friend."

"Well, *I'm* her friend, and just because you're too obtuse to notice how great she is…and how she feels about you…"

His stomach dropped. "What the hell is that supposed to mean?"

"She told you that despite the fact that you don't speak and you have staring problems, she's attracted to your assets for some reason," Austin said, with a slow grin.

His face burned. He needed to stop attending Sunday night dinner every week.

Callie pointed the tip of her beer bottle at him and lowered her voice. "See? Everyone sees it, even Austin and Brody, and they notice nothing."

"We're all in the same room, you know," Austin said.

He ran his hands through his hair, not liking how they

were all talking about him. "Stop trying to invent things that don't exist. You want a new BFF, great, go for it. I don't need another wife, so back off."

He saw the sympathy flash across his sister's eyes; that made him even angrier. He hated sympathy. He'd rather she be pissed at him. "I'll back off," she said.

"I say we ask her to fill in next weekend," Austin said, clearly not giving a crap about what Cooper had just said.

Callie clapped. "Perfect."

He glared at her.

She gave him a big, smug grin. "One day, big brother, you're going to thank me. Just try and talk a little more."

He clenched his teeth and turned and walked out of the room just as the doorbell rang. Ignoring his sister's squeal, he walked into the dining room, hoping his mother would put him to work or something. She was straightening the cutlery as though expecting royalty.

"Can I help with anything?" he asked, knowing full well she wasn't going to trust him with her table arrangement.

She gave him a smile not unlike Callie's. "Not at all, my dear. We both know I'd never let you anywhere near my perfectly arranged table, just as we both know you are trying to ignore the beautiful, sweet woman at our door. Now, be on your best manners and try to make it look like you comb your hair every once in a while." She patted him on the arm, and when he didn't move, she turned it into a pinch. "Get out into the hallway and greet our guest," she hissed, still smiling, though it now seemed closer to a snarl.

He knew his mother wouldn't relent. He made his way out toward the entrance, where the rest of his siblings and his father were all standing around and greeting Emily like they hadn't just seen her the other night.

He stood on the sidelines, hands in the pockets of his Sunday jeans, wishing the sight of Emily didn't make him so damn *happy*. Her glossy brown hair fell in waves over her shoulders, and the pale-blue sweater she was wearing highlighted her curves as it fell over her hips and the top of her dark skinny jeans.

Worse was the undeniable fact that she wasn't just a gorgeous woman; it was her sincerity, her laugh, her warmth. She was smiling and joking with his family as though she'd known them for years. She handed a bouquet of flowers and a bottle of wine to his parents, and they gushed over the gesture.

Emily glanced at him, and for a second he forgot that he didn't want a relationship again. But when her smile faltered and uncertainty danced across her green eyes, he found himself walking forward, not wanting to be the man who took her spark away.

"Hi, Emily," he said, trying to pretend he didn't notice his family all but lean in and grab front row seats. It felt like he was about to take her to prom or something.

She let out a small breath, almost like she was relieved, like maybe she didn't think he'd come forward and greet her. "Hi. I hope you don't mind that I'm joining your family for dinner tonight," she said, taking off one of the tall leather boots she was wearing. He felt the sound of that zip scrape along his nerve endings, and dammit if he didn't have to turn away. His attraction to her was becoming inconvenient—especially when his stupid brothers were grinning because they knew exactly what he was thinking.

He cleared his throat. "Not at all. Our Mom makes the best Sunday night dinners in the county."

His mother beamed at him and patted his cheek as she walked by. "Good boy. You should have shaved, but your compliments make up for your whiskers. Come in, Emily, don't be a stranger."

Callie linked her arm with Emily's and guided her

toward the kitchen. “Come on, I’ll show you to the wine,” she whispered.

Emily laughed, and he turned to talk to his brothers but then decided against it, since they were watching him with stupid grins on their faces. His family was great, but this was overstepping. He didn’t need them interfering in his perfectly…*okay* life.

But interfere they did. Two hours later, he was seated beside Emily, trying to ignore the lemony scent of her perfume whenever she leaned over to reach something on the table. She fit into Sunday night dinner as easily as the pumpkin pie his mother would serve later.

“And what about your family, dear?” his mother said.

He glanced at Emily when she didn’t answer right away. Her face went slightly red, and one hand clenched in her lap. “My parents both died in a car accident almost a year ago.”

Silence fell over the table, and he had the overwhelming urge to reach out and put his arm around her. He wouldn’t, of course. She seemed alone and vulnerable, telling all of them she was basically on her own. It wasn’t good to have no one around. He placed his arm on the back of her chair, not touching her but hoping it made her realize she wasn’t alone.

“I’m so sorry to hear that, dear,” his mom said. They all agreed, mumbling out condolences.

“But she has a cat now. How’s your cat, Emily?” he asked, inwardly cringing at his conversation. Who was he? He was a guy who didn’t talk and stared at people apparently. He didn’t want to be that guy anymore.

“Um, she’s so cute,” Emily said, shooting him a wobbly smile. Even she knew he was acting weird. “Her name is Buttons. She’s a gray and white long-hair cat.”

“She’s adorable. Like a puffball,” Callie agreed, topping up his wineglass with a suspicious gleam in her eye.

“How wonderful that she’s found a good home. Hopefully

she doesn't get into too much mischief," his mother said.

"She will definitely keep me busy. Tonight I have her set up in my bedroom with water and food to keep her away from the construction. I think I'll have to gradually allow her into different rooms once they're cat-proofed."

"Well that's a very good plan. If you need any help at all Cooper loves animals," his mom said with a smile that was a little too wide to be natural.

"I do?"

Her smile dipped. "Remember that animal you brought home in the first grade?"

His brothers burst out laughing. "You mean the class gerbil I had to take care of for a week?"

She nodded. "You did a fine job with that."

He leaned forward. "Mom, the gerbil died on day three. Austin ran him over with his bike."

"You guys are sick," Callie said. "I'm so glad I wasn't born to witness this stuff."

"It was an accident. Not one of my finer moments as a four-year-old. I didn't know Cooper had brought the hamster out to the driveway, and I was practicing riding a two-wheeler. I had no control over that bike," Austin said, his face red.

"That sounds very tragic," Emily said, her eyes swimming with laughter.

"Life with three boys," his mom said, placing her napkin on the table and leaning back in her chair with a sigh.

"Do you have any other family?" his dad asked, brows drawing together along with a deep frown.

"I have a brother back in Toronto. We're…not that close. He's twelve years older than me."

There was hardness to her voice when she spoke of him that reminded him of the night he'd heard her on the phone. "Oh, well, hopefully he can get out to see you sometime soon. Or are you planning on going back to the city?"

She toyed with her napkin, and he fought the urge to tell his family to stop giving her the third degree. "I think I'd like to settle down here. It's not that far from Toronto that I can't visit. Besides, it's nice to be in my grandmother's old town," she said with a smile.

"Your grandmother was highly regarded here. I'm sure she'd be proud of you, what with opening an inn. That's a big project you've got there."

"She's doing a great job on it, too," he said before he could second-guess himself, or before he could contemplate the implications. Everyone turned to him. He shrugged and finished off his wine.

"Well, thank you," she said, her cheeks turning a pretty shade of pink. Ah, damn. The fact that he was noticing things like the shade of pink her cheeks turned when she blushed was a bad sign. "I have big plans, but it's all of you working on that house that are making it happen."

His dad folded his hand on the table, his chest puffing up slightly, as did each of his brothers. She'd charmed them all. Including him. She laughed and joked with everyone, and clearly they were all in love with her. He glanced at her and found himself smiling involuntarily.

• • •

Emily tried to quell the onslaught of emotion that had threatened to overwhelm her through the night. This was family dinner like she had never known. There wasn't any tension—well, except from the man sitting beside her—but there wasn't any *angry* tension. The entire family joked and laughed, and when they teased there wasn't any underlying hostility. They all seemed genuinely happy to be sitting and enjoying each other's company. It wasn't about the food, even though it was all delicious. It was about being together.

Sure, she knew families like this existed, but she'd mostly witnessed that on television. If it weren't for the man sitting next to her, this would have been the most relaxing, enjoyable night of her life. Cooper took away the relaxing part of the night, though. She couldn't quite relax around him—she was a bundle of carefully controlled nerves and excitement. "I'll help clear the table," she said when the siblings all stood and began gathering dishes.

"Oh now, I can't have a guest do that," Mrs. Merrick said. "But since you're more like family, if you want to help, then I suppose that's okay. Usually the kids take care of the dishes on Sunday nights."

Brody walked by and gave his mother a kiss on the head, and Emily spotted Cooper trying to trip him as he walked into the kitchen, almost sending the platter of leftover roast flying across the room. Emily bit back her smile as she stood, gathering her dish and then scraping and stacking some more. She joined the others in the large kitchen and felt like an outsider—an outsider who desperately wanted to be an insider. Callie was prepping two different pies while coffee brewed, the aroma filling the already fragrant kitchen. Brody and Austin were loading the dishwasher and Cooper was at the sink, his sleeves rolled up as he washed the platters.

The Merrick house was large but warm and homey. The kitchen had an oversize chestnut-stained island with a butcher-block top, while the rest of the kitchen had white cabinets with white quartz countertops and an enormous white farmhouse sink.

Emily stood there and wanted to just join in on the chatter and banter, stand beside Cooper and rinse the dishes and dry them. She wanted so badly to belong to a family like this one.

"Hey, Emily. Do you want to grab the mugs and creamer and sugar?" Callie said, shooting her a smile over her shoulder.

She nodded and walked over to her friend.

"Emily, are you a baseball fan?" Austin asked.

She smiled. "Absolutely. Our company always had season tickets." She picked up a small tray holding the coffee condiments. Callie shot Cooper a strange smile.

"Perfect. Next weekend we have our end-of-season tournament. We have a long-standing rivalry with the other team. Our first baseman is out with a broken arm. Any chance you want to take his spot?" Austin asked.

Emily felt all the blood drain from her face, and she was pretty sure she was as white as the cream on the tray she was holding. She glanced around at the other Merricks, mostly interested in Cooper's expression. But his jaw was doing that ticking thing and his eyes weren't exactly warmed by the idea of her joining the team.

For a second she wanted to readily agree, but with confidence. She wanted to be the woman who'd grown up playing sports, who was comfortable joining any kind of sporting event, but she wasn't. She had never been allowed to play. Coupled with her insecurities, something like this was a nightmare. She searched for something to say that wouldn't make her sound inept. "I'd love to. Thanks so much for asking, but um, I'm not a great player. Big fan, no talent."

Callie frowned and walked over to her. "You don't have to be a great player. My brothers can barely catch a ball," she said, smiling.

"Hey," Austin said, attempting to swat her on the head, but Callie ducked in time.

"Seriously, it's just a fun game," Callie urged.

"But it's end of season and against your rival," she said, shifting from one foot to the other. She couldn't do this. She'd humiliate herself.

"No one takes these games seriously except Cooper. Really, don't worry about it," Brody said, walking past them and back into the dining room.

She glanced at Cooper, but he didn't deny that he took it seriously. No way would she add this pressure to her life and make a fool of herself in front of her new friends. "Well, I'm busy on weekends, and I um, have my cat."

Callie frowned at her, clearly not buying her feeble excuses. "I'm not going to let you become some under-thirty, crazy cat lady. You're on the team and I'm not taking no for an answer. If you haven't played in a while, I'll come over and help you practice, okay?"

"You should join," Cooper said, and before she could answer he walked past them, back into the dining room. Her heart raced and she almost broke out into a sweat. She should do this. It would be good for her, another way for her to break out of her shell, out of the mold she'd been forced into. She smiled at Callie. "Okay. But you have to come over and help."

Callie squealed and put her arm around her. "You won't regret this."

Chapter Six

Emily decided that her lofty goal of giving up Cheetos and Diet Coke was going to end this weekend. With all the stress in her life—the latest being the upcoming baseball game in which she was certain she'd make a fool of herself—this was precisely the time *for* Cheetos and Diet Coke. Wasn't the whole 'stress-eating' term exactly this situation? She hadn't busted open a bag since Cooper had mentioned the Cheetos-dust and she hadn't touched a Diet Coke since moving here. But this baseball game was seriously trying her resolve. Peach Perrier wasn't going to cut it. She could eat the Cheetos on the porch so it wouldn't attract any mice in the house.

She adjusted her ponytail and crouched, picking a few random weeds near the front walkway to her home while going back and forth on her resolutions. She was waiting for Callie to come and give her baseball lessons, but her friend was clearly running late. Everyone had gone home for the day, and she was exhausted and seriously questioning why she ever agreed to this.

She glanced up, squinting against the sun setting over

the barn, as the sound of tires crunched against gravel. Her stomach dropped when she realized it was Cooper's truck pulling into the driveway instead of Callie's jeep. She stood slowly, pulling her Blue Jays cap lower over her eyes. She prayed frantically that maybe Callie had borrowed her brother's truck. She held her breath to see who would emerge and then she tried not to cry as Cooper rounded the corner, stopped at the cab of his truck, and pulled out a bat, two gloves, and a bucket of something.

He walked toward her, and she reminded herself this was her new life, the life where she had oodles of confidence. Except she was about to make a fool of herself in front of him, and no amount of confidence could fix that. Cooper was the problem, maybe. He was too…much of everything. Too intense, too attractive, too…much. If it hadn't been cool out, she was pretty sure she'd have broken out in a sweat just watching him make his way over to her. She had already memorized the way he walked; it wasn't a swagger, but it might as well have been, because it had the same effect on her. He was wearing a battered Blue Jays cap, worn jeans, and one of those soft, shoulder-hugging T-shirts with their construction company name in white letters on the front.

"Hi," he said as he put the bat down along with a bucket full of baseballs.

She forced her lips into what she hoped was a carefree smile, not the smile of a woman about to disgrace herself. "Uh, hi. What happened to Callie?"

"Both of the girls working the shop canceled, so she had to fill in."

Great. What were the odds? She crossed her arms in front of her chest. "Oh. Well, you don't have to do this. I'm sure you're wiped after working all day on this old place."

He handed her a glove. "Not a problem. It's our final game of the season and I'd hate to forfeit due to lack of players. So, what do you need help with?"

She swallowed hard and winced. "Um, everything?"

He gave a laugh but then stopped when she didn't join in. "Seriously?"

She clutched the glove tightly, trying to hold onto her pride. "I told Callie I've never played. I believe I tried telling all of you that at your parents' house on Sunday. I'm a baseball nerd in the sense that I watch every game and know the rules and all that. But…actually playing, um. No."

She watched what she assumed was irritation flicker across his eyes, and she had to fight the urge to just leave. She didn't need to be made fun of. She'd been shamed and told she was stupid one too many times in her life; she didn't need that from him. This was her new life. In her new life, she wasn't inferior anymore. In her new life, she was enough, just the way she was. In her new life, she wasn't afraid to admit she didn't know how to do something. In her new life, she tried new things. She lifted her chin and tried to act like the person in her head she wanted to be. "Ya know, I was there when you said I should join. Maybe you should do a better job of scouting prospects before you ask them."

He grinned and ducked his head momentarily. When he looked back up at her, his eyes were filled with warmth that made her toes curl and her breath catch. "You're right."

She nodded, trying to play it cool. "If you don't have time for this, that's okay. I'm sure you guys can find someone else to play this weekend."

"I'm a great coach. You'll catch on in no time. No pun intended."

She attempted a smile at his humor, but her initial concern of looking stupid came back quickly. "Funny. Great. Let's get started."

"Okay. What do you want to start with? Batting or tossing the ball around?"

Both were going to go epically bad, but hitting did seem like more fun whenever she watched a game. "Batting. I think I'd be good at batting."

"Perfect. I brought Callie's bat, it'll be the right size and weight for you. Be right back."

She wasn't so nervous that she didn't notice the very fine view he provided as he turned around and jogged to his truck. A few minutes later she was breaking out into a sweat as he handed her the bat and then positioned himself a few yards away. "Okay, so I'll start off really easy. All you have to do is swing."

"Oh, great. No problem. Just hit the moving target," she said. Why had she said she thought she'd be good at batting? She turned slightly, holding the bat over her shoulder like she'd seen the MLB players do hundreds of times. It looked easy enough.

Cooper was facing her, ball and glove ready. "Ready?"

"As I'll ever be," she choked.

True to his word, the ball came toward her gently, and she swung a home-run swing, but the ball landed with a *thud* on the grass behind her. "Oops," she said, grabbing the ball and tossing it back to him underhanded.

He rubbed a hand over his jaw. "Your swing is good. Just uh, try keeping your eyes open when the ball approaches."

She inhaled sharply. She'd closed her eyes? "I did. I'm pretty sure I would know if I closed my eyes."

"Ya' closed them, Em."

It was either the softness of his tone or the "Em" that sent a rush of warmth through her body and made the fact that she closed her eyes sting a little less. "Okay, I'll keep them open this time. Promise."

He threw the ball and this time she kept her eyes open, but still missed. Ugh. How hard was it to hit a slow pitch? "Maybe we should have started with catch?"

He shook his head and walked over to her. "Nah. You'll get the hang of this. I'm going to help you correct your swing, though. You're kind of doing a tennis serve thing."

That was almost funny, especially since she'd never even played tennis.

"I'm just going to fix your form a bit," he said, placing his hands on her shoulders gently and turning her.

"Sure," she croaked, pretending like his hands on her weren't causing some kind of massive spark throughout her body.

"Okay, now pick up the bat, and I'm going to adjust your hand position," he said, standing behind her.

She followed his instructions and stopped breathing when his arms wrapped around her from behind and his hands settled on hers.

"Just so we're clear, this is all about baseball. I'm not practicing my ladies' man moves." His deep voice was laced with laughter.

She let out a strangled laugh. "The thought wouldn't have crossed my mind at all."

"That these are my moves or that I'd be practicing?"

Her heart raced at his nearness, the feel of his hands on her, the intimacy in his voice. "That you'd practice on me, obviously."

"Right," he said in a thick voice. "I'll try not to take it personally that you think I need any practice at all."

She didn't move for a second as he took a step away from her, and something clung in the air between them, glittered in his blue eyes as he stared at her. "It's not personal."

"How 'bout we try a few more pitches?"

She nodded, relieved the moment was gone. "I'm ready. If I miss, it's your fault."

He grinned and her heart skipped a few beats. "Done."

His smile fell when she missed the next three pitches. Her

face grew warmer and warmer, and their banter died. "Maybe we should try catch now?" she suggested, desperate to move through all this as quickly as possible. There was no way she'd be a great ball player after only one practice anyway.

"I'm not giving up. Let's end on a high note. I pitch until you hit one. You're a homerun run-hitter, I know it."

Her heart swelled at his determination and the unexpected patience he was showing her. "Okay then."

"Also, the other team's best pitcher is out with a sore shoulder. The rest of the guys can pitch well, but not as fast as him. Remember if the pitch is coming too close to try and get out of the way, and if you can't, and it's an inside pitch, turn your shoulder so the ball hits you in the back."

"Oh great. I love getting hit by a baseball in the back," she said.

He gave a short laugh and got back into position. "Don't worry, it'll sting, but at least it won't be a serious injury."

Ten pitches later, she had the thrill of making contact and watching the ball fly toward the barn. "I did it!" she said with disbelief.

He grinned. "Hit one like that and you'll be batting clean-up," he said. She knew he was exaggerating but he'd managed to make an otherwise uncomfortable situation into something rewarding and positive.

"Ready to toss the ball around?"

She swallowed hard. She'd never even put her hand in a baseball glove before, let alone toss a ball around and then somehow catch it again. But if she could hit, how hard could it be to catch? "Sounds great!"

He was moving away from her, tossing a ball in the air and catching it effortlessly. He kept walking backward, and the farther he went the more panicked she felt. She took a deep breath. *You've watched baseball. How hard could it be to throw a ball in the direction of his glove? You take chances now, remember?* And just because she hadn't actually caught a ball in a glove didn't mean she couldn't catch. Of course she had caught things in her lifetime. Bags of Cheetos from a friend at school. Diet Cokes across the university dorm room. C'mon. She could do this.

"Ready?" he yelled, when she hadn't moved an inch or even put the glove on.

She shoved her hand into the glove he'd provided and nodded. The moment he released the ball it seemed to fly through the air at a dangerous speed, but she forced herself to keep her eye on it and lift her glove in the general direction. But it was too close, too fast, and instead of making the catch as all her favorite players did, she yelped and shielded her head.

A part of her really wished the ball had hit her in the head and she could fake some kind of concussion. That would take the focus off the fact that she had just screamed at a ball instead of catching it. Emily Birmingham was not a stranger to humiliation, but this was a new kind. For one, it had happened in front of one of the hottest men she'd ever met. Two, this was her new phase of life, the one where humiliation wasn't supposed to follow.

The ball hit the ground with a *thump* and rolled into the shrubs. She didn't dare look in Cooper's direction, because he was probably staring at her in horror or disgust.

"The sun was in my eyes!" she managed to yell as she crouched, searching for the ball. That was a great excuse and she gave herself kudos for thinking of it on the spot, while at the same time reflecting on how humiliation seemed to follow her everywhere. She wasn't a kid anymore, she wasn't even around the same people or in the same place anymore, so how could her insecurities still exist, how could they still be relevant? At what point in her life would she finally be able to be rid of past hurt?

As she knelt on all fours and extended her hand under the prickly evergreens, she psyched herself up to stand and face Cooper again. She wouldn't quit. On the bright side, it would be her turn to throw. Throwing had to be easier than catching. *You can do it, Emily.* She grabbed the ball in one hand and brushed off the dirt with her glove on the other as she stood. She turned around and yelped when she ran into Cooper's wall of a chest.

"Sorry," he said, sounding worried. Like maybe he was wondering if there was something wrong with her.

"Oh, no problem. Okay, my turn. Go, run out there," she said, pointing in the direction of the large maple tree in front of the barn. He didn't move, though. Instead, that weird expression flickered across his face. Oh, *pity.* Maybe that was it.

"Let me just fix something first," he said in a voice that wasn't mocking, but rather, sympathetic.

She shifted from one foot to the other. "Sure. Whatever you think is best."

He took the glove from her and gently shoved her hand into the glove—having the good manners to not say out loud that she'd had the *wrong hand in the glove*—which made her want to run and hide. She winced and made eye contact with him.

"No worries," he said, without a hint of sarcasm or gloating. It was such a nice thing, such a character-revealing expression, that the back of her eyes stung. Where had men like this been all her life? "Okay, let's do a light ball toss from a closer distance. We can switch sides so that the sun isn't in your eyes."

She rolled her lips inward and nodded, stifling the urge to groan with embarrassment when he only moved about five feet away and then tossed her the ball underhanded, as though he were throwing to a five-year-old. She managed to open her glove in time and then close it awkwardly. The ball didn't fall. She had done it. She wanted to do a happy dance or throw her hands in the air or something, except that seemed sad. Like, she'd be advertising her weaknesses. She'd learned long ago to never do that.

"Nice catch," he said, moving back a few more steps. They continued like this for what seemed a long time, with her making awkward catches and him throwing silently then moving farther away when she caught the ball. The sun had set a while ago, and the faint sound of rolling thunder echoed through the forest around them. She was hoping he'd suggest they quit and avoid getting stuck in the rain, but evidently he thought she needed help so badly that it was worth the risk of getting struck by lightning.

Maybe an hour later, he was back to where he originally started, and she stood there, deciding it was time to make a real throw. She needed to test her skills and not be afraid of missing the target. She drew her arm back past her shoulder, and when she brought it forward again, the ball left her hand with the force of a pro ball player. She watched proudly as it soared over the long distance between them. Alarm filled her as she realized it was way too high, way too wide. Cooper may have been a college-level ball player, but there was no way he'd make that catch, and it was heading straight for the living room Gothic windows.

She heard him curse as he made an impressive jump to attempt to catch her wild ball, but he missed it by five feet too wide and about five feet too low. She squeezed her eyes shut as the sound of glass shattering filled the otherwise quiet yard.

She forced herself to run over to where he was standing, just as the sky decided to dump the rain it had been threatening the last hour. Cooper didn't even flinch. "Sorry," she said, stealing a sideways glance.

He turned to her, and she braced herself for the sarcastic remark that was inevitable. "It was a pretty impressive throw. I think you have a future in the outfield."

As cold rain plastered her hair to her head and ran down her face, she stared at the man she decided she wanted to keep. She opened her mouth but didn't know what to say, because Cooper had just inadvertently helped her overcome one of her biggest insecurities. She had put herself out there, had attempted something she'd never done before, had displayed her vulnerability for him to see…and the world had gone on. No one had mocked her. No one had laughed at her. She felt…free, light, giddy.

He turned around and stared up at the gaping hole in the one window that hadn't needed repairing before now. "That's going to be a problem."

"I'm so sorry. I can't believe I just added to the work around here," she said, cringing.

"Don't worry about it. It can easily be fixed next week."

She knew he was just being nice. "Thanks. But if you need to get going, that's fine," she said, taking off the glove and pretending like everything that had just happened was normal, and that she'd be fine dealing with the giant hole in her house.

"As if," he said, before heading toward his truck. He was staying. He wasn't going to take off on her. Everything about him had been different today, as though he was giving her a glimpse of the man he really was. Staring at the broken window, she cursed her bad aim. The floors in the living room had just been refinished. She needed to figure out how to seal the window and get rid of the broken glass and dry the floors before they were damaged. She turned to leave and spotted Cooper pulling his toolbox out of his truck and walking toward her. "Let's go deal with that window," he said, not breaking his stride.

She turned on a few lights as they walked through the quiet and dark house. As soon as they entered the living room, the draft from the window hit her body, chilling her through her wet clothes.

"I'm going to go see if I can find some wood to board up this window," Cooper said, taking out a measuring tape. She shivered from the dropping temperatures and her wet clothes but didn't say anything because he was soaked as well. His shirt clung to him, highlighting his muscled form to perfection. Not that she was noticing.

"Okay, I'll get something to deal with the glass and get the floor dried while you do that," she said, trying to be useful.

"Great," he said, his back to her as he continued measuring the window. She was not going to stare and admire him. That would be rude. He was here because of her screw-up.

She paused in the doorway. "Do you want a coffee?"

"Uh, if you're having one, I'd love one," he said, glancing over his shoulder at her.

"Definitely," she said, before leaving the room. Buttons, her cat, bolted down the stairs, and Emily closed the living room door. The last thing she needed was the cat getting her paws cut on glass.

She started a pot of coffee and went to find her broom and dustpan along with a garbage bag while the coffee brewed. She buzzed around with a nervous sort of energy. This afternoon had not gone the way she'd intended. She'd made a fool of herself, of course, but in doing so, she'd gotten a glimpse of the man Cooper was.

As she poured the coffee into mugs, she tried not to let any of this mean more than it did. Like, what kind of person was actually excited by their contractor having to stay late and fix something? Especially damage she was responsible for. Maybe it was because said contractor had wrapped his arms around her and joked about his moves. Or maybe it was because he'd been all solid muscle and had smelled crisp and clean and oh-so-masculine. She covered her face and groaned. Get a grip. He was being friendly and making it clear that he was only helping with baseball and not coming on to her.

Just focus on acting normal. She tucked a garbage bag into the back pocket of her jeans, tucked the broom and its attached dustpan under her arm, and then grabbed the coffees and made her way back to the living room.

Cooper wasn't back yet from cutting the wood in the coach house. She set their mugs on the radiator ledge and got to work cleaning up the glass. If she could finish before he came back, at least he'd have a clean place to work. Rain drizzled through the window and she was shivering by the time she'd collected all the glass.

She stood as Cooper entered the room. He was holding a large wooden board and was disheveled and…something else she couldn't quite figure out. Or maybe it was the look in his eyes. A nervous tremor ran through her that she knew wasn't just a shiver from the rain. Maybe it was the flash of something in his eyes, or maybe she was just imagining that his gaze had flickered over her. She dragged the broom out of the window area. "Your coffee is on the radiator. I picked up the glass, but be careful, there might be some little pieces still there. I'll be right back to finish," she said, shooting him a smile.

"Great," he said, not sounding great as he walked back into the room.

She left with the tension in the room increasing somehow. It was like things had suddenly changed. It was the wet clothes. Or maybe it was that he knew she was attracted to him. Had she stared? Had she given something away? No, of course not. She needed to keep it that way. Cooper had made it clear he was her contractor. He was also her new BFF's brother. Which was why it was really ridiculous of her to stop in front of the powder room mirror and fix her hair.

• • •

Cooper cursed himself as he realized the board was about an inch too short. He just wanted to get the hell out of this house and the hell away from Emily and this crazy tension between them. Hell, he would have even welcomed one of his brothers here right now.

Emily was currently wiping up the floor while humming. He was trying to get his head screwed on straight and his mind off the woman beside him. He had known she was attractive the minute he'd met her.

But lots of women were attractive.

But it was Emily who turned on a switch that had been turned off in him for years. She wasn't what he'd consider his classic type, not that he'd ever really had a type. But she'd felt so damn good, like she fit in his arms. She'd smelled like spring flowers and he'd wanted nothing more than for her to turn around and kiss her. Today he'd been able to make light of it all, but it was getting harder to pretend that he wasn't attracted to her.

But she carried around some kind of hurt and vulnerability that affected him. Maybe because he understood hurt.

But then she was independent and smart because she was taking over a massive project and building a company all on her own.

But she couldn't throw a ball to save her life.

He took the board down and leaned it against the window. It was the only wood remotely close to fitting as a temporary fix. He didn't want to just tarp the opening. That would make the house too easy to break into, and he wouldn't sleep well knowing Emily was here by herself with only a piece of plastic as a barrier and Moose knowing where she lived.

"Everything okay?" she asked, coming up to stand next to him.

He glanced at her and tried not to notice how gorgeous she was, even when her hair was a messy heap around her shoulders and her clothes wet and clinging to her. He wished he hadn't noticed that, but he had, as soon as it had started raining. "I'm going to need your help," he said.

"Sure!" Her enthusiasm was commendable, despite the rain coming in.

"I need to drill into the window frame, which is fine, since these frames haven't been restored yet, but the board is too small, so it's going to fall out. Basically, all I need you to do is stand in front of the window and hold it in place until I can secure it. Then along the edges I'm going to use tarp and duct tape. What do you think?"

"That sounds easy enough," she said with a nervous smile.

He moved aside so she could stand in front of the window, and she shivered as a gust of wind blew through the opening. "Do you want to go change first?" he asked. A part of him—his head—hoped she would go throw on some oversize, shapeless sweatshirt while other parts were happy to have her in clinging clothes.

"Nope, I'm fine."

He hadn't realized how close he'd have to stand to her, but as they were in the nook of the bay window and he hoisted the large wood board, she shuffled to let him pass. "Okay, can you hold that?" he asked, hating that it all of a sudden felt very intimate in the gigantic room.

"Got it," she said, spreading each hand on the top two corners. He picked up his drill and grimly realized he'd be standing almost directly behind her, so there would be inevitable body contact. This was the last thing he wanted with the woman he needed to avoid. They had already done this today. It was torture.

"Okay, hold on," he said, bracing himself against one hand and leaning in and up to drill into one side of the window.

She moved her head and bumped into his chest. "Sorry, was just trying to see what you were doing," she said, her voice laced with embarrassment.

Embarrassment was the furthest thing from his mind. He was close enough that he could feel the shiver from her body, could smell the almost sweet scent of her perfume. "No problem. I'm almost done."

She nodded.

He worked in silence, his awareness of her increasing every time his body brushed against hers. "Okay," he said, clearing his throat and securing the last of the tape. "I'm done."

She turned around quickly, and her soft curves grazed his body enticingly, setting his teeth on edge. She stepped back, bumping into the wooden makeshift window. "You okay?" he said, taking a step back to collect his drill, needing to get out of there. Standing so close to Emily made it impossible for him not to notice her mouth or her eyes, or how much he wanted to kiss her.

She rubbed the back of her head. "Yup. Thanks for setting this up. I, um, I guess I'll see you at the game tomorrow?"

He nodded and walked out of the living room. He needed to remember that a relationship wasn't in the cards for him anymore. Emily was a woman who did relationships. "Sure. See you tomorrow."

Chapter Seven

Emily took a deep breath of the fresh fall air while wishing for courage. She'd really love to be one of those people who didn't care what others' opinions of her were. But Cooper hadn't ridiculed her—not when she'd put the baseball glove on the wrong hand, or when she'd been unable to catch…or when she'd overthrown by a mile and sent the ball crashing through her living room window.

As she made her way from the parking lot to the baseball diamond, she tugged at her Maple Hill Warriors T-shirt in a futile attempt at not having it be so clingy and tried to look like she belonged at this game. She scanned the people in the dugout but didn't see anyone she recognized yet. She pretended to tie her shoe and wished Callie would hurry and get here so she wouldn't have to hang out with the guys on the team without her.

"You're Callie's friend, right?" a male voice said.

Emily looked up to see a guy around her age approaching her. She smiled then pretended to tie her other shoe. "Yup."

"You're new in town?"

She sighed and then straightened. "Uh, yeah. Nice to meet you, I'm Emily."

He smiled at her. He seemed nice, not creepy or anything. But he wasn't Cooper. That was basically the only thing wrong with him. "John. So what position are you playing?"

"Hopefully I'll be warming the bench, if I get my way."

He laughed. "I'm afraid that won't happen, since we're short on players. Don't worry. How about we get out there and throw the ball around while we wait for everyone to arrive?"

She nodded. "I might as well. I need all the practice I can get."

She picked her glove up off the ground and walked with him out to the field. "I hope your team isn't super competitive or anything."

"Besides Cooper and his family, the rest of us are pretty normal," he said with a wink.

Her stomach churned with dread at the upcoming humiliation. There wasn't a cloud in the sky, so she couldn't even pray for rain. Though, they'd probably opt to play in the rain. She put Callie's loaned glove on and moved away from John, mentally psyching herself up to catch. He tossed her a couple of easy throws while talking, and she missed four out of five, but he was very kind and kept reassuring her.

"Emily!" She turned in the direction of Callie's voice and waved to her friend, who was walking with Cooper. She tried to quell her nerves as Cooper gave her a wave. He looked... hot. His ball cap was pulled low and his T-shirt hugged his athletic form, as did his pants. How had she actually gotten herself into this situation? This was her contractor. Now she was joining their baseball team? Playing baseball was a childhood dream, now it was turning into some kind of adult nightmare.

The ballpark started filling up and the other team started

spilling out onto the field, and dozens of people started to crowd the stands. This many people actually came to watch an adult league play?

She walked over and joined the rest of the team, and Cooper started reading off names and their various positions. When he came to her name he said, "First base or outfield?"

Her mouth went dry. First base. Their conversation, when she'd said she'd always envisioned herself as a first baseman. Was it a coincidence? It couldn't be; she was horrible. There was no way he'd give someone as bad as her first base unless… he felt sorry for her. But he was also giving her an out by offering outfield. First base would have so much action and would require her to make really fast plays she wasn't good enough for. She'd be responsible for catching and making quick outs. Unless the team they were playing against had huge hits, she might be able to just fly under the radar in the outfield.

She stared at him, a part of her wanting desperately to take first base, but also knowing it would be suicide. She'd also be letting the team down because there was no way she could play that position effectively. "Uh, I'll take outfield," she said, pulling her cap down a little so he wouldn't catch the expression in her eyes.

"Done," he said and then turned to the rest of the team. His brothers were having some kind of an exchange, but he ignored them, and Callie was smiling at her as though she'd just won the lottery. "Okay, everyone, let's do this. We've gotta beat these guys because if we don't, we'll have to listen to their obnoxious victory chant," Cooper said.

Everyone laughed. John walked with her out onto the field until Callie came running up to her.

"My brother offered you first base," she whispered, walking beside her.

"Is that bad?"

"No, it's very good. Cooper is the most competitive person in our family. He's, like, insane when it comes to baseball. Do you know he was the only team captain in this just-for-fun league that actually held tryouts? The fact that he was actually willing to put you on first base says everything about his feelings toward you."

She felt nauseated and excited all at the same time, which was a new one for her. "What?"

Callie put her arm around her. "Yup. He doesn't care that you'll screw up the game and we'll lose. That means he's interested in you."

"Um, how do you know that I'll screw up the game and we'll lose?"

Callie tilted her head and patted Emily's arm. "Sweetie, you already told me you can't throw a ball."

She narrowed her eyes on her friend. "Did Cooper say anything about the day he came to help?"

Callie shook her head. "Why? Did something happen?"

Emily stared down at her cleats. "Uh, I couldn't catch a ball and then made one big showman attempt at a throw, and it went right through one of the Gothic living room windows, which he then had to repair."

Callie slapped a hand over her mouth, but not before Emily saw her laugh. Tears formed at the corners of her friend's eyes, probably from repressing her laughter.

"Hey, Callie, we're playing a game out here!" Cooper yelled from the pitcher's mound. Callie gave him a salute, and then the two of them ran to the outfield. Emily said a hysterical prayer that no balls would be thrown her way, that she wouldn't have to throw any balls, and that she'd be at the bottom of the batting lineup and would hopefully only have to go up to bat once.

"Well, good luck," Callie said as she walked out to center field. "Drinks are on me tonight for forcing you to do this!"

Emily nodded and forced a wobbly smile. This whole having female friends thing was proving to be a lot more problematic than she'd imagined.

• • •

Cooper had known this was going to be bad, but he hadn't realized just how bad until now.

Thankfully there hadn't been too many plays in right field, so the five balls that Emily missed weren't too deadly for them. They'd been getting runs in, and he just hoped that Emily's last at bat might yield at least one hit for her. She was standing in the dugout, her fingers coiled around the metal fence.

"How the hell did you get such a hot fill-in?" John said, standing beside him.

Normally he liked John. Today…not so much. "She's Callie's friend."

"Oh, well, that's good. I assumed she might have been dating you. Now that I know she's not, I'm going to ask her out."

Cooper looked up from his chart and frowned. "I didn't say that she's not dating anyone. Like you said, she's hot. I'm sure she has a boyfriend."

Josh glanced at the stands. "Well, there's no harm in asking."

Cooper tried not to let his irritation show. "She's from Toronto. I'm pretty sure there's someone back home."

Josh shrugged and looked over at Emily. Cooper knew exactly what he saw in her; she was gorgeous, and despite her obvious discomfort, she'd managed to be nice to everyone, to cheer along with every at bat, and to engage in conversation. She also filled out the baseball uniform really nicely. Her Maple Hill shirt clung to her full breasts and small waist, the white pants highlighting her curvy hips. Not that any of that should matter. He was team captain, not the team player—that was Austin's role. Or, evidently, John's.

He clenched his teeth and stopped that line of thinking. "I've got to go see if anyone needs help," Cooper said.

Despite needing distance from the conversation, he glanced at Emily, who was putting on her batting helmet. She walked over to where the bats were leaning against the dugout fence, and he knew she was scoping out Callie's.

He moved closer to the diamond and clapped for Emily as she approached home plate. He fought the urge to remind her of the pointers or how to avoid getting hit by a pitch, but that would only embarrass her. She tapped the end of her bat on the ground, a very common image of the major-leaguers. She got into position, exactly like they'd practiced, and like someone who watched baseball. Her lack of confidence out there was her biggest problem.

Emily raised her bat above her shoulder. The pitcher threw a fast one and she shut her eyes when she swung, missing it by a mile. The pit in his stomach grew until it was the size of a cavern. Her timing at bat was horrible and they were in a bases-loaded situation, where a strikeout would be awful and also embarrassing.

Maybe what bugged him the most was that she seemed to care. It would have been different if she'd brushed off yesterday's lesson or hadn't been interested, but her vulnerability had been palpable, and it had triggered his protective side. But she'd toughed it out, she'd held her chin high...and she'd trusted him with her ego, and he'd felt strangely protective of her, like he'd do anything not to be the person that knocked her down. He'd assumed at first she was this privileged, rich, educated woman without any vulnerability, but the more he got to know her, the more he sensed it was just an image she projected.

"Strike one!" the umpire yelled, a little louder than necessary.

Emily rolled her shoulders, stepped out of the batter's box, and took a practice swing before getting back into position, her eyes on the ball. Then she struck out…again.

This time the idiots in the bleachers on the opposing team's side clapped and cheered. He caught a tremble in her chin as he picked up his own bat and got ready, because he was next in the lineup. He tried to focus, but the gnawing in his gut prevented him from turning away.

"C'mon, Em, you got this!" Callie yelled from first base.

He walked out to the on-deck circle, knowing he should be concentrating on practice swings, but his eyes were on Emily. She made contact, but the ball bounced behind her in a weak foul ball. Well, at least she was staying alive. Emily would be the second out of the inning, and then he'd be up to bat and could bring everyone home. Except he didn't want that for her. He wanted her to have the satisfaction and the pride that came from batting in a run. He actually held his breath as Emily took a swing…and struck out.

Her pretty face turned bright red, and she slowly turned and walked back to the dugout. She made eye contact with him briefly, and he caught the embarrassment flashing in her green eyes before she disappeared to sit on the bench.

He rolled his shoulders and focused on the field. There were now two outs and bases were loaded. He knew this pitcher and he knew he'd be able to crank one out into the outfield, driving the winning run home. He knew that as he walked by the team bench were Emily was standing behind the fence. She had been the only one to strike out time after time tonight. She'd been the only one to miss any ball thrown her way. And yet, she'd given it her all.

He stepped up to the plate, tapping his bat on the ground, getting into position. He made eye contact with Callie, seeing her confidence, seeing her determination. Despite his better judgement, he glanced behind him and saw the woman who was the complete opposite of his sister but deserved to have that same confidence. He drew his bat back slightly behind his shoulder and faced the pitcher. His head was in the game. It was his damn heart that was on the woman who couldn't play ball to save her life.

He swung and missed. Deliberately. And then he did it two more times. And then for the first time in his adult career, he struck out, and it was on purpose. He'd made the decision that letting his team down was less painful than letting Emily be the only one who struck out tonight. He registered the shock on everyone's faces before his brothers started yelling at him.

He turned and spotted Emily with her fingers still curled around the metal fence, and he walked over to her, ignoring the rest of his teammates and family as they approached. "That was a good try," she said with a wobbly smile.

He ducked his head for a moment and then looked back up at her. "Thanks."

"What the hell? Are you freaking kidding me? You can't hit a ball anymore?" Austin said before shoving him.

"Bad luck," he said, walking back to his equipment bag hanging on the other side of the fence.

He needed to get out of there as fast as possible, before either of his idiot brothers figured out what he'd done tonight. Hell, he didn't even know why he'd done what he'd done. Well, he did know, but he wasn't sure what to do with that knowledge. Emily was a woman who could get under his skin. He swung his bag over his shoulder and glanced back, smiling slightly as his sister put her arm around Emily and made her laugh. He walked to his truck and swung his bag into the cab then swore under his breath as Austin and Brody came over to him.

"You struck out on purpose," Brody said flatly.

He didn't affirm or deny.

"You did it because you felt bad for Emily," Brody continued.

He crossed his arms over his chest and leaned against his truck, not saying anything.

"So you going to finally get up the nerve to ask her out?" Austin said.

He frowned at them. "What makes you think I'd want to do that?"

"Because you have never struck out on this team. Ever. Then, just as our gorgeous *client* strikes out after a very adorable and earnest but very sad display at the plate, you come up to bat with a dumb-ass expression on your face and somehow can't manage to even get a base hit so that one of us could run home to score."

"I don't know what you're imagining, but I gotta get going," he said, opening his door. He hated that they knew him so well.

"We're going out for wings," they said.

"Not in the mood." He wanted to be by himself. He hopped into his truck, shut the door, and put the key in the ignition, not letting his brother's thunderous expressions guilt him into joining them. He wanted to go home, shower, and then go over all the reasons he would never ask Emily out. He pulled out of the parking lot, but not before spotting his sister and Emily walking toward Emily's SUV. His sister waved frantically at him, but it was Emily's smile, maybe the light in her eyes, too, that made him turn away from everything that existed between them and leave.

Chapter Eight

Emily adjusted her laptop screen so the glare from the sun wouldn't prevent her from seeing what she was typing. She was working on the front porch because her house was filled with men ripping out walls and floors and installing bathroom fixtures. There was dust and noise everywhere, which made it virtually impossible to get any work done. She'd have gone to the Sleepless Goat, but she needed to stick around here because someone usually had a question or two for her throughout the day.

She may have also been on the porch because of Cooper. Ever since he'd thrown the ball around with her and then repaired that window…and according to Callie, had struck out on purpose at the game, things had been different. Something had shifted and become almost awkward. At first she assumed it was just her, because she was attracted to him in a way that made her not know how to act. But then at the baseball game…she'd sensed it from him, too. This week they had both been avoiding each other. It seemed that it was always one of his brothers coming to ask her questions and

Cooper was always off by himself, working in a part of the house that she wasn't.

Reminding herself that she had way bigger problems than the fact that she couldn't play ball was a great way to get her mind back on the big picture. She focused on her computer screen, giving the pages one last glance. She had just finished her deposition for tomorrow night's council meeting and was quite pleased with herself. Her business plan was complete, and she'd printed enough copies for each town council member, just in case they were needed. Her strategy was solid, and she had the experience to back up her dream.

She glanced up when she heard the old screen door squeaking as it opened. Cooper was standing there looking like she was used to him looking—hot and disgruntled. It had never been a look she'd appreciated on a man before, but he pulled it off well. "The kitchen guys are here and have a few questions."

She nodded, snapping the lid on her computer shut. "Sure. Is there a problem?" she asked as she followed him back into the house. She sidestepped the ladder the electrician was standing on and gingerly walked across the tarped floors.

"I think it's just last-minute stuff," he said, moving aside and letting her walk first into the kitchen.

She smiled at the two men from the small family-run custom cabinetry company. They were rushing the project for her and so far had been very pleasant to work with. They were standing there with worried expressions on their faces. "Morning," she said with a smile.

"Good morning, Emily. Everything is right on schedule with the cabinetry. Tim and I were just discussing the reservations we had with installing the cabinetry directly against the brick because it is fragile and uneven," the father, Dillon, said.

Cooper was running his hands along the exposed brick.

"I don't think it's going to be too much of a problem, Tim. It'll take a bit longer than your standard installation, but I'm confident it'll hold up. I've done this before and I'll be here when your guys are installing, if they need a hand."

Emily breathed a sigh of relief. The red brick was beautiful, and she knew it would be a great contrast against the white cabinetry. "Great," she said, shooting Cooper a smile. But he was focused on the two men in front of them.

"All right, Coop. We're going to do a few last-minute measurements and then we'll be out of here. Next Monday, we start the installation," Tim said.

Emily beamed and couldn't resist a little hand clap. The men smiled at her before leaving. "This is so exciting," she said to Cooper, her mind racing at the thought of finally having a working kitchen and finishing the transformation from run-down to a modern farmhouse kitchen. "I've already taken before shots of the room, so when the house is all done I can send the pictures to some different home magazines. Maybe I can get some extra—and free—publicity if they feature this reno. Of course, I'd give you credit."

He smiled. "Thanks. I think you're doing something special here. Speaking of, are you ready for the council meeting tomorrow night?"

She shrugged. "Pretty much. I don't think this should be that much of an issue."

He shoved his hands in the back pockets of his jeans, and she tried not to pay any attention to the way the motion stretched his shirt across his broad shoulders or the fact that he'd revealed he liked what she was doing with the house. "I hope not. Just remember this isn't the city. A lot of people here have big opinions about seemingly little things."

She frowned. "I haven't heard anything. Have you?"

"Not exactly, but a few people have been grumbling to my dad about how they don't want a big inn on a little street."

"Big inn? I'm not making this place any bigger! I'm just changing its primary use. Okay…well, thanks for the heads-up."

"Coop, we're heading out to the Sampson job now," Brody said, poking his head in the room from the servants' staircase.

"Sure," Cooper said. "I'll walk you guys out. I need to pick up a few supplies in town."

Brody nodded and left the room.

Cooper turned back to her. "Well…I'll see you tomorrow as usual."

"I'll, uh, yeah, see you later," she said. Now she was nervous about tomorrow night's meeting, and she was not liking the awkward tension between her and Cooper or the fact that he seemed to be purposely trying to get away from her. Embarrassment stung her as she wondered if he might be aware of her attraction to him and that it might be completely one-sided.

• • •

Emily frowned as she took in the packed room. The large chamber in the historical city hall building was impressive, with its domed ceiling and paneled circular space. Unfortunately, she couldn't dwell on the architectural features of the place because it was packed to the brim. All these people couldn't be here because of her case, could they?

She clutched her file to her chest and forced herself to calm down and look serene and confident as she searched for an empty seat. Panic bubbled inside her as it became very clear no one was making eye contact with her.

Then she saw Cooper's parents waving her over. She gave them a thankful smile and made her way to them.

"Come sit with us, dear," Mrs. Merrick said, sliding to

make room on the bench.

"How are you doing, Emily?" Mr. Merrick said.

"I was fine until I saw how many people are here," she whispered, wincing.

Mrs. Merrick gave her a sympathetic smile. "Let's hope they're here for some of the other issues on the table tonight." But she didn't sound convinced and her husband didn't back up her opinion.

"You're doing nothing wrong," Mr. Merrick said. "When it's your turn to speak, you just get up there and be confident and tell them all the improvements you're making to your grandmother's old house."

"Cooper and his brothers are standing in the back," Mrs. Merrick said with a wink that made Emily shift in her seat. She had no idea why she was winking at her like that and there was no way Emily was going to turn around and see exactly where Cooper was standing. She turned to face the front, focusing on the meeting that was being called to attention.

She sat on pins and needles, clutching her file as council and town staff went through different agenda items, hers, of course, being last on the list. When they finally arrived at her zoning application, chatter erupted, and the mayor had to remind everyone to keep quiet.

Mayor Burton was in his late sixties, she guessed, with gray hair and a firm demeanor—not exactly the warm and fuzzy type.

She'd never had to sit through one of these meetings for her family's company. Usually it was their lawyers and planners who were involved at this level. Surveying the room, she tried not to let the wave of loneliness fog her focus. It didn't matter that she was an outsider, that she didn't have a family, that she didn't even have any old friends here. She was here as a business person.

Her eyes widened as the line at the microphone grew and she had to turn in her seat to see how far it wrapped around the room. Surely all these people couldn't be opposed to her little inn, could they?

"We will begin hearing all the comments on the application to change zoning on 10 Maple Hill," the mayor said.

She held her breath as her neighbor took to the microphone. "Yeah, I don't want a damn inn beside my farm! I drive my tractor up and down that road, and I don't want to be competin' with some fancy sports cars going to that fancy inn."

Emily shut her eyes and sank a little in her chair. This was what she'd feared, that the townspeople wouldn't see the value in it, that they'd just see it as a threat to their way of living. She watched as, one by one, people who lived on her street took to the microphone, stating their similar grievances. Mrs. Merrick patted her knee and gave her a sympathetic smile.

"I think you'd better get up there," Mr. Merrick said, pointing to the line that only had one person left.

Emily shot him a wobbly smile and stood just as the mayor called her forward. The silence in the room wasn't comfortable and she had never felt so much like an outsider as she did this very moment.

She had never really fit in at the family business—as much as she loved it—because she was the boss's daughter. People treated her with courtesy and respect, but she never knew if it was earned or if it was because she was seen as daddy's little girl. She wasn't invited to the impromptu drinks after work or ladies' nights. She had told herself it didn't matter, that she'd be running the company one day and should just concentrate on that and working late. No guy had even dared show any romantic interest in her and, mixed with her brother's constant remarks about her appearance growing up, she'd waffle between thinking no one would ask her out because she was the boss's daughter or because she just wasn't a very attractive person.

She fumbled with the microphone, staring at it a moment, willing all those old memories to recede deep down into the vault she usually kept tightly locked. She hated being weak, she hated feeling exposed, but that was exactly what was happening tonight. She glanced over her shoulder, not really knowing why, not really needing to, and sought the gaze of the one man who'd seemed to capture her attention from day one. Her breath caught in her throat as she made eye contact across the crowd, with Cooper. She couldn't quite read that expression in his blue eyes, but it was his face, that handsome face, that wasn't with its usual disgruntled expression. Instead it had softened, and there was almost a look of...maybe sympathy, maybe pride.

She turned away quickly and opened her notes, rummaging through the folder as she cleared her throat. "Good evening," she began, hating that her voice wobbled. *Focus. You're Emily Birmingham, you used to run a multi-million-dollar company. You gave speeches and presentations hundreds of times.* She took another deep breath and lifted her chin, remembering her father's words to never look down when you faced a rival or an opponent.

"My name is Emily Birmingham and I'm the owner of Ten Maple Lane. This was my grandmother's house and I'm very blessed to now own it and become a member of this wonderful community. Over the years, my grandmother's house has been neglected. It is my goal to see that this great heritage home is meticulously restored to its original beauty. My intention is not to take away from the character of the home or its heritage features but to restore it to its former glory. Any renovations that are being done are those that involve plumbing and electrical and things of that nature to bring the home up to code."

"Well, if you love it so much, why are you making it an inn?" someone yelled out.

"Because it is too big a house for one person alone. I want to share the estate's beauty with everyone. We will be open for breakfast, lunch, and dinner, and anyone is welcome, not just guests of the inn. I will be providing tourism publicity to the community as well as jobs. It will be a boutique inn, so it will be very small, and the increase in traffic will be negligible, especially during the slow season. It is my great hope that my neighbors and community can see that this inn will only enhance the neighborhood and bring vibrancy to the tourism of Maple Hill. Thank you."

She took her seat as quickly as possible, while trying to not appear as though she were running from center stage. As soon as she sat down, Mr. and Mrs. Merrick each gave her a thumbs-up. She turned to the front of the room to listen, holding her breath as the mayor addressed the room.

• • •

Emily stared at the menu as she stood in line at the Maple Hill Dairy Bar near the pier. Rocky Road and Peanut Butter Swirl were the top contenders at the moment. She fished through her purse, taking out cash and hoping to avoid eye contact with anyone who might know her. Tonight wasn't going to be pretty and she didn't think she could fake being okay. Since she'd somehow managed to still not cave on the Diet Coke and Cheetos, clearly ice cream was her only alternative. She took a deep breath, clutching her ten-dollar bill with one hand and lowering her baseball cap so she could barely see if she looked straight.

"Miss, can I help you?"

"Hi, I'd like your largest size of Rocky Road, please."

"Sure," the teenager said, seeming completely disinterested in her, which was perfect. She needed to get her tub of ice cream and then go wander along what she hoped would be a deserted pier so she could sit on a bench and try to figure out how she could be so stupid.

A few minutes later she was holding her half pint of Rocky Road and hating it. Maybe it was good she hated it, because it took the attention off the fact that the entire town, the council, and the mayor decided against her zoning amendment.

She found a bench near the end of the pier and collapsed with an ungraceful *thud*. She sat cross-legged and stared out at the vista in front of her. The choppy, bluish-gray waters of Lake Erie were as miserable as she felt. Normally she knew this was a picturesque spot and the nicest sunset around. But tonight the water was angry, the waves crashing furiously against the rocks. There wasn't even one of the usual fishermen out on the pier with a lawn chair. They were probably all still gossiping about the inn outside the town hall.

She stabbed her plastic spoon into the dense ice cream and wished she were home. But she hadn't felt like going back to the house that she now had no idea what to do with. She shivered and zipped her sweater as far up as it would go. Ice cream probably wasn't the best choice for the rapidly falling temperature, but drinking alcohol on the pier was illegal, so that left her with this as the only option.

Spoonful by spoonful, she took in the sights, the sounds, the smells of the beach in the distance and the pier around her.

Emily stared at the father and daughter walking hand-in-hand on the pier, the little girl smiling up at her dad as she licked her ice cream. Her heart constricted at the adorable sight, and inevitably she remembered her father, the man that she had looked up at like that little girl. Maybe she'd always known, somewhere deep down, that she wouldn't matter as much to him as her brother did. Maybe that's why she'd tried so hard to please her father. Instead of following her dreams, she'd followed her father's dreams, and in the end it had gotten her nowhere. How could she have not seen it coming?

The little girl's peal of laughter floated over as her father scooped her into the air. Emily's throat tightened painfully, and she couldn't even manage to swallow the hunk of ice cream slowly sliding down her throat. Had she ever had that kind of relationship with her father? No, of course not. If she'd wanted to spend time with him, it meant following him to the office. If she wanted to see his smile, it meant getting a perfect score on a test, or later on it meant getting into the top business school in the country. After that, it meant joining his team at the hotel and staying up all night, putting together new marketing directions and stellar presentations.

Had she ever held her father's hand? Now he was gone, and the opportunity was lost. Her ability to ask him why, why he'd shut her out at the end, was ripped away from her.

Too much ice cream pooled in her throat and she coughed, choking.

"Easy there. You wouldn't want to cause a scene, or it'll be on Facebook by morning," Cooper said, a corner of his mouth tilting upward.

As she coughed up an almond, he sat down beside her, much to her mortification. Why did this man only seem to catch her at her worst? She snatched a napkin from the bundle hanging out of her pocket and wiped her face, trying to not cough too loudly as a cluster of almond and marshmallow finally eased its way down her throat. She didn't even like Rocky Road; she'd just been lured by the tempting similarities between her life and the name of the ice cream. Now she was paying for it by being humiliated in front of Cooper for what had to be at least the third time—and she'd only known the man for a month. "I'm fine, thanks," she choked.

He managed to pull off end-of-day exhausted very well. For her, end-of-day exhaustion meant a hot mess. For him it meant a delectable five o'clock shadow, mussed up hair that made her fingers want to continue mussing it up, and clothes that were rumpled, reminding her of how physical his job was. All things she didn't need to be thinking about for many reasons. The most obvious being that he was her new—and her first—BFF's brother. That wouldn't be good because if she and Cooper were a train-wreck, Callie would be caught in the middle. Also, Cooper seemed detached. Like, just when she thought the chemistry between them was mutual, he'd close up and distance himself. Sort of like the way you'd be nice to an animal at the shelter. You'd smile at the animal, maybe give it a pat or two, but then you'd leave, knowing you had no intention of taking the animal home. But since you had a heart, you felt bad for the poor thing.

"So what are you doing out here tonight? Definitely not beach weather," he said, turning his head from the swirling pink horizon to face her.

She forgot about her ice cream, she forgot about the original reason she'd come out here tonight, because when he looked at her he made her wish things could be different, that there was more between them. She turned her attention to the half-eaten tub of ice cream and wondered what to say.

People here didn't hide. You knew who they were, and if you didn't know, someone would be able to tell you their entire life story in under five minutes. Except Cooper, he didn't really talk about himself, and no one had told her anything about him. But really, they didn't hide behind suits and designer clothing, expensive cars, or houses. In some ways it was reassuring and in others it was disconcerting, especially when you didn't really know who you were or what you stood for. "I just wanted some peace and quiet."

"Does this have something to do with the zoning meeting?"

She shrugged. It had to do with everything. Her family. The zoning. The inn. Her life here. The fact that she was more alone than she'd ever been. "Obviously. Everything I've planned is now going up in smoke."

"Not necessarily," he said gently. "You know you can take this up to the next level. Builders do it all the time when they don't like what the county votes."

She twirled her spoon around in the ice cream. "I know, but if I do that, I'm going to make enemies. Do I want that? This town is so small I can't walk around with everyone hating me and talking about me."

He stretched out his legs in front of him. "People will talk no matter what you do, so you might as well do what you believe in. Your speech was pretty damn good. Your vision for that old place is something I think your grandmother would be very proud of."

She was staring at him. "It doesn't matter if I can't even start this inn. All the money, the time, what, for nothing?"

He ran a hand over his jaw, and she waited patiently. She had never been around anyone who could calmly assess a losing situation. He wasn't telling her it was her fault for running ahead with renovations without getting all her zoning approved first. He wasn't telling her she was an idiot for trying to turn an old house into an inn in a small town. "I don't think it's for nothing, and I don't think it's over unless you want it to be over. Those renovations are moving faster than even I believed was possible, because you're able to make on-the-spot decisions and you know what you want. I know that place is going to be amazing."

She held her breath for a moment, relishing his words. She wasn't used to that…to someone believing in her like that. She put down her cup of half-finished ice cream and crossed her arms for warmth. She hardly knew her grandmother. She wasn't doing this for her, though. She was doing it for revenge, for pride, for ego. She wanted to prove that she could run her own line of boutique inns. She wanted to show them all, to show her brother that even though their father never had confidence in her, she had confidence in herself. If she gave up now, she'd be proving him right. "Thank you," she said, turning to Cooper and forcing a smile. "We weren't that close, but I hope she would have been."

"Well, I think your point about the restoration was dead-on. It's one of the oldest homes in Maple Hill, and you're doing the community a service by restoring it and making it a public place for everyone to have access to."

"Right? I'm glad you see it like that."

"A lot of people do." He held her stare for a moment and her mouth went dry. It was as though the wind brought with it a change in mood, and suddenly she was very aware of his proximity, of the heat emanating from his strong body, of the light in his blue eyes. For a second, she hoped that maybe he felt the same way, that maybe she wasn't crazy thinking they had some kind of a connection. But then he stood. "Can I walk you back to your car? I've got to get going. We have an early start tomorrow."

And just like that, the moment was broken. Cooper was back to being gentlemanly and friendly and nothing more. She stood, the weight of all the day's disappointments on her shoulders. That loneliness that had begun to seep inside as she stood at the town hall meeting tonight dug a wider hole in her heart, as did the realization that to Cooper she'd always be just a friend and client.

Chapter Nine

"All right, Buttons, it's time we go up to bed," Emily said to her cat, who ignored her and kept on walking. Cats, she'd realized, didn't listen at all and they didn't even try to fake listening. Emily was okay with that, though; she respected the fact that Buttons was independent and operated on her own schedule. Buttons was affectionate and would often approach her during the day to be picked up and snuggled, and just about when Emily got her hopes up she could hold onto her furry friend forever, Buttons would jump off and leave her for parts unknown. Everyone in the house knew not to let Buttons outside, and so far her cat had managed to stay out of trouble because Emily had been diligent in keeping her confined to different areas of the home.

It was the end of a long day and she walked around the large house, turning off lights and double-checking the doors were locked. Though so many people said they didn't even bother locking their doors in Maple Hill, there was no way Emily would ever go to bed without making sure the house was secure. There were some city habits she had no intention of breaking. It was way earlier than she normally went to bed, but she was so exhausted—or maybe defeated—from the town hall loss two nights ago that she was ready to turn in.

She walked up the stairs slowly, spotting Buttons heading down the basement staircase. She quickly showered in her newly finished en suite, and as usual, she admired the marble herringbone tile in the large shower. Every day this week she was trying to focus on the positive things in her life and not on the growing suspicion that she had made one of the biggest mistakes of her career. She towel-dried her hair and quickly dressed, anxious to get to bed because she was tired and the crew would arrive early tomorrow.

A creepy meow that almost sounded like a loud moan echoed through the empty house, and she ran out into the hallway and peered over the banister. "Buttons, you okay?" she called out.

Of course, Buttons didn't answer, and Emily's heart started hammering. But the house was gigantic, and from the upstairs it wasn't always possible to hear if someone was entering from the back door. She gingerly made her way down the stairs, searching for signs of trouble. Buttons was nowhere to be seen. When she reached the kitchen a shiver stole through her body and her gaze scanned the room.

Her adorable, affectionate, fluffy cat came tearing through the kitchen with something black with a long tail hanging out of her mouth. A mouse.

Emily screamed, and the horrifying little creature escaped from Buttons's mouth and scurried across the kitchen. Emily kept screaming, not caring that her reaction was way over the top, and climbed onto the island as though her life depended on it. "Buttons!" she yelled, her voice a shriek and narrow whisper all at the same time.

Buttons didn't pay her any attention. She was all stealth and on a mission to get the mouse. Emily watched in horror as her previously adorable cat—now bloodthirsty killing machine—tore through the kitchen again in hot pursuit of the mouse. While Buttons was doing exactly what a cat was supposed to do, exactly what she had hoped her cat would do, Emily was not prepared to witness this.

She needed to leave the scene. Ignorance would be bliss. She spotted the leftover paper cups from the Sleepless Goat when Callie had surprised them all with coffee today, and a bag of Cheetos on the counter and knew what needed to happen. Tonight was no time to deal with her addictions. Tonight was about survival. Her heart hammered painfully in her chest and she scanned the room for Buttons or the mouse, but thankfully they were nowhere to be seen. This was Emily's only chance to leave. It was now or never. She counted to ten and then jumped off the island, paper cup in hand, running, not even slowing down. With one hand she snagged a bottle of wine from the counter like a baton in an Olympic race, and with the other she snatched the Cheetos, then kept running down the hall, up the stairs, and into her bedroom, shutting the door behind her.

Mice.

She couldn't deal with mice. Didn't Cooper say they'd dealt with rodents? She tightly squeezed her eyes shut and clutched the bottle of wine to her chest. Logically, she knew mice were harmless, but they were nasty and they had no business in her home.

She heard that horrible moaning sound from Buttons and held her breath. What was happening down there? Was Buttons murdering the mouse? She poured a glass of wine and chugged it like a university student at a keg party with their peers chanting *chug, chug, chug.*

She leaned her head against the back of the door again and closed her eyes as the sound of Buttons skidding into the wall, jumping, and meowing echoed around the house likes sounds from a horror movie.

She poured another glass of wine as her phone rang. Who would be calling her at this time of night? Sadly it wasn't even ten o'clock, she realized as she glanced at the phone. It was Cooper. She took a deep breath and answered, "Hello?"

"Hey, it's Cooper. Can you check something down in the basement?"

She took a deep breath and tried to sound normal. What did she think the man would be calling for? To ask her out? To spend the night on the phone with her, having a heart to heart discussion? Just because he'd sat on the pier with her two nights ago didn't mean he had feelings for her. The next morning it had been business as usual. "Excuse me? Why the basement?"

"I need you to make sure the boiler is off."

She barely even knew what the boiler looked like. "I can't do that."

"Sure you can. Leave me on the line and I'll tell you exactly what to do. That thing hasn't been inspected yet and I just found out one of the guys turned it on earlier today. If it wasn't shut off again it's a fire hazard, Emily."

A fire at this point wasn't a bad idea. Really, she couldn't turn it into an inn, and it was now infested with rodents. She could collect her insurance check and walk away from all of this. Let it burn. "I avoid the basement at all costs. Most days I live here pretending this house doesn't even have a basement. It's like a dungeon."

She wasn't sure if his muffled response was a laugh or a curse. "Go down to the basement, please, so that I'm not held liable for damages."

Well, if that wasn't an honest declaration of a man's feelings or lack of feelings then what was? She gasped and shivered as a crash sounded from downstairs. "Hold on," she managed to choke. She put the phone down and poured another glass of wine.

"All right, where are you?" he said when she picked up the phone again.

"Uh, in my room, drinking wine and about to open a bag of Cheetos."

"Why did you put the phone down? I thought you were walking downstairs?"

"Nope. I was pouring more wine."

"Okay, I'm missing something. You can have wine after you go to the basement."

"Nope, I'll need more wine before I can be convinced to go to the basement."

"Emily." His voice sounded strangled, like he was trying to curb his frustration.

"I am unable to go downstairs at this time."

"Why not?"

"There is a situation happening downstairs that I'm not capable of dealing with."

There was a long sigh. "Well, you're going to have to force yourself."

"I'm not doing anything. I'm actually going to stay in my room tonight on an elevated surface and finish this bottle of wine and pray for daylight." She was slightly aware that the wine may have started having an effect, because the urge to laugh and cry simultaneously at the situation was becoming impossible to fight.

"I don't know what's going on, but it doesn't sound too good. Do you need me to come over there?" he said, the frustration leaving his voice. Now he almost sounded…sweet. Maybe tender. Possibly worried. Kind of like the night he taught her how to play ball, or at the pier. She squeezed her eyes shut and finished her glass of wine.

"I don't need anyone," she whispered, wishing so desperately that it was true. She needed people. She needed her father. She needed a normal brother. She needed a mother who had her back and understood her. She needed real friends. She needed a family. A real family. And maybe she needed a man exactly like Cooper. Or maybe she needed Cooper.

"I'm coming over," he said before ending the call.

The giant crash downstairs made her jump and she stared at the half-empty bottle of wine, telling herself to wait before she drank more. Her tolerance was low because she rarely drank and any more of it might not be wise.

She should really open the door and assess the situation, but the thought of that creature, in Buttons's mouth and then scurrying around, made her pause. She would never be able to think of Buttons the same way again. But Cooper was on his way over, and if she didn't want to humiliate herself for the five thousandth time since she'd met him, she should force herself to go downstairs like a sane person.

She opened the door carefully, hoping like hell she wasn't going to collide with her cat or a mouse. Seeing nothing, she took a wobbly step forward, slowly walking to the stairs. When she reached the top step she gasped and covered her mouth, but not before the hideous sight took root in her mind. She would never be able to wash the image from her eyes—it was a bloody massacre. Half a dozen black mice littered her hallway; heads and tails were in different areas.

She closed her eyes and clutched the railing, swaying slightly from the panic, from the wine, from the exhaustion, from the fear. Some days felt like too much. This week was too much. Her brother, and the town hall meeting in which basically everyone opposed her plan, making it abundantly clear she didn't fit in this small town. She wasn't one of them, she didn't see things the way they did. She didn't belong in the city and she didn't belong here, either.

She'd always been able to weather the storm, bear the

insults, and keep going. She'd always held out hope that she'd find her place in the world, that she'd find her people, she'd find her man, she'd have a family, children whom she'd love and protect. But right now, more than anything, she wanted someone to lean on, someone to protect her, to tell her it was all going to be okay. Right now, she didn't want to do any of this alone. What had she been thinking?

She clutched the handrail tightly at the sound of knocking on the front door. It was straight ahead. All she had to do was walk straight down the stairs and open the door. But anxiety gripped her without warning and held her still. She took a deep breath and tried to move but couldn't.

What was the point of drinking wine if it didn't make you brave?

She was going to make a further fool of herself in front of Cooper. First the baseball situation, then the town hall, the ice cream, now this. What kind of adult couldn't deal with mice? Or maybe it wasn't the mice. Maybe it was everything.

She wanted to sit down, she wanted to crawl into bed and just wake up a new person.

"Emily, are you in there? I'm getting kind of worried, open the door!"

She took a deep breath and tried not to cry like a baby as she descended the stairs. She shielded the corner of her eyes with her hand and then ran down the stairs and into the door before whipping it open. Cooper stood there frowning. He had the best frown she'd ever seen.

"What the hell is going on?"

• • •

Cooper walked into Emily's house, knowing immediately that something was wrong. Her face was white and had a few red blotches and she wasn't even pretending to have it all together. She was like a different person. A very hot, very sexy different person, which presented another problem entirely. She was wearing some flimsy camisole top with spaghetti straps and a lacy neckline that showed way too much creamy cleavage for him to not notice, or for him to keep lying to himself and pretending that he wasn't insanely attracted to this woman. But right now the glimmer in her eyes had nothing to do with attraction. She looked slightly crazed and extremely panicked. "It's…Buttons."

She clutched his forearms, and her bare hands on him sent a searing jolt of desire through him. They never touched. Well, rarely. Especially after the baseball lesson day when he'd figured out just how attracted to her he was. After that, he went out of his way to make sure he never touched her. Her hands were soft, even though her nails were digging into his skin. He forced himself to remember they were talking about her cat.

"What happened to Buttons?" he asked, his voice sounding choked. He tried to remind himself he was here because something was wrong, even though all he wanted to do was kiss her.

"She's a serial killer."

"What?"

She squeezed her eyes shut and jacked a thumb over her shoulder.

He glanced that way. Damn. That cat was impressive. At least a half dozen mice—though, it was hard to get an exact body count since there were no fully intact bodies—were littered down the grand hallway. Buttons had been such a lazy-looking thing, he hadn't had high hopes, but this was the work of a very fine predator. Emily made a gagging noise as she quickly peeked over her shoulder. That's when it registered. Somehow the scattered mouse bodies, heads, and tails must have been disturbing to her. "Buttons did this?"

"No, I did. I ripped their heads off with my bare hands."

He laughed out loud. She was pretty funny. She also hadn't removed her hands from his arms, and he liked that. Buttons came sauntering toward them, purring.

"Good job, Buttons," he said as she entered the vestibule, not even a piece of fur out of place.

"I don't even know who you are anymore, Buttons. You should be ashamed of yourself," Emily said.

He laughed again, and she glared at him. "This is what we wanted her to do, remember?" he said. "Come on, let's deal with this bloodbath."

Her eyes widened and she clutched his forearms tighter. He was dying a slow death. Her mouth was slightly open, and her lips were full and so damn soft-looking that he had to focus on something else. He'd been in denial, thinking he could do this, that he could get through this reno and then leave her, but he knew it wasn't going to be that easy. He knew he wasn't going to just be able to walk away from Emily. Her hands were soft and smooth on his skin, it was dark and late, and he wanted nothing more than to spend the night with her, not cleaning up mouse carcasses, but in bed.

The last woman he'd been in bed with was his wife, five years ago.

While he'd missed sex, while he knew he couldn't go the rest of his life without it, there had never been one woman who'd made him want it again, on a personal level. Emily made him want all those things again. He liked talking to her, hearing her voice, hearing her thoughts. He loved that she was smart and strong and brave, but he was intrigued by the vulnerability he caught glimpses of every now and then.

That night of the council meeting, he'd hated that the town had turned against her. He'd hated that even though she presented valid and beneficial ideas, no one was open to change. And that's when the irony of it all had hit him—

he couldn't handle change well, either. The woman in front of him was evidence of that. He'd followed her down to the pier because he hated thinking of her being alone and disappointed. When he saw her sitting there staring off into the distance, her shoulders slouched, completely defeated, he'd wanted to pull her into his arms. He'd wanted her to know she had his shoulder whenever she needed it. Instead, he'd clung to the status quo like a lifeboat.

"I *can't*. I can't deal with the murdered bodies and random pieces of rodent," Emily hissed, her statement making him remember why he was actually here.

His eyes narrowed on her face and noticed how pale she was, not at all like she was joking. "All right. I'll deal with it. First I need to check on that boiler," he said, trying to sidestep her.

She pulled on his shirt, stopping him. "Wait."

He forced a tight smile because he really needed to put some distance between them. His attraction to her was getting difficult to keep under control. "Yes?"

"I can't let you help me."

Her eyes were slightly glossy and her cheeks were flushed. "How much have you had to drink?" he asked, really hoping that was the problem.

She winced and looked away. "A half bottle of wine, but that has nothing to do with my current situation."

"Okay, I thought I was here to help you solve your crisis of the day."

Clearly, that was not the thing to say, because she glared at him and perched her hands on her hips. Lord help him, he was a weak man, because he used that as an opportunity to glance at her cleavage.

If he had a sweater on he'd have taken it off and draped it across her.

"I don't have a daily crisis, and even if I had, you haven't been called in to deal with all my catastrophes. You called me, remember? About some boiler issue that you failed to resolve before the end of your work day? Yeah. I've been dealing with my own drama all on my own. Fine, maybe you have dealt with house drama, but you're getting paid for that. This…this is why I can't accept your help tonight. This idea that you're solving my problems…that I need a *man* to solve my problems for me."

Oh, hell. This was going sideways fast. He didn't even know how to counteract this kind of logic. "I'm not a man solving your problems. Don't even try to make this a guy-girl thing. I'm a person who's dealing with a rodent situation because you're afraid of mice."

She held up a hand. "I'm not afraid."

He folded his arms across his chest. "Then turn around and let's go get a shovel and a garbage bag. You can either hold the bag or scoop the body parts."

She made a gagging sound and clutched his arm. He tried hard not to laugh. "Fine," she croaked, then turned in the direction of the mice again and shielded her eyes.

"Emily?"

She blinked furiously. "I can't be weak. I've been strong for so long. I can't let the mice break me."

It dawned on him, perhaps belatedly, that this wasn't about mice. This really was about the fact that he was a man. She really saw him helping her with the mice as a sign that he might have some kind of upper hand or as a symbol of the fact that she couldn't cut it.

"Hey," he said, crouching slightly and holding her bare arms, her soft skin making it very clear to him that they were very different, in the best possible ways, in ways he would only ever intend on relishing, not exploiting. He had never viewed femininity as inferior, just different. Just like he couldn't deal with half the shit women had to. "If you think that needing me to help you with mice means I'm proving I'm the superior sex then you don't know me at all. I'm your friend. I knew something was bothering you, so I came over. Yeah, I called about the boiler, but the truth is that you sounded upset. Now I'm helping you. That's it. There's no score sheet. There's no—" He paused and racked his brain for a synonym of *tit for tat*, because his mind went straight to the gutter and he couldn't say it. "There's no…way I'd lord this over you. If I were a woman, would you bat an eye at asking me for help right now?"

She shook her head slowly. "I just…wanted to do all this on my own."

"Why? Why the hell would you want to do this on your own? What do you have to prove to anyone?"

She opened her mouth like she was going to tell him, and it became very clear that she did have something to prove to someone. The more he got to know Emily, the more he realized just how many layers she had. She might drive an expensive car, wear designer clothes, and come from money, but there was no denying she was made of steel. And there was no denying he wanted to know more. Damn.

She gave a nod of defeat and swept an arm in the direction of the mice. "All right. Go. Deal with Miceageddon. You win."

"Let's be clear about something," he said as he walked by her and into the mice-ridden hallway. "Cleaning up dead mice isn't exactly what I call winning."

That earned him a half laugh. "How about while you do that, I get you a drink? I might have to walk outside to get to the kitchen, though."

"I can get my own beer once I'm done with this. I'm just going to check out the boiler in the basement first. I'll meet you in the family room."

"Okay. Can you also pull out my steam cleaner so I can

disinfect the floors when you're done?"

"Sure."

"I'll need to find rubber boots, maybe a hazmat suit or something. Mice carry the hantavirus."

He was halfway down the old wooden stairs to the basement when he laughed at her antics. As he reached for a shovel, garbage bags, and the steam cleaner, he realized that being at Emily's place, cleaning up dead mice, was the most fun he'd had in a long time.

An hour later, he watched Emily wash her hands and scrub them down like she was a doctor heading into surgery. The mouse situation had been dealt with, and they were standing in the laundry room, using the only functioning sink on the main floor. He tried to hide his disappointment as Emily took an oversize hoodie from the dryer and wrapped herself in it. He had turned into a teenage boy.

"So do you think that's it?" she said. "It's over?"

He leaned against the counter. "I'm sure Buttons is pretty tired out. I'll call the wildlife guys again and maybe have a few more traps set in the basement."

She rolled her eyes. "Isn't that what they were supposed to do in the first place?"

"You're right."

"Oh, I promised you a beer," she said, walking past him.

He reached out and caught her wrist, grasping it gently. She turned to him, her face becoming pink. He had no idea why he'd just done that. He knew why he wanted to; he just didn't know why he'd given in. This could go either way. He could drop her wrist, pretend like nothing happened, and walk out of there. Or he could be the man he used to be, the one who didn't hide from life, from emotion, from love.

She stared at him expectantly, like there had to be a reason he'd reached out and touched her. He saw all those moments since he'd met her flash before him, reminding him that he couldn't keep hiding. He saw her that first day at the Sleepless Goat, and he remembered that feeling in his gut, the one that told him there was something special about this woman. He saw all her expressions of wonder as they walked through the house, he saw her bravado the night she and his sister decided to take on Moose. He saw her embarrassment when he taught her how to throw a ball, the day she'd struck out at the game, her vulnerability and strength at the town hall, and then her dejection on the pier later. He saw all of it and knew it wasn't enough.

He knew he wanted more. He wanted to step back into the land of the living. He wanted back in on life. He had tried to tell himself it was just because she was sweet and beautiful, but he knew deep down it was more.

"I don't need a beer. I'll just head home."

Her face fell, and he knew that wasn't the answer she wanted. He hadn't moved away, and he hadn't dropped her wrist. It was as if, now that he'd touched her, he couldn't make himself go back to that place without her. "Do you have plans next Saturday night?"

Her mouth dropped open. "Uh, um. Besides hiding from mice in my room? No."

He smiled—despite these crazy life revelations, she made him smile. "Maybe I can give you a break from the mice. There's a steakhouse restaurant in a town not too far from here. It overlooks a gorge. I think you'd like it."

He didn't dwell on the fact that it was the first time he'd asked a woman on a date in over a decade, or what that meant. But he knew he couldn't keep living on the sidelines, not now that Emily had come into his life. The tension between them grew, more intense than it had ever been, because he was finally doing something about it. But what he really wanted to do was tug her over to him, to hold her body against his, and to bury his hands in her hair and kiss her until she couldn't stand on her own.

It took him a minute to realize she didn't exactly look… thrilled. She actually took a step back, and her neck was turning red. "I don't think that would be a good idea. I mean it would be bad, really. Awful, most likely. You and me? Nope." She even shook her head at the end, to add more insult to injury.

He straightened his shoulders. "Why?"

She waved a hand in his direction. "You work for me. How awful will it be if we're a disaster couple? Then you'll get all offended and walk off the job—"

"I'm not like that. Also, I'll try not to be offended that you've already decided you'll be writing me off."

She gave him a sheepish smile. "Fine. Then we need ground rules. Some kind of agreement. A contract."

He stilled. "A contract?"

She crossed her arms. "Yes."

He rolled his shoulders, determined not to get thrown off track by her odd request. There was no denying his feelings for her anymore. How bad could this contract be? "Fine, I'm good with contracts."

Her mouth dropped open. "Oh."

He grinned and pulled out the notepad and small pencil he always kept in the back pocket of his jeans. He had no idea who the hell he was anymore, but apparently he was the guy about to sign a contract with a woman for a date. Not just any woman. Emily, the only woman in five years to interest him in a relationship. "All right, go."

She cleared her throat. "Okay, fine. No getting your family involved. No details, nothing."

"Hell no, we don't want them involved. Fine, done." he said, jotting it down happily. This was easy. He could do this. His family was already over-involved. "But that includes Callie."

She sucked in a breath. "But she's my best friend."

"As much as it pains me to admit this, Austin and Brody are my best friends. I'm not telling them anything."

She leaned against the counter. "Fine. I'll just tell Callie we're going out and nothing more."

"That's fair. Okay, what else?"

She pointed to the paper. "No commenting on what I order for dinner."

He glanced up, unable to resist teasing her. "Like Cheetos?"

Her eyes narrowed. "No taking me to places that offer Cheetos as an entrée."

He laughed as he added that. "Fair enough."

"No sharing of childhood stories."

Perfect. Childhood stories were too personal. "Absolutely. I second that."

"No downplaying my successes to make you feel like more of a man."

He stilled momentarily then wrote it down, making a mental note to go over all this stuff later at home, by himself, with a beer in hand. He should have known it wasn't going to be simple. "Fine."

She bit her lower lip and then pointed to the list again. "You have to teach me how to play baseball for real. Catching, throwing, hitting, and if I'm really awesome, then pitching."

"Done," he said, his voice sounding gruff from the unexpected emotion in his throat. What the hell was happening to him?

She exhaled. "I'll take you to any Jays game of your choice in Toronto. I choose the seats."

"Hell, yes."

Her eyes sparkled, and she smiled at him as though she'd won the lottery. "We eat hot dogs and drink beer."

"Obviously."

"No asking personal stuff. Especially pertaining to Darth."

Dammit. He wanted to know about him. He held her stare, and hell if he was not going to give in. "Fine. No Darth and no personal dating history."

A strange look passed across her eyes. "Fine. Um, I'll add one more thing—if I have rodent issues, you have to deal with them, since you're so talented."

She smiled triumphantly, and he fought the urge to pull her to him and kiss her. He also fought the urge to question out loud how he was getting into this mess. But she kept smiling at him, and he knew he wasn't going to say no. He just might not make it that obvious. "So, if we only ever go out once, I'm stuck dealing with your rodent issues for a lifetime?"

She drummed her fingers against the countertop. "It's do-or-die time, Cooper. I've got to get to bed."

Bed. That was exactly where he wanted to be—but with Emily. He cleared his throat and lifted the pen, writing the last condition on this crazy-ass contract. "Done."

She peered at the list. "Wonderful. It looks like you got everything. I'll walk you out," she said, handing it back to him.

He walked beside Emily, through the corridor that just over an hour ago had been filled with mouse guts, and into the vestibule where she'd tried to refuse his help because he was a guy, and he wondered what the hell he was getting into. He wasn't a complicated person. Emily was…all sorts of complicated. She opened the door and turned to him, those gorgeous green eyes holding onto him, tugging at the heart he'd given up on, making him believe that this was all worth it, that she was all worth it. He cleared his throat. "Okay. So, I'll see you tomorrow."

"Yup. Just hold on a second," she said, and pulled her phone out of her pocket. "Can I see the contract again?"

"You mean the notepaper?" he asked, teasing her but taking it out again.

She rolled her eyes. "Would you mind signing the bottom?"

He laughed.

She didn't smile. "It's a *contract.* Without a signature it's just a *list.*"

Sighing deeply, he obliged.

He watched in silence as she took a picture of the "contract."

She smiled up at him, a smile that reminded him how beautiful she was, and how much he wanted her. It was the same smile that had roped him in that first day at the Sleepless Goat, the one that had the power to make him sign a contract in which he was now responsible for Emily's pest-control issues for life.

Chapter Ten

I, Cooper Merrick agree to help Emily Birmingham with rodent removal services for the rest of our lives.

Emily stared at that line again on the contract, just as she had every night since they wrote it. That whole mice catastrophe had changed her life. She stared at her reflection in the bathroom mirror and decided against blow-drying her hair because she was too tired. She was wearing her favorite pink-and-white striped pajamas and planned on watching a movie, fantasizing about her date with Cooper tomorrow night. She still couldn't believe it was happening. The week had been filled with this nervous tension between them, almost like neither of them knew how to act around each other—or in front of his brothers. She hadn't seen Callie this week, but they'd exchanged a series of texts, and Emily had told her about their date.

She had reread the contract every night since they wrote it. She believed the contract was for the best, that she'd be able to avoid any future heartache if she got him to agree to those minor points. Sure she'd felt silly at times, but it was the only way to protect herself. She would never let a man hurt her again. The new Emily was strong and decisive and self-confident. The contract solidified that.

The doorbell rang just as she was about to flop onto her bed. She peeked out the upstairs hall window and was relieved to see Callie's jeep parked outside. She ran down the stairs and opened the door. Callie was standing there in yoga pants, holding a bottle of wine in one hand and a bag of organic something in the other.

"Have I ever told you that you're the best friend I've ever had?" Emily blurted out.

Callie laughed and walked inside. "Because I bring a new replacement for Cheetos? I promise they taste way better, and despite the high fat and calorie content, they should bring no guilt because technically you're not going back on your no-Cheetos rule. Also, organic wine from one of the local wineries."

"Wow, yes, because all of the above," Emily said with a laugh. Callie marched into the room she was now calling the TV room and sank into the one couch. Furniture had started arriving this week, and the house was actually beginning to turn into the country inn she'd hoped for. Callie pulled two paper cups out of her purse and avoided eye contact.

"Uh-oh. Are you breaking up with me?" she half joked as she sat down across from Callie, sensing her friend's sudden uneasiness.

Callie handed her a glass of wine and winced. "No, but you might break up with me. I'm sorry I've been so busy. I missed your night at town hall, and I had no idea my brother was actually going to ask you out. I mean, I hoped he was, but I had no idea he'd actually do it."

"What do you mean?"

Callie rolled her eyes. "We all knew he had feelings for you. It was obvious to all of us—except him."

She toyed with a damp strand of hair, trying to appear casual. "Really?"

"Uh, yeah. You didn't notice?"

She tilted her head. "Well, sometimes I'd think, maybe… but then it was like he was going out of his way to avoid me."

Callie took a sip of wine, her blue eyes turning serious. "Yeah, that sounds like Cooper. He hasn't even told anyone. I only know because *you* texted me."

"Is this going to be awkward? Should I not have told you?" She loved having a female friend to confide in. Sitting on this couch with Callie and talking about life was what she'd always wanted, but maybe the fact that Cooper was her brother was going to make things weird between them.

Callie leaned forward and clutched her forearm dramatically. "Uh, of course you should have told me. You can spare me the details that involve…my brother's *skills*. But other than that, tell me everything. I won't tell him a thing. Unless he's being idiotic, then I'll tell him."

Emily laughed and tried not to get too hung up on the mention of Cooper's *skills*. She had no skills, so she was pretty sure his skills would be better than hers. Something about him told her he had very advanced skills. But she didn't want to think about that too much because that would mean another one of her confessions in which she admits to never having done something. What was the point of worrying about any of that anyway? What if their date was horrible? What if he turned out to be a secret jerk? She'd deal with that if it came up. Somehow. "Okay, fair enough."

"So, um, there's something I think you should know. It's not that we've all been hiding it on purpose, but I'm acting as a friend here, not as Cooper's little sister. He might hate me for telling you, but I don't want you being blindsided."

Her stomach dropped. "Why? What is it?"

Callie's eyes widened above the rim of her paper cup as

she gulped some wine. Emily couldn't even drink because she was dying of anticipation. She braced herself for the worst but still tried to remain rational. Maybe he'd gone to jail for something. Or maybe he'd been involved in some kind of torrid affair…

"First, you need to know that I'm thrilled you're going out with Coop…it's just that you don't know everything. At first, I was just his sister and we were sort of friends. But now…now we're like, so close, and as your BFF in Maple Hill I need to tell you the whole truth about Cooper, because I'm afraid he's going to blow it tomorrow night and I don't want either of you hurt."

Now she was drinking the wine. "You're freaking me out. What do you mean the whole truth about Cooper? This sounds like some kind of bad made-for-television movie."

Callie shut her eyes for a second, all humor disappearing from her pretty face. Emily's heart pounded as she tried to be patient. "I wish. He's a good guy, Emily," she whispered, her voice filled with emotion.

Emily nodded slowly. "I…know. I mean, I think so."

Callie nodded rapidly, her eyes wide. "He is. Okay, I'm butchering this and you're probably thinking he's some axe murderer or something. He's not, obviously. He's the best. It's just that Cooper…he was married before. I mean, he hasn't been married for the past five years, but he was married."

Her mouth dropped open. He was in his early thirties, she'd guessed. It wouldn't be unheard of that he'd been married before. It wasn't exactly the shocking secret she was expecting. He didn't exactly seem like the marrying type, not that she really even knew what type that was, but still. She took a sip of wine and drew her legs up, sensing there had to be more. "Okay…"

"He's… She died. Cooper's wife, Catherine, died."

She gasped. The image of Cooper, that expression she

sometimes saw, the one where it almost seemed like he was somewhere else, somewhere far away, floated across her mind. She had assumed at first that he wasn't interested in her, or just standoffish. But then sometimes he'd do things for her...he'd act a certain way that led her to believe he had feelings for her.

But it wasn't until the night of the mouse catastrophe, standing in the laundry room, that she realized she hadn't been imagining it. When he'd reached for her, the expression in his eyes had made her want to jump into his arms. She had read the desire, but it was more. It was like a longing—for her. He'd stolen her breath away, and she had tossed and turned all night, thinking of him, of laughing with him as they wrote up that contract. Now she felt stupid because... she hadn't expected this. She hadn't even imagined he might be a widower. Her heart ached for him. And for Callie, too. For the whole family that his wife had been part of. "I'm so sorry," she softly, her chest aching.

Callie nodded and leaned across to give her a hug. "I know. I... It's not my story to tell, so I won't say any details, but I wanted you to know where he's coming from. I see the way he looks at you, the way he talks about you without even realizing he's talking about you. The little things he does, like at the baseball game."

"He struck out on purpose," she whispered. She hadn't wanted to think he'd done that for her, or what it could mean, so she'd just brushed it off. Then he'd been business as usual on the following Monday.

Callie scrunched up her nose and nodded. "He never strikes out. But he did. For you... Hun, he hasn't been out with anyone in five years."

Emily's eyes widened. None of this was what she'd expected; it wasn't anything she could ever even be prepared for. She remembered her contract and groaned, putting her wine down so she could place her hands over her face. What an idiot she was. A contract, stipulating mouse removals and hot dogs and…all for a date. The man had lost his wife, had buried his wife, and she, like an immature, self-centered idiot, had handed him a list of terms and conditions. Like life had terms and conditions or guarantees. What had he thought of her? He must have regretted asking her out at that point, or certainly once he read over the contract again later. He was just too polite to cancel on her.

He hadn't been out with anyone in five years, and he'd asked her, the woman incapable of dealing with mice.

"Say something," Callie whispered.

She forced her gaze to her friend. "I don't even know what to say. I want to ask you so many things, but I want to respect his privacy and your loyalty to him. I guess he'll tell me when he's ready. I mean…if there's a second date. Or anything. Is this weird that he's your brother? I have a thousand things to say right now, and I don't even know if it's okay anymore."

"I'm so happy he's going out with you. I know you would never hurt him. He's been through so much, and the Cooper I grew up with…he's nothing like the man you know. He was… funny. Like, all the time. He was carefree and a prankster and everyone loved him… Wow, I'm talking too much," she said, wiping her eyes with her sweater sleeve.

Emily was having a hard time breathing normally. She clung to every word, every tidbit of information about him. None of this… She couldn't even picture him like Callie was describing him, which made her ache for him even more. "Thanks for telling me," she managed to say.

Callie poured herself more wine. "You can't let on that you know. I mean, if he even *thinks* I said anything, he'll kill me. Like this, right now?" She gestured toward Emily's face. "You can't look like that tomorrow night when you open the door. You have sympathy stamped all over you. He'll take one look at you and know."

Emily nodded. "Okay. Then maybe we shouldn't talk about this anymore."

"Okay. What are you going to wear? That's normal conversation."

"I made him write up a contract," she blurted out, unable to keep it to herself, desperate for her friend to tell her it was still okay.

Callie sprayed wine from her mouth. "What?"

Emily held up her cup and signaled for a refill. Callie obliged and asked, "What kind of contract?"

She cringed, having a hard time making eye contact. "A well-intentioned but horribly lame kind that I'm regretting immensely and am so humiliated by right now."

"Was it like a kind that a person has to sign?" Callie choked out.

Emily rolled her lips inward and nodded.

"Did, um..." Callie coughed. "Did Coop sign this document?"

"He did. He wrote while I dictated."

"*My* brother, Cooper, did this?"

She nodded again, not able to elaborate due to the terms of their contract. Callie patted her knee. "It's okay. Really. I'm sure it's fine. The bright side is, if you actually got Cooper to sign something like that, it must mean he's really interested. Now, tell me, where's he taking you?"

"He mentioned some place in some small town that has a view of a gorge or something..." Her voice trailed off as Callie inhaled sharply.

"That's the Anson Mill. It's stunning. It's... Okay, I'm not going to tell you any more. It's just really...that's really sweet. Major points for Coop," she said, clearly proud of her brother's choice.

"So what should I wear to a place like that?"

"It's not dressy-dressy. Like, some people might dress up, but you don't have to. It's not like a suit-and-tie kind of place. Cooper would never pick a place he'd need to wear a tie to," she said with a short laugh.

"Okay. So I could wear a casual dress and heels?"

"Definitely." She let out a squeal. "I don't know which one of you I'm more excited for."

She almost laughed, but the revelation that Cooper had been married before...and that he'd experienced a loss like that...left her unsettled, sad for him. It also made her regret ever making a contract with him.

• • •

Cooper stretched out on the couch in his living room, opened his beer, and stared at the folded "contract" on his lap. He didn't know what the hell he'd gotten himself into.

Couldn't he just take a woman out on a date anymore? He'd basically signed his life away in exchange for dinner. He never would have thought Emily would make them write up a contract before going out. There were things in there that set off alarm bells, but she'd cleverly even prevented him from asking about Darth.

He shut his eyes and leaned his head back on the sofa, and his thoughts went to where they'd often been going the past month...to Emily. He had no idea what was happening to him—well, no, he did know. What he didn't know was why. Why now? After five years of not being remotely interested in anyone, how did this complete stranger enter his life and fill him with a longing he couldn't ignore?

He sighed loudly and leaned forward, snatching the contract, and reread it, a mix of anger and sadness washing over him again. He'd first assumed her whole contract thing had to do with money or something, because he knew she came from wealth. What kind of jerk had she dated in the past that she needed to make some kind of contract to protect herself?

He tossed the paper onto the coffee table and put his feet up on the ottoman, thinking back to their conversations, their time together, namely the baseball thing. He could still see the embarrassment on her face when they'd practiced. Every move she made, every throw, every attempted catch had looked as though she was bracing herself for mockery.

And then the whole mousecapade thing, like she had serious issues asking him for help. Again, like she assumed he was going to interpret that as weakness.

Growing up, he and his brothers had been taught to look out for the women in their lives—not because they were inferior or incapable, but because they were incredibly important people and the world could be a really shitty place filled with really shitty people. But there was never any doubt their mother was an equal to their father. While his parents had taken on traditional male and female gender roles in the house, they both viewed what the other did with admiration. They would always say it was the sum of their mutually important jobs that made the household run. His dad always treated his mom with respect and adoration. He and his brothers had done the same. When Callie had come along—the *oops* baby—his parents' long-forgotten dream of having a girl had come to fruition, and she'd been a cherished addition to their family.

Their father had lectured that they couldn't roughhouse with a girl the same way they did with one another as brothers. Unfortunately, once Callie had figured that rule out, she'd used it to her advantage. She'd been younger than them, though, and it had been fun to watch her turn into a spunky, independent young woman. They'd been overprotective, maybe to a fault, but they'd always treated her with respect, too.

He glanced at his wedding picture on the fireplace mantel and smiled, thinking of Catherine. They'd had a relationship similar to his parents', except that Catherine had a career as a teacher and loved working outside the home. She and Callie had been very close… Catherine had been close to his entire family, and both their families had gotten along well.

He frowned, realizing he didn't know that much about Emily's family. He would ask her on their date.

He swore when he heard pounding on his front door. One of his brothers. They were the only people that didn't use the bell and the only people who came by uninvited. If his door hadn't been locked, they would have walked right in. He'd gotten in the habit of locking it just to have some warning before they infiltrated his home.

He stood, stretched, and then slowly made his way to the entrance, his pace completely contrasting the urgency of the knock. He opened the front door, and Austin barrelled in. "Took you long enough. I have other places to be, Coop."

"Well, you should've gone directly," he said, taking a sip of his beer casually.

He went back to the couch while Austin headed to the kitchen in search of a drink. Moments later, his brother sat in the chair across from him, propping his feet up on the ottoman and sipping a beer. "So, what are you doing?"

Cooper frowned at him. "Why are you here?"

"Because I may have heard something about you going on a date, and I happened to see your truck in the driveway, so I thought I'd see if it was actually true."

Dread pooled in his stomach. "Who told you?"

"I know things. I also know that you were at Emily's house last Saturday night by yourself."

He was going to play this cool and not get lured in. "What, are you stalking me?"

"No."

He took another drink and propped his feet up on the coffee table, hoping his brother wouldn't notice Emily's contract. "I already told you, she had a mouse problem."

"So she called you?"

"No, I actually called her, warning her to turn off the boiler."

"Huh."

"What?"

"That boiler was serviced properly."

Cooper shifted in his seat. His brothers were really irritating. "Well, I was double-checking. I wouldn't want anything bad to happen."

"Or, more likely, you wanted a reason to talk to her."

He rolled his eyes. "I talk to her every day."

"With us around. Maybe you wanted to talk to her by yourself."

"I'm not sixteen, calling a girl on the phone."

"So, then, how did you end up at her house, again?"

"I told you, there was a mouse situation."

"She told you?"

"Something like that. She sounded…upset, so I thought I'd see if I could help."

His brother smiled a stupid smile. "I bet you did."

"I don't even know what that means or why you're saying it like that. There's nothing going on. She's our client."

"Our hot client for whom you threw a baseball game. You, the king of competition, actually struck out for the first time in your adult league baseball history, against your most detested team. Then you ran out of the town hall meeting after her. Oh, and don't forget you're going on a date with her on Saturday."

He shifted in his seat. "I didn't run out of the meeting. It was over."

"But you didn't go home."

"Again, why are you stalking me?"

"Someone has to keep tabs on you."

"Have I told you lately how irritating you are?"

His brother cackled. "Only when I'm right. I have to say, though, this date really threw me for a loop. I didn't expect that. I expected months of you denying your attraction to her and us having to take turns at convincing you to go out with her."

He blinked. "What?"

His brother nodded. "Yeah. We had a big family discussion about this."

"When?"

"When you were late last Sunday for dinner. Everyone knows. Even Dad, who has no idea what's going on in our personal lives most of the time. Oh, we all love Emily, too."

He leaned forward, bracing his elbows on his legs and running his hands through his hair. He hated when they did this, acted like he was this pathetic loser who couldn't get his life back on track. "Well, you don't need to be talking about me behind my back. I'm fine."

"Well, I'll be sure to put in a good word for you and let them all know you're not denying your feelings and that you're actually moving on with your life."

"Thanks," he said drily.

"What's that?" Austin asked, leaning forward and snatched the contract up before Cooper could hide it away.

He watched as Austin's eyes widened comically. What was even more surprising was that his brother didn't even laugh. His reaction appeared very similar to how Cooper felt when they were writing up the contract.

Austin looked up at him a minute later. "What *is* this?"

He settled back onto the couch and finished the rest of his beer. "I know. That's exactly what I thought. You can't tell anyone about that."

"Don't worry. I can keep a secret."

Shit. They both knew very well that *no one* in his family could keep a secret. "Obviously, she's been out with a loser or two, and I don't want it getting around. You shouldn't have even read that."

"I know. You're not even technically supposed to be talking about this according to rule number one."

Cooper dragged his hands down his face. "Then stop talking."

His brother grinned and stood. "Good. I'm glad to see my work here is done."

"Uh, to be clear, you did nothing. No work was done here. I already signed and agreed to the terms anyway."

"Well, then, I reassured you that you're doing the right thing."

"You did?"

Austin frowned at him. "Clearly."

He shrugged. "Fine. Bye."

Austin paused at the picture frame on the mantel and then looked back at him with that expression he had whenever he mentioned Catherine. "She would have liked Emily, you know."

Cooper avoided his gaze. "Yeah. I know."

"And it's okay to want someone again."

He ignored the jab in his stomach. "I know that, too."

"It's okay to want to be married again."

He straightened his shoulders. "Hey, this is a date, you know, like what all you guys do? I'm not looking to get married. Are you?"

Austin took a step back, his eyes wide. "Hell no. But I'm not you."

Cooper narrowed his eyes. "What's that supposed to mean?"

"You just have that marriage vibe about you."

"Time for you to go," he said, walking toward the door, ready to kick Austin out. He didn't want to hear about the family discussion about him being a marrying man.

"Well you're not just going to sleep with her and leave. You can't actually do that when you see the woman the next day and for the next few months because you're renovating her house."

Cooper took a deep breath and resisted the urge to tackle his brother. "I'm not an ass. As if I would do that."

"Fine. Just offering advice, in case you'd forgotten the rules."

Cooper opened the door. "You are the last person I need rule advice from."

"Clearly you're wrong since you just signed a contract in which you have to pick up rodent carcass for the rest of your life, just for taking a woman out to dinner."

He shut the door in his brother's face, hating that Austin was right, and hating that he'd do it all over again for Emily.

Chapter Eleven

Cooper shifted from one foot to the other as he waited for Emily to answer the door. He wasn't going to concentrate on the fact that this was the first date he'd been on in over a decade, since that was just pretty damn sad.

But he didn't have to worry about any of that, because Emily opened the door a moment later, looking like a woman he didn't deserve to have. Her brown hair fell in loose waves around her shoulders and the deep wine-colored sweater dress hugged her curves. But when his eyes met hers, his gut clenched, and he cursed his family. She knew. Sympathy and pity were shining in those green eyes, and he wanted to smash his fist against the brick. He didn't want Emily's sympathy. He wanted to be Cooper and not the poor widower that everyone felt sorry for.

"Hi, you look beautiful," he said, manners forcing him to be polite.

"Thank you," she said, tossing him a smile.

He held the door for her while she gathered her purse and some kind of pale-pink wrap. After she locked up, they walked to his truck in silence, and he held the passenger side door open for her. As he rounded his side of the truck, he knew he was going to have to say something and get it over with, because if he didn't, the whole damn night was going to be ruined. He climbed into the driver's seat beside her and pulled out of the driveway.

"Is everything okay?" she said when they'd been driving a few minutes.

He glanced at her and cursed himself for being distant. "I don't know. Why don't you tell me why you were looking at me like you wanted to cry?"

She let out a little moan. "It's… I'm sorry. Callie is going to kill me."

He gave a short laugh. "Callie. I should have guessed."

"She meant well, she really did. She didn't tell me much, and she emphasized it was your story to tell. She just said that you'd been married before…and that your wife had died." Her sentence ended on a whisper.

He glanced at his rearview mirror and then he pulled the truck over onto the shoulder. It was a quiet country road, but he put his hazard lights on to be safe. There was no way he was having this conversation while he was driving. He was just going to get it out there and done. "I met Catherine in high school. Her family had just moved here from Vancouver. We became friends right away. She was into sports and a lot of the girls' and boys' teams hung out after games and practices. We had a lot in common. We were friends for a long time. We went to senior prom together and…were together ever since. Everything with Catherine was easy. We were so similar. We hardly argued. We jogged together. We played co-ed sports together. We were inseparable. Everyone loved Catherine, she was everyone's favorite. Just so easygoing and happy."

Emily's smile was wobbly, and her eyes were filled with that same kind of sympathy he'd seen on her porch…but they were filled with something else, too…something he couldn't deal with right now because he was talking about something he hated talking about. He'd never really had to tell what had happened to Catherine. Everyone who knew him already knew their story. He turned away from the questions in her sad eyes, staring out the windshield and into the black night.

"We decided we wanted a baby after we were married a couple years and, uh, were trying for a few months. I thought that it would just take longer but Catherine insisted something was wrong." He turned to look at her because she would keep him grounded in the present, and because he wanted her to know he was here. He wasn't still living a life that didn't exist. He had come to terms with his past and with saying goodbye to the woman he'd planned on spending the rest of his life with. There hadn't been anyone else, because he just didn't want to go down a road that could ever bring that kind of pain again…which of course made him question what he was doing here now with Emily.

"What happened?" she whispered, tilting her head.

He cleared his throat. "They found a tumor on her liver, and that was the beginning of the end. It was the most unfair thing I've ever witnessed. She didn't have any hope of surviving. It was like one of those things you see on TV where a person is given months to live. We went everywhere. We wanted more than one opinion, but it was all the same. It was too fast."

Emily's hand went to his knee, and he stared at it, felt the impact of the compassionate gesture ripple through his body. "I'm sorry," she said in a raw voice that cut through him.

He didn't want to talk about any of this any longer. He wanted to be rid of the injustice of Catherine's cancer instead of living in the haze of loss for the rest of his life. He didn't want to be a man Emily pitied. He wanted to act like the man he was before Catherine. "It was five years ago, Em. I'm not there anymore. I'm right here."

The windows were fogged from their body heat, and it almost felt like the rest of the world didn't exist, and that was what he wanted. He slowly grasped Emily's hand in his, his thumb running over her fingers, enjoying the softness, until that wasn't enough. He slowly brought her hand to his lips, and her soft gasp ricocheted through his body. He turned her hand over and kissed the inside of her palm, and she watched him with an expression he knew, one that he was feeling, too. He held her hand in his and then raised his other one to cup the side of her face, leaning toward her, wanting to taste her, wanting to hold her in his arms, wanting to show her that she was the woman he was thinking about now.

A loud horn and lights from an eighteen-wheeler had them both jumping, and he checked his mirrors to make sure they weren't in immediate danger. The truck roared past them, robbing them of their moment. He hung his head for a second. "I think that was our warning. I'd better get us off the side of the road," he said.

She nodded. "Of course."

He started the engine again and took her hand in his as he pulled back onto the dark road.

• • •

Emily laughed as Cooper told her a funny story about his childhood antics with his brothers. She was sitting across from him at the restaurant at a corner table that had a full view of a gorge. There was a suspension bridge over it, lit with twinkling lights. The restaurant was charming and cozy, and all the tables had white tablecloths and flickering candles. It couldn't have been a more perfect evening.

She never would have expected Cooper to be like this the entire night. Her first surprise had been seeing him out of his usual work clothes—which he pulled off exceptionally well. Most of her daydreams were about him in the worn jeans and fitted T-shirts. But the clean-shaven, button-down-shirt–wearing Cooper was mouth-watering.

She didn't know what exactly she'd expected him to be like, but after that moment in the truck when they'd almost kissed, there had been a change in him, almost like a relief, and then he'd become this man who was affectionate and caring. She loved the rough texture of his strong hand in hers, she loved the way he'd graze his thumb across her hand every now and then, and she loved the ripple effect it had throughout her body. She had believed him to be so hard and indifferent when she'd first met him, but now she knew. When he'd told her about Catherine, when he'd reached for her, and now, sitting across from him, she knew the truth—he was a man who felt deeply, who loved deeply. And somehow, he had found something in her that made him want to trust her with his heart. She believed he was ready to move on, but she also didn't think it could ever be that simple.

"Can I get you anything else?" their waitress asked a moment later.

Cooper looked at her. She shook her head. "I really can't eat anything else."

"Coffee?" he asked.

She nodded, smiling. She didn't want tonight to be over, the magic of it. She didn't want Cooper to go back to being the guy who viewed her as just a friend. Maybe tonight was her own Cinderella night, and she wanted to enjoy it for as long as she could.

"Do you miss Toronto?" he asked after the waitress left.

She thought about that for a moment, absently admiring the orange and burgundy roses on the table. "Not…really. I didn't belong there. There was a different kind of energy, and it was easy to get caught up in the hustle and bustle and excitement of the city, but it's also really easy to get lost in it and forget what's important."

"How so?"

He was easier to talk to than she'd expected. She had always had a hard time opening up to people, trusting people and letting them in. She was so cautious, never wanting to get hurt or be vulnerable, but somehow Cooper made her feel safe and warm. "Maybe it was just our social circles, but it was like I was always so busy trying to be the person everyone else thought I should be. I hate shopping. I hate makeup. I hate getting my hair done. I resented that I had to do those things to keep up appearances. I couldn't go to work dressed casually. I couldn't go for brunch in jeans, unless the outfit had been carefully planned out. If I had a day off I'd rather sit at home and drink coffee and read a book, but my days off were spent doing things that other people thought I should be doing."

The warmth emanating from his eyes made it clear that he liked her answer or that he felt the same way. "I know we haven't known each other very long, but I can't see you living that city life. Maybe when I first met you, but I think I know you better now."

She swallowed hard. "Sometimes it takes distance to figure things out. I just went along with everything and never questioned it, until something snapped. It's like a huge weight has been lifted off me. There are no expectations of me, because no one knew me."

"Your family...you said you have a brother, right?"

She shrugged but nodded and took a deep breath. She really didn't want to talk about her family. How did a person get into all that? Technically, they'd be breaking the Darth rule, too. She was from a dysfunctional family, and he came from the most high-functioning family she'd ever seen. "I think I needed space from him. We all worked together, and it was just too much."

He nodded politely like he understood, but she knew he didn't. His family worked together, and they drove each other crazy, but they were all in it together. They were all close. "Sometimes space is what we need. Would you ever go back?"

She shook her head, knowing the answer without even thinking about it. Their waitress brought their coffees, and she was adding cream to hers when a man and woman walked over to them.

"Cooper?" the woman said with a slight smile. They were an attractive older couple. Cooper's smile fell slightly, and his gaze slipped from hers as he stood to kiss the woman on the cheek and shake the man's hand.

Cooper turned to her. "Bernice, Frank, this is Emily…"

She stood out of politeness and shook their hands.

"Emily, these are Catherine's parents," he said softly.

Goose bumps prickled her flesh, and she struggled to find words, but the awkwardness of the four of them standing there made it impossible to think. "It's very nice to meet you," she said, unable to come up with anything else. She wanted to shrink away and hide.

Bernice gave her a small smile and nod and then turned to Cooper. "Well, it was nice to see you. It's been a while," she said.

Cooper nodded. "It has. I've been busy with work, but uh, I'll stop by one day for a coffee."

Frank grasped his shoulder, warmth and familiarity spilling from his eyes. "You do that, son."

"It was nice meeting you, miss," Frank said. Bernice nodded again, and then they left. She and Cooper sat back down, and she couldn't quite tell what the expression on his face meant, but whatever warmth and openness had been there before was now gone. He seemed hard and closed off, very much like the man she'd first met.

Emily took a sip of her coffee, but it was now cold. “They seem like very nice people,” she said, trying to break the silence. He didn’t say anything for a moment, and she looked away, her gaze wandering the restaurant. Couples laughed and talked in soft voices, candlelight flickered, and her heart squeezed as she realized she had never really been one of those people. Cooper had, with his wife. But she’d always kept her distance; she didn’t even know how to be open with another person. Cooper had, and he’d lost it all.

The waitress brought their check, and Cooper quickly put the cash in the black leather billfold, obviously trying to expedite their exit. “They are very nice people,” he said finally, as the waitress left. “We were pretty close. They were a second set of parents to me. Catherine was an only child, and they took me in like one of their own.”

She cringed at the injustice those people had suffered. And then to see Cooper tonight on a date with a new woman must have been heartbreaking. For all of them. They all shared this past, this love of a woman that had died too young, and they could never reclaim that life. It was like a different world, or maybe a dream.

Cooper stood, the hard lines of his face taut and unyielding. “I guess we should get going,” he said.

Wow. That was a sad end to their first date, and she couldn’t even blame him. She nodded, her throat clogged with emotion, not wanting to speak. She grabbed her purse, and they made their way out of the restaurant, the faint touch of his hand on the small of her back reminding her that before they’d met Catherine’s parents he had been affectionate and warm, and now…he was distant and polite and nothing more. If she’d been in his position, she didn’t know what she would have done. Maybe cried. She was getting the distinct impression that maybe this wasn’t right.

They drove in silence, and she didn’t know what to say.

She wanted to retreat within herself, to go back to her new home and just be alone. Their easy conversation was gone, and she didn't think there was anything she could say that would make it better. The truck jerked slightly, and Cooper cursed under his breath as he decelerated and pulled onto the shoulder.

"I have a flat," he said, running his hands through his hair.

Her mouth dropped open. This was almost laughable. Like, of course this was the way her first day with a man like this would go. Oh, wait until she told Callie. This was a disaster. "Oh no, do you have CAA?"

"What?"

"You know, roadside assistance."

"Nope. I'm going to change it myself."

"Oh," she said.

"It'll take me a bit," he said. "You can stay inside and stay warm."

"Sure." She sat back and crossed her arms.

He hopped out of the truck, and the force of the wind slammed it shut. She heard the sound of clanking, and all her hope at a relationship with Cooper faded. Tonight was going all wrong. This man had lost his first wife. He'd stood by her. He'd been everything to her. He hadn't been out with anyone in five years. Then she came along, and she knew from the moment she'd met him at the Sleepless Goat that he was someone special. And, despite everything, he'd seen something in her.

He'd never made fun of her when he taught her how to throw a ball. He'd struck out on purpose because of her. He'd cleaned up dead mice for her. He had made reservations to an elegant restaurant and dressed up for her even though she'd only ever seen him in jeans. He had signed her damned contract without asking her a question. And now, after a ruined night, he was outside in the cold changing a tire, probably regretting everything.

She opened the door, the cool air making her shudder, and walked around the side, her heels sinking into the soft gravel. He was pulling things out of the cab of his truck. "You should go back inside, Emily. It's cold and damp out here. No point in both of us getting chilled," he said, not really looking at her, just chucking tools onto the ground. She'd never changed a tire in her life or even seen anyone change one.

"That's okay. I'll keep you company," she said, trying to sound chipper as the wind blew her hair off her face, making a mockery of the perfect beach waves she'd managed. Her mouth went dry as he began unbuttoning his shirt. She shouldn't stare. Unfortunately she just couldn't make herself turn away.

He shrugged out of his button-down shirt and dropped it into the cab of his truck, not paying her any notice, which was good because she didn't really want to look away. Sure, she'd seen him around the house in T-shirts, but this wasn't the same. This was a fitted white undershirt that was plastered to his body, highlighting all of his muscles as they rippled. If she'd had a lawn chair and popcorn she might have pulled up and watched the show. That was juvenile of her. "Can I do anything?" she asked, knowing she actually had no way of helping.

He was now under the truck and hoisting it up. Her breath caught as his shirt rode up, revealing what she'd suspected were taut, perhaps six-pack abs. Not that it mattered. That was vain and silly. Very silly. But she still didn't turn away.

"Nope," came the muffled reply.

She ignored him. He stood abruptly and hauled the tire off the back of the truck, and she tried not to look like she'd been watching him like a fangirl as he paused and made eye contact with her.

"I'm sorry," he said flatly.

Emotion and adrenaline clogged her throat as she stared at the man in front of her. His hair was as disheveled as hers. He was dirty and hard and frustrated, and he was the best thing she'd ever seen in her entire life because he was real. He was staring at her as though he'd just committed a crime, as though it hurt him, because their date hadn't gone like it was supposed to. He was concerned for her. Maybe that was it. Maybe it was because Cooper was a man of so many gifts, so much heartache, so much integrity. Maybe that was why she didn't just stand there on the sidelines and accept that as her fate in life.

Life wasn't fair, and he was living proof of that, but the winners kept going, they kept pushing through the pain and the heartache, they pushed to see if they could get to the other side. That's what she wanted. She wanted him. She wanted to join him, to find that other side, that new life.

Maybe he got that, because instead of going back to fixing the tire, he let it fall to the ground, and as he approached, he dropped the tool he was holding and kept walking toward her with an expression that made it impossible to breathe. He stood in front of her, maybe an inch from making contact, and then he raised his hands and cupped each side of her face, and she was pretty sure that her entire life she had never experienced something so intoxicating and overwhelming as having Cooper's hands on hers, his gaze on her, telling her things without words. He was speaking to her heart, and no one had ever done that. "I'm sorry tonight didn't go as planned. I wanted to do something special for you," he said, his voice low and gruff, his gaze going from her eyes to her mouth.

"This…right here…you, this is all I want," she whispered. She didn't have a minute to second-guess being so candid and so vulnerable, because he lowered his mouth and took hers in a way that made it perfectly clear he wanted her just as much. His mouth was firm and intense and everything she dreamed of. Her hands roamed over his hard chest, and he kept one hand on her face while the other pulled her into him, and the feel of his hard body made her whimper against his mouth.

He backed her against the truck, and she finally experienced what it was like to lose control. She had never imagined how all-encompassing, how consuming it could be to be with someone. But she knew it wasn't just *someone*, just *anyone*, because no one had ever managed to evoke complete abandon like he did. It was like she was herself, but without inhibitions, like she was looking at herself from outside.

This woman, the one in Cooper's arms, the one kissing a man on the side of the road against a truck, wasn't sensible Emily. This woman was the real Emily.

She clung to him for dear life, for this other version of herself that he brought out. She didn't want her to go away, she didn't want Cooper to ever stop. One strong hand ran down her side and stopped at her bottom. He cupped one cheek, and she raised her leg so that he could step in closer. He made a noise that sounded like approval as his hand went to her breast, and that was the moment she contemplated how bad it would be to have sex with someone on the side of the road.

But strong headlights drew them both from the haze they were in. Cooper raised both his arms so she was huddled against his chest, blocked from view, until the large truck barrelled past them. Neither of them moved for a moment, and then he pressed his lips against her forehead before he pushed off of her gently. She shivered.

"I guess I should apologize about this, too," he said with a small smile that seemed only slightly apologetic.

She laughed. "No, I think this made up for our bad luck tonight."

His eyes darkened and something flashed across them. “I should get this tire on, and you should get in the truck, or we’re both going to be sick on Monday.”

She shrugged. “I think I’d rather keep you company. You’re a lot more fun now that you’ve worked on your bedside manner.”

Chapter Twelve

The sound of Emily's teeth chattering made Cooper get up off the couch and put another log on the fire. "There, that should heat this room up in no time," he said. They were back at her giant house, sitting on the sofa in the family room, waiting for the fireplace to warm up the large space.

"I thought you said the boiler was more than adequate for heating up this house," she said, shooting him a teasing look.

"It is, except you actually have to turn on the heat to make it work, and it takes longer than ten minutes to warm a ten-thousand-square-foot inn."

"Details," she said over the rim of her wineglass.

He laughed. He hadn't intended on coming in after he drove her home, but after the night they'd had, he couldn't just leave her. And if he were really truthful, he didn't want to leave her. He wanted more. For the first time since Catherine, he wanted everything. He wanted to know her secrets, he wanted to know her past, he wanted to hear her laugh, he wanted to hold her, he wanted to kiss her, he wanted to spend the night with her.

Emily was so different from Catherine. What he felt for her was different, too. Not that he wanted to go through his life comparing women to his deceased wife, but she was the only woman he'd given his heart and soul to. Catherine had been fearless. She'd had an easy self-confidence that had come from an upbringing that was solid and positive. She hadn't been afraid of anything or of trying anything.

On the outside, at first, that's what he'd assumed about Emily. She'd been polished…except for their first encounter. But she was poised and knew her way around a business. She was educated and sophisticated, but when he started spending more time with her, some of the layers stripped away to reveal a vulnerable side that left him with the unfamiliar need to watch out for her. "So can I ask you about that contract that I signed?"

Her gaze darted from his to the wine bottle. "Uh, sure. But you really should have asked for clarification before you signed."

He laughed. "Noted. But I think I would have signed just about anything to go out with you."

Her shoulders relaxed, and the panic left her eyes. She smiled at him, almost like she was seeing him in a different way, and he wondered at that. At what it was she was so afraid of. "So which points did you want clarification on?"

He thought back to the contract and tried to keep the mood light. "Maybe not the points in detail, but maybe the reason behind the entire list."

She pulled the plaid blanket tighter around herself, and he fought the urge to pull her onto his lap and lie down with her, to feel her body next to his again. "So, I've had people in my past that made me insecure about myself. I decided I was going to start a new life, and anyone who tried to put me down or make me feel inadequate by their standards didn't deserve to be in my life."

"Who was he?" he asked in as soft a voice as he could muster. He already knew it was some guy, but he wanted to know more. He wanted to know what he did, wanted to know who she was before she became the woman sitting in front of him.

"We're breaking so many rules. So many personal stories. If I tell you, that'll nix the Darth rule, too."

She was right. He didn't care about the contract anymore. Hell, he didn't even care about the lifetime rodent removal he'd agreed to, because he wanted to know more. He couldn't get enough of Emily. "I won't let anyone know we're in breach of contract if you don't."

She made a sound that was almost a laugh. Her gaze left his, and she drew her knees up under her chin. "I guess I have to talk, don't I? You managed, and your…heartbreak is one I can't even imagine living through," she whispered, her eyes shining. Maybe that was one of those things he liked most about her—the compassion that appeared without warning, without qualifiers. They were talking about her, and she was still thinking about him and Catherine.

"We all have our own stories, our own pain," he said. "This isn't about who had a worse life or who suffered more. My experience doesn't make yours any less bad."

She picked up her wineglass again. "It was my family, I guess. There was a very strange family dynamic in my house. My brother is twelve years older than me, and my father was often working and not really involved in the day-to-day at the house. My brother took over as a sort of pseudo-father figure, except he wasn't a very nice person."

He tried to hide his surprise, because this hadn't been what he was expecting. He had thought the guy was an ex, a boyfriend or husband. He'd come from a very normal, stable family, as had Catherine, and he had no idea what it would be like to grow up in a dysfunctional home. "How so?" he asked when she didn't continue.

She gave a small shrug. "I have a lot of early memories of fearing him. Like he had this uncontrollable temper. I remember once when I was six, I laughed at something he did when a friend was over, and he just went crazy and started kicking me and yelling at me. He had a violent streak that would come on without warning. Or like other things, like destroying my favorite toys in a fit of rage. I remember running to the bathroom to lock myself in because I was afraid he'd hurt me. When you're little and you're growing up in a house like that, you don't really realize there is something wrong until you get older and see how other families function. Because he was so much older, it wasn't just a brother and sister tormenting or teasing each other. He was *twelve years* older than me.

"Anyway, as I grew up, I really became close with my father. I'd go into the office with him, and I'd want to know everything about the family business. Those were my favorite days. No one mocked me, no one hurt me."

She took a long sip of wine and blinked a few times. "When I started going through puberty, my brother would make constant remarks about how fat I was getting, what I should be eating to lose weight, or how ugly I was. This is where the whole baseball story fits in," she said, choking out a laugh.

He couldn't even bring himself to fake a smile.

"I really wanted to play baseball. I was a huge fan and watched so many games. I was asking my mother one day if I could play. My brother overheard and said that I should play something like soccer, instead, because it burned more calories than baseball."

He ran a hand over his jaw, keeping his remarks to himself. "What did your mother say?"

"She never corrected him. I think at some point along the way she became afraid of him—when he didn't get his way, he would lash out and be verbally abusive. So she just told me that it was for boys, anyway, and I should sign up for piano lessons. I started becoming more and more self-conscious and would try to cover myself up as much as possible. I had a lot of issues with my body and had a very distorted image of who I was. When I look back on pictures, I'm sad for that girl, because I actually wasn't heavy at all. But in my mind I was obese. I grew up hiding all my accomplishments because whenever something good happened to me, he would lash out even more."

"Didn't he ever move out?"

She gave a short laugh. "No. I went away to university hours away just to be free of that house. But the saddest part was that it was him who drove me away. I missed my parents, even my mother, who I saw as someone who didn't help me fight against him. But I had no choice—I needed to get away to preserve my sanity. He would call me all the time."

"Why?"

"A way to control me, maybe? He had no friends, no lasting relationships. He had a volatile relationship with our father, and even though he was always arguing with him, he joined the family business. I would have to talk to him on the phone just to try to preserve some peace and not have him lash out at me and create problems with our mother. When I graduated, I started working with my father right away. I worked so hard, and we saw eye to eye on so many things.

"But that, unfortunately, also brought out my brother's jealous side. My father saw and knew exactly the kind of man my brother was, but confronting him made my mother very upset, so my father always backed off. My father knew I wanted to run the company one day, and I thought…I thought I would. He shut me out, though," she said, her voice breaking.

He took her hand, and it felt cold and small in his. "I'm sorry," he said roughly.

She shot him a wobbly smile, but it was the look in her eyes that gutted him. "He gave it all to my brother. Instead, I inherited this place," she said, spreading her arms wide.

Hell. The betrayal. He got it now; he understood it. "Did you say anything? Could you contest the will?"

She shrugged. "It wasn't even about the company, in the end. It was that my father betrayed me. He would rather jeopardize everything he'd worked for rather than give it to a woman. My brother said they'd discussed it and they agreed that it was more fitting for a man to have a career that demanding."

"He's Darth?"

"Yep." She gave him a wry smile that made his stomach twist. "Darth."

"Come here," he said, tugging her over to him. She came willingly, like he was exactly what she needed. He reclined on the plush sofa, taking her with him, her body against his as he smoothed the hair off her face and stared into her eyes. He wanted more for her. He wanted her to have the childhood his sister had had.

The women in his life brought out a different side of him, a better side, and he was very well aware that they made him a better man. So, holding Emily in his arms, knowing how smart, how hardworking, how compassionate she was, and hearing her treated like that made him angry.

Emily was very different from Catherine. He and Catherine had been like high school sweethearts. Looking back, he saw that they had been practically children. Emily was a woman. She was strong in different ways, and she made him alive and excited. She made him into a different man.

He gently grasped the nape of her neck, threading his

fingers through the silky hair, and reached out to kiss her. Slowly. Not like before, not like their first kiss, when he didn't think he'd ever get enough. This kiss was about her, about letting her know how amazing he thought she was. "I'm so happy you moved here," he said against her mouth. "And I think, if it doesn't make me an evil person, that I'm glad I'm the one who taught you how to throw a ball, because I think that was the day I knew I was falling for you."

She didn't say anything for a moment, and then she kissed him. She kissed him and clung to him like he was a lifeline. Her fingers were in his hair, and he flung the blanket off her, letting his hands roam down her curvy body. He slid one hand up her leg, loving the warmth of her skin under him.

He knew that there was no going back to the way they were after tonight, and he didn't care. He didn't care that it was risky because they worked together and his family was involved. He didn't care about any of it, because the woman in his arms was worth all the complications. He didn't want to think of all the reasons they should stop or he should leave. For the first time in five years, he just wanted to feel. He wanted to feel alive again, wanted to feel a woman's body again—not just any woman. Emily. He wanted it all with her, and that was the scariest thing, because he'd sworn he would never go down that road again.

A pounding on the front door made them both jump. "Oh my gosh, did you hear that?" Emily asked, slowly raising her body away from his, resting her hands on his shoulders.

She appeared flustered and flushed, and he was pretty sure he was going to kill whoever was on the other side of that door, especially if it was one of his brothers. "I should get that, shouldn't I?"

He ran his hands through his hair as she scrambled to her feet and smoothed out her own hair and straightened out her dress. He sat up, painfully aware he needed a few more seconds before he stood. "Whoever it is, they really should think about calling before showing up at midnight," he said.

He took her hand, and they made their way to the door. His stomach dropped when Moose's daughter stood there with a backpack and a black eye.

• • •

"Can I crash here, or were you lying about helping me?"

Emily felt like she had the wind knocked out of her. Going from lying on top of Cooper a few minutes ago to answering the door to a poor girl who was in rough shape, was too much to process. Adrenaline kicked in a second later and she opened the door wider. "Of course I wasn't lying. Come in."

The girl shot Cooper a nervous glance but walked over the threshold and stood in the entryway, her gaze darting around jerkily. "This is impressive, even though it's old."

"Thanks. It's a work in progress, but I think you'll like it. Do you need some food? Can I get you some ice for your eye?" she asked, leading her down the hallway. Cooper was already walking toward the kitchen, and she was grateful he was here tonight.

"Food would be good. Ice, too, I guess," she said, still looking around, her eyes wide. Even though she tried to sound tough, Emily could tell she was putting up a front. The girl looked terrified and her voice held a faint tremble.

Cooper had already set a bunch of ice cubes in a tea towel and handed it to her. The girl flinched, and immediately he handed the bundle to Emily. "Here, sit down at the island and put this on your eye. How about a turkey sandwich and a glass of apple juice?"

She thought for a second that the girl was going to make a smart-ass remark about the apple juice being childish, but her chin trembled, and she shrugged but nodded.

"Does your dad know where you are?" Cooper asked gently, standing across the island.

She frowned. "He doesn't care, and I'm old enough to do what I want."

"Okay. What's your name, hun?" Emily asked, trying to keep her tone light as she pulled out some lettuce, sliced turkey, mayo, and cheddar cheese from the fridge. Cooper had already put sliced bread in the toaster.

"Morgan," she said. "You know, after the captain?"

The bread popped out of the toaster, the only sound echoing in the large space. Emily couldn't even make light of that comment, and when she looked at Cooper, she could see he was fighting the same urge to yell at someone. "Okay, so, how about you eat up, and I'll go get your room ready?"

Morgan put down her makeshift ice pack and stared at her with disbelief. "You mean you're actually letting me stay here?"

Her heart squeezed. "Of course. I said if you needed help, I'd help you. I have lots of rooms and a big old empty house. So, you eat, I'll go get you set up."

Morgan's eyes shifted warily from her to Cooper. "Do the rooms have locks?"

Emily winced. "Not yet, because we're still renovating, but no one will bother you. It's just me and—"

"I would never hurt you," Cooper said, his voice thick with emotion. Emily didn't turn around to look at him, because she didn't know what he was saying, why he was implying he was staying here. But she didn't want to cause any more confusion.

After a minute, Morgan shrugged and picked up her sandwich. "Okay. I'll stay if you insist."

Emily shot her a smile, and she and Cooper left the room. They took the back staircase from the kitchen. When they were upstairs and out of earshot, they stared at each other.

"Oh my gosh," Emily whispered.

Cooper was shaking his head. "I don't even know what to say or where to start with this."

"What was I supposed to do?"

He shrugged. "I don't know. I would have done the same, too. I don't blame you, but this is going to get complicated, fast."

"She is of age. It's not like it's illegal for her to leave home," Emily reasoned out loud.

"I know, but you're about to involve yourself in a heap of family problems."

"I can't deny a person with a black eye a safe home," she said, getting riled up again.

Cooper nodded grimly. "I know. I wasn't going to turn her away, either, and somehow she got it in her head that you're trustworthy."

She narrowed her eyes. "That doesn't exactly sound flattering."

He flashed a smile. "It came out the wrong way. I meant it as a compliment. She must have sensed something in you to make her want to come here over anywhere else."

Her heart squeezed. "I don't know what I'm doing."

Cooper rubbed the back of his neck. "Maybe you don't have to. Maybe all she needs is someone she can trust, someone who is kind and can offer her a warm bed and food."

She took a deep breath. "Well, I can do that. I'm going to get bedding for her and some toiletries and towels."

"Okay, I'll double-check the en suite and see that everything is up and running."

A few minutes later, they met back in the bedroom that Morgan would sleep in. Cooper was helping her with the sheets. "This is some luxury bedding," Cooper said as the bedsheet billowed over the queen-size mattress.

"Part of my hotel collection. I got a great deal on it."

He gave her a look she couldn't figure out, and for a second she didn't think he was going to say anything. "You're pretty amazing, Em. You're taking this girl in and giving her five-star hotel treatment."

She had never been good at taking compliments. She never really received any. Her parents had never been big on praise. Certainly not her mother, because that would have angered her brother. From him, she'd only ever received criticism. She fluffed a pillow. "It's not a big deal."

"It's a big deal."

"So are you really staying here tonight?" she asked, straightening up.

"I don't trust Moose. I can't leave you here, knowing that guy might show up," he said, taking a step closer to her. She shouldn't be surprised, because that was the kind of man Cooper was, but she was relieved and…happy that he was staying.

"Do you have a blanket or something I could borrow?"

They glanced over to see Morgan standing in the doorway with her arms crossed. Her face was very pale, and her bruise seemed more pronounced. Emily forced a bright smile. "Here you go. You can sleep here. Fresh sheets, warm blankets. There's a bathroom right through that door," she said, pointing to it. "Toothbrush, toothpaste, soap, and all that are in there. Oh, and towels and a bathrobe, too. We'll give you some privacy. Let me know if you need anything, okay?"

Morgan frowned, but it wasn't an angry one. She blinked rapidly, and her eyes were watery as her gaze roamed the room. The large windows and window seat already had floor-to-ceiling, pinch-pleat silk curtains, and the hardwood floors gleamed. The crystal chandelier was dim, and the matching crystal bedside lamps cast a comforting glow. The restored mantel had a watercolor landscape hanging above it, painted by a local artist. "You mean *this* is my room?"

Emily gave her a gentle smile. "I would have turned the fireplace on, but our contractors are really slow at getting the gas line in."

"Hey," Cooper said with a short laugh. "That's only because someone changes her mind a lot, so we've been waiting."

Morgan's chin was trembling, and her arms were crossed in front of her thin body. "It's just, uh, it's okay…thanks."

Cooper shot Emily a look; she gave him a small nod, and then they left the room, neither of them saying anything as they walked down the stairs. "I think this hallway needs wallpaper, Cooper. Do you guys hang wallpaper?"

When they reached the bottom of the stairs, he kissed her, making her breathless, making her want more.

He pulled back a second later. "You know full well we don't," he said, smiling and then kissing her again. "And you're trying to avoid having a real conversation about the fact that you're letting that girl stay here."

"We already discussed it. We both agreed there were no other options." She realized that he was kissing her as though it was perfectly natural to do so. She wondered if that was what he was like when he was in a relationship. Was he affectionate like that? Would he just reach out and kiss her or hug her?

"Why do I sense you're contemplating way more than wallpaper or Morgan?"

She placed her hand over her heart. "You don't know me at all."

He grinned. "I know you."

"Yeah? Then what am I thinking?"

"You're wondering where I'm going to sleep tonight."

Her heart started hammering and laughter bubbled in

her chest, because she had a hunch she was going to love bothering him. "Oh, I know exactly where you're going to be sleeping. On that lovely couch in the family room."

He laughed as he put one hand around her waist and tugged her closer. "Is that right?"

"Yup. I'll see if I can find you a blanket or something." She ran her hands up his hard chest and gladly moved close to him. She liked this fun side of him and that he seemed to be able to bring out the fun side in her. She wasn't worried about doing or saying the right thing. She was just being herself. And she liked teasing Cooper.

For a second she was distracted from what they were talking about, and her gaze went over his features. She had never been this casually close to a man before, let alone a man as handsome as Cooper. She resisted the urge to trace his jawline with her fingers or run her hands over his chest and shoulders. He was magnetic and masculine, and she was so out of her comfort zone, in the best possible way.

Chapter Thirteen

"Morning."

Cooper pulled away from Emily and silently cursed his idiot brothers, who were standing in the doorway of the kitchen, barely containing their pleasure at walking in on him and Emily kissing. It was like they were all in high school. Emily's face was bright red, and she immediately walked over to the coffee pot.

"Aren't you early?" he snapped at them when they walked in.

"Nope," Brody said with a chuckle.

"I'm going to go upstairs to check on Morgan," Emily said, holding a mug of coffee and walking across the kitchen. "Help yourselves to coffee," she said, not making eye contact with anyone as she left the room.

"So let's stop pretending we didn't just see you inhaling Emily's face like the Hungry Man's Special at the Sunshine Diner," Austin said with a grin once Emily was out of earshot.

"You have the maturity of a twelve-year-old," Cooper said, getting a mug and pouring himself a coffee, being sure not to offer any to either one of them. He also hated they were right. He was different. He was like his old self, but different. He couldn't get enough of Emily. He'd slept here the entire weekend—on the couch, sure, but he'd been here—for late-night wine and cheese, for early morning coffee on the porch…to Morgan gloomily walking around the house like a lost soul.

The weekend had been almost surreal. Neither of them talked about what was happening, what they were doing, or where this was going, but both of them knew it was something. He wasn't prepared to analyze what that meant. He didn't care. Right now, he knew that he was insanely attracted to Emily. He was turned on and charmed. He didn't do charmed, yet here he was, infatuated by her. A part of him wanted to stop before he couldn't turn back, before this became an actual relationship. But the other part of him, the one that was winning out, didn't want to ever go back to the way he was before Emily walked into his world.

He didn't want the weekend to end. He hadn't enjoyed a weekend and dreaded a Monday in over five years. He lived for work, for the distraction, for the physical exhaustion that came with it and enabled him to fall asleep exhausted. He didn't want it to be Monday morning with his brothers and a whole bunch of tradesmen intruding on their time together.

Cooper scowled at Brody and Austin then walked out of the room, determined to start the day and get this house done for Emily. He took the stairs two at a time, ready to work on the last bathroom that needed to be finished. Emily was at the top of the stairs, and she tugged on his shirt and dragged him into her room. "Come here," she whispered.

"I like where you're going with this," he said, leaning down for a kiss.

She laughed against his mouth. "I need to talk to you about us."

He leaned against the door, pulling her with him. "What about us?"

"Well…now that the weekend is over, what happens? Your brothers are here. How do we act? Was this just…"

"Maybe we should refer to the contract."

She playfully punched him in the stomach, and he laughed, pulling her close. He kissed the soft skin beneath her ear, loving the way she fit against him so easily. "I don't know. All I know is that I'm mad the weekend is over. I'm mad I have to share you with the rest of the world, and I just want to lock that front door and spend the day in bed with you."

She sighed against his mouth and kissed him. "That was the best answer ever."

The soft knock at the door had them both standing up and pulling away from each other.

"Hey, Emily, are you in there?" Morgan said. "Can you give me a ride to school?"

Emily's eyes widened. "Sure, when do we need to leave?"

"I dunno. Ten minutes?"

"Okay, I'll meet you downstairs."

"Okay."

Emily clutched his waist, her eyes panicked. "We still don't have a plan. I need to talk to her seriously. I'm driving her to school…I don't even know where she *goes* to school."

He kissed her forehead. "There's only one high school in town."

She nodded. "Okay, that's good. I can do that. She's going to need help, more than just a roof over her head and food in her stomach."

"Just take it a day at a time. Maybe right now all she needs is a safe place to stay. You don't need to have qualifications to help a friend, and that's what you're doing right now. Eventually you're going to have to come up with a plan, but right now, just give her a roof over her head, a safe place to come home to, and someone she can trust."

She took a deep breath. "You're right. That's all I can do. Don't you think it's weird that Moose hasn't been by or tried to contact her?"

"I've known Moose for a long time. We went to school together, and he was always trouble. He came from a messed-up family, and it showed. He always had anger management issues and was kicked out of school so many times. It doesn't surprise me that he isn't searching for his daughter. He may be happy he doesn't have to deal with her. Her mom is long gone, and he's stuck raising her."

Emily winced and shook her head, and he was falling for her a little more. "I feel so bad for her. I mean, what's worse, your jerk father trying to make you go back home, or him not caring enough to even try?" she whispered.

He leaned forward and kissed her softly. "This is amazing, what you're doing. Concentrate on that and how you can help her. I better get to work. How about when this place clears out tonight we go into town? Get some dinner?"

She smiled and nodded. "Perfect."

She walked out of the room, and he rolled his shoulders, surprised for the first time in a long time that they weren't stiff or weighed down by his past. He was actually looking forward to his day and then his night with Emily.

• • •

"So were you guys, like, having sex?"

Emily choked on her coffee and coughed as she drove Morgan to the local high school. She glanced at her younger friend, unable to hide her shock. The girl was slouched in the front seat, her brows drawn tightly together. She was the epitome of teenage anger and rebellion. Emily couldn't really relate to that. She'd never gone through a rebellious stage because she'd been a people pleaser. Then again, she hadn't had a drunk, abusive father, either. She still didn't know what she was going to do with Morgan.

All of a sudden, her life was changing fast. Her weekend had been filled with Cooper and Morgan. It was probably the best weekend of her life. While Morgan hadn't been exactly chatty, Emily could tell the girl liked her room. They'd ordered pizza, and Morgan had joined them, not really contributing to conversation but not making an effort to leave the table, either. Emily wanted to give her space, but she also wanted to help her.

Then there was...Cooper. He'd been amazing. She hadn't expected him to just move in without complaint or without being asked. Not that she would have asked. But he'd sort of taken up residence and was making no mention of leaving anytime soon. It was as though they were falling into some kind of new routine. Or a relationship. Their date had changed everything. He'd opened up to her, and she was falling in love for the first time in her life. If that's what it was. It had to be. She had openly talked to him about her family and her brother, and he hadn't made fun of her or belittled her. It had been a life-changing experience. She trusted him.

"Um, *no*," she finally answered. "We were talking about our plans for the day."

Morgan shrugged and smirked. "I wouldn't think you were a slut if you were."

Emily tried frantically to think of something to say and not give away the fact that she was a panicked, unqualified person to be talking about this kind of stuff. She glanced at her from the corner of her eye while driving. It was morning; she couldn't deal with stuff like this in the morning. She needed friends who had teenagers.

She cleared her throat and tried to sound like she was an

authority and yet also somewhat cool. She kept her eyes on the road because this wasn't a conversation where eye contact would be comfortable. "Well, I'm not a fan of the word slut. I don't think it's a nice word."

Morgan snorted. "Tell that to my dad. Everyone talks like that anyway."

Emily squeezed the steering wheel tightly. "You don't have to. No one can force you to say things."

"What if someone is?"

"We don't need to label people, period."

"Well, your boyfriend seems decent. He's hot, too, for someone older. If you don't put out, he'll leave, so don't let me being around stop you."

If she could safely close her eyes and drive, she would. In fact, maybe she should. If only plowing into a tree would solve her problems. "He wouldn't do that. And if he did, then he wouldn't be a guy worth having."

Morgan snickered. "Are you, like, from the past?"

That was *almost* funny, but she wouldn't laugh. "Uh, *no*. But I wouldn't stay with someone who pressured me to do something I didn't want to do or who assumed I owed him something. That's not a real relationship, so it wouldn't last, and I'd consider him a douche."

Morgan plucked an imaginary piece of lint from her shirt. "Wouldn't that be labeling him?"

Emily clenched her teeth. She had such newfound sympathy for parents of teenagers. "I was trying to make a point."

Morgan didn't say anything, but her smirk held its position.

Emily frantically searched for something to say that had nothing to do with sex or relationships. "So, how's school? This is your last year, right?"

"Yeah. It's okay," she said in that same despondent sort

of voice. "I don't really care anyway."

"Do you have any favorite subjects?" Emily asked, desperate to draw her out.

Morgan scoffed. "No."

Emily fiddled with her travel mug, wondering if it would be too much to ask her what her plans were after graduation. But who knew if she was even going to graduate? She knew nothing about her. One thing was clear: she was going to have to get the girl some help. There was no way she would stand by and let Morgan flounder and suffer. She would help her however she could, even if it meant more excruciatingly painful conversations. "I didn't really have a favorite, either," she said, trying her best to sound nonchalant.

Morgan scoffed. "I bet you went to private school and were on the honor roll and had your pick of universities. Your parents were probably loaded, and you were the perfect daughter. I don't want to be mean to you, because you didn't actually have to help me out, but you probably shouldn't compare our high school years."

Emily flushed, embarrassed and hurt, as Morgan turned from her and picked up her backpack. She pulled her car up outside the front of the high school. Students were milling around the front yard, but Morgan didn't make a move to get out. "So, um, you have a good day, okay?" Emily said in a gentle voice.

Morgan nodded, picking up her backpack but not making an effort to move.

"Everything okay?" Emily asked when Morgan's face turned red.

Morgan nodded again, and this time opened her door. Emily realized she was in way over her head. She needed some help if she was going to have Morgan in her house for an indefinite amount of time. She was also going to have to tell Moose that his daughter was staying with her. "Wait!"

Emily called out just as Morgan was about to shut the door.

Morgan turned to her.

"Do you have a lunch? Oh my gosh, I didn't even think of that," she said, not waiting for a reply and reaching into her wallet. "Here." She shoved her only bill at Morgan. "Will ten be enough for lunch in the caf?"

Morgan stared at the bill then up at Emily. "For real?"

Emily nodded, not knowing if it was enough money or not. "Is that enough for a drink, too?"

"Uh, yeah, thanks," she said, taking the money and shoving it into the front pocket of her jeans. "It's more than I've ever had."

Her heart squeezed, but she was relieved that she'd done something right. "Okay. Um, maybe I can pick you up after school and we can go do some shopping? You can pick up some of your favorite foods? I'm not much of a cook, but I'm sure we can figure it out. Then maybe we can get you some extra clothes, since you didn't bring too much. Who wants to have to do laundry all the time, right?" she said, forcing a smile, trying to hide how sad she was for this young girl. Morgan's expression of disbelief was enough to make her want to cry.

Morgan gave her a small nod; she didn't even make one of her sarcastic remarks. She shut the door, and Emily watched the girl walk across the lawn. Her chest was heavy. She let out a long, deep breath, almost feeling as though she'd just run a marathon. What had that girl been through? How was she supposed to even concentrate on school when she'd just left her father and was living with a virtual stranger?

Emily covered her face. Morgan had entered her life for a reason, and she was going to do everything she could to see that she was okay.

She took a deep breath and pulled away from the school, taking the quiet, tree-lined streets to downtown Maple Hill.

She needed another coffee and a chat with Callie. As she passed the quaint family homes, she thought of Cooper and Catherine and wondered about their life. Had they lived in one of these houses? She drove past a mother pushing a bright-red stroller, and her heart clenched, thinking about how Catherine had wanted children. It was all so unfair... and now she was falling for this man who'd lived an entire lifetime before her.

She tried to shake off the worry that she was getting in over her head, that things were moving too fast, that she was falling too hard. She was inexperienced in this whole thing. She'd never been in love, and she had no idea if Cooper even wanted that again. What if he only wanted her physically? Or just for a little while? Then what? What was her plan? Sure, she'd made him sign a contract to basically promise not to be a jerk, but her contract didn't exactly guarantee that she wouldn't end up with a broken heart.

The Darth Vader ringtone blasted loudly in her quiet car, ripping her away from her current thoughts and dragging her into the past. She pulled into an empty spot outside the Sleepless Goat and parked, relieved when the ringing stopped. She grabbed her purse just as the ringing started up again. She squeezed her eyes shut and knew she should answer and get it over with, just as she'd always done. Or maybe she should block his number and be rid of him forever. But guilt seeped through her when she thought of her parents. She slowly opened her eyes and answered the call, vowing to herself she wouldn't take any insults.

"Hi," she said, holding the phone in front of her, focusing on the cute downtown, on the shops that she wanted to visit soon. Maybe she could focus on the adorable little cheese boutique or the flower shop with the potted mums outside and only have a half-assed conversation.

"I'm willing to make you a partner," came the reply. She

could already tell from her brother's tone that this was the last thing he wanted to do. But he needed her. He didn't have the people skills that she had. He also needed someone to control now that their mother was gone. His voice was low and filled with an anger that she knew all too well. She'd heard that voice so many times growing up; she'd seen the effect it had had on her family. She wanted no part of it anymore.

"I'm not coming back. I have my own life," she said, leaning her head back on the headrest.

"That's gratitude for you. I am doing you a favor—"

"No," she said, sitting up straight and cutting him off. She had never been able to cut him off growing up because it would result in terrifying anger and then him manipulating the situation until she was forced by her mother to apologize. Those days were over. "You're doing *you* a favor and disguising it as a good deed. You are incapable of leading a company, and you want me to bail you out."

She happened to glance at Callie's and saw Austin and Brody walk out, laughing, as Callie yelled something to them from the door. They would never talk to Callie that way. Her brothers doted on her. She couldn't imagine Cooper ever speaking to a woman the way Emily's brother spoke to her.

"Ever since you went away to school, you got this nasty edge to you. You changed. You're depressed and angry. You can't speak to me like that. You're an ugly, little—"

Emily ended the call and dropped the phone on the passenger seat. She clutched the steering wheel and rested her forehead on it, trying to shake off the insecurities that were drowning her in a past she desperately wanted to forget. She wanted to be her own person, and she wanted to be surrounded by people who loved her and treated her with kindness. She counted to ten slowly and then thought of Morgan. She needed to focus on getting that girl help.

A few minutes later, once she'd composed herself, she

pulled open the door of the Sleepless Goat and was greeted by the delicious smell of fresh coffee and a scream from Callie, who ran over to her. She hugged her and laughed. "How are you? I was expecting a call, like, Sunday morning!"

The coffee shop was bustling, so they moved to the side. She was relieved that Callie's all-or-nothing personality enabled her to forget the phone call with her brother almost entirely. "Crazy. Everything is crazy."

"Okay, I'm going to get us coffees, and then I want all the details about your date with Cooper! And I want to know why he didn't show for Sunday night dinner!" she said with a squeal that made Emily laugh.

"Fine. I'll go grab the table by the window," she said, already walking toward it before someone grabbed it.

A few minutes later, Callie joined her, handing her a steaming cup of coffee. "Okay. Spill. But nothing explicit, because I can't handle hearing that."

Emily took a long sip of coffee, trying to hide the fact she was blushing. "Trust me, nothing explicit. I think I just had the craziest weekend of my life," she said, leaning forward.

Callie's eyes widened comically over the rim of her coffee cup. "No. Way. With my brother. What did Cooper do?"

She couldn't help the laughter that bubbled up at Callie's dramatic outburst. "I'm pretty sure not what you're thinking. Okay, let me see. Saturday night seems so long ago at this point. Well, our date kind of had a rocky start. We were driving to the restaurant, and he pulled over to talk about Catherine," she said softly. Her friend's eyes filled with tears.

"I'm glad he told you," she said.

She nodded. "Me, too. And thank you for trusting me enough to tell me, because I would have been a wreck hearing that story if I were unprepared. It's devastating, what he went through, what you all went through. She sounded like an amazing woman."

Callie nodded. "We were close. She was everything to him. She was the perfect package, the perfect family."

Emily wrapped her hands around the cup, the warmth seeping through her hands as she tried to quell her own feelings of inadequacy and the worry that Cooper would never love anyone as much as Catherine. "I know. That's the other thing. Catherine's parents were at the restaurant."

Callie groaned. "I'm heartbroken for them. I don't think they ever recovered. Not that you could, but it's just, they have no other kids, no grandchildren. They seem so alone. Her mother especially seems so lost still. I know Cooper still sees them, and my parents invite them over every now and again, but they don't come that often. Did you guys talk to them?"

She glanced out the window for a moment, remembering that moment she realized who they were, and the sadness in Catherine's mother's eyes. "Yes. They walked up to us to say hi. It was…tense. I felt guilty to be sitting there with Cooper, you know?"

Callie leaned forward. "I can't imagine how awkward that must have been for all of you. As sad as it is, though, Cooper *should* be out on dates. He's too young to not get out there again, and he waited. It's been five years. Well, he should be out on dates with you, I mean," she said with a small pat on her hand.

Emily forced a smile. "Thanks. He was great. I mean, he was worried about me. That he'd ruined our date with all this baggage. He's amazing, Callie. I've never met anyone like him."

Callie gave a little squeal. "I'm so happy. Okay, what else?"

She let out a small laugh. "His truck got a flat as we were driving home."

Callie slapped a hand over her mouth, her eyes wide and

sparkling. "Talk about bad luck."

Emily shrugged and tried not to smile at the memory of when Cooper had kissed her against the truck. It had been one of the best moments of her life.

"Uh, I'm sensing something here that you're not sharing," Callie said, waving her index finger around in a circle in front of her.

"Details I probably shouldn't share," she said, raising her eyebrows as she tried to hide her smile.

Callie clapped and did a little cheer. "Okay, say no more. But I am happy. But I kinda wish he wasn't my brother because I really want to know how a flat tire could have resulted in anything I can't hear about."

"I know," Emily said softly. "I…just. Something changed in me." She felt silly even speaking like this, but she had never let anyone close before. She was breaking her own rules, letting herself become vulnerable.

"Cooper, too, I'm sure," Callie said. "Okay, what else?"

Emily took another sip of her now lukewarm coffee. "Well, he came back to my house for a bit"—she quickly skirted over that memory so that neither of them would be awkward—"and then Moose's daughter showed up."

Callie sucked in a gulp of air. "No. Oh, God, he's such an ass. What happened?"

"She stayed. I gave her a room, and she's staying at my house indefinitely."

"Wow. What was Cooper doing during all this?"

"Helping me. He slept at the house—on the couch—because he was worried Moose would come over in an angry rage."

"That's why he didn't come over Sunday. Okay, so what's the plan? Can I help?"

Emily leaned back and crossed one leg over the other. "I don't know. I just dropped her off at school. I mean, I have no idea what I'm doing. All I know is I had the empty room, she was in need, and she has nowhere to go. But she has issues, understandably, and I need to get some help."

Callie was nodding and scrolling through her phone. "Okay, one of my best friends from school is moving back to Maple Hill. She was a social worker, and she just got a psychology degree. She's worked with at-risk teens in Toronto. Let me call her and get you some answers."

Emily breathed a sigh of relief. "That would be amazing. Give her my number. I was thinking about Morgan, and I know I offered her help if she needed it, and I'm glad she remembered that and came to me, but it made me think about other women who might need a place to go. Are there any other women's shelters around here?"

Callie tilted her head in thought. "Not close, that's for sure. I think the nearest one is in Binbrook, and that's about an hour's drive from here. I know we've donated to them before."

"That's a long way to go, especially if someone is trying to escape."

"I know they have arrangements for pickup, but last time I was there, that place was operating at full capacity. It's not ideal, for sure."

Emily leaned forward. "It's so sad to think of these kids and women in situations like this, you know? Like, Morgan is so vulnerable. She has this tough-girl act, but she is clearly scared, and she must have so many issues to work through."

Callie nodded. "Of course. And where is she going to go eventually? Like, Moose isn't exactly the type of guy to get help and want to rebuild a relationship with his daughter. She can't stay with you forever."

Emily didn't know what to say. She had a business she was trying to open, a reno to finish, and her own past to deal with. But the thought of telling Morgan to leave at some point didn't seem right, either. "I don't know. I guess we'll just take it day by day. The house is still empty. I still don't have zoning for the inn, so I might as well let her have a room."

Callie smiled at her. "You're making a huge difference in that girl's life, you know. I think what you're doing is amazing."

Emily shrugged, uncomfortable with the praise. "I just want to help her… I should probably get back to the house. The final kitchen pieces are getting installed today, and they're starting the last of the floors that needed refinishing. Things are actually nearing the end. I have an errand I want to run, too."

"And Cooper is there," Callie said with a smug smile as they stood.

Emily laughed. "Well, there's the Cooper factor."

Callie linked her arm through hers, and they walked through the busy coffee shop and stopped when they reached the door. "I'm so glad you came into our lives, Em," she said, surprising her and giving her a hug.

Emily hugged her back tightly. As she left the little coffee shop and walked down the quaint Main Street, the unfamiliar sensation of belonging swept through her. She had never felt so at home, so true to herself, as she was right now.

Chapter Fourteen

"This kitchen is even more beautiful than I'd imagined," Emily said, running her hand over the new quartz countertop. Cooper knew the countertop looked good, but he'd moved past that after it had been installed a few hours ago. Really, he was just happy she was happy.

Now his thoughts were on the woman talking about the countertop. Emily's hair was pulled up in some kind of knot that highlighted her glossy hair and long neck. He'd found himself watching her this week—not that he hadn't before, but it was different now because he knew her on a deeper level. His gaze ran over her curves in her pale-blue sweater and skinny jeans. She was effortlessly beautiful and feminine, and he couldn't get enough of her.

She frowned at him. "Seriously, Cooper, look at these counters. Aren't you paying attention?"

He crossed the room and pulled her into his arms. "I was distracted by you," he said, leaning down to kiss her.

She kissed him back and then jabbed him in the stomach. "We can't do this here. Aren't your brothers still in the house?"

He lifted her by the waist and placed her onto the counter. "What are you doing," she whispered. "What if someone comes in here?"

"You're testing the counter," he said.

She burst out laughing.

He smiled, loving the fact that she seemed to have no idea how attracted to her he was. "Hopefully they'll have enough common sense to turn around and leave," he said, leaning forward and kissing her, half expecting her to shove him away. Instead, she melted against him and opened her legs for him to step closer. Something had changed in him since the night of their date. He was done ignoring his instincts, his desire for Emily. He was alive. He kissed her soft lips, loving her body against his, the soft pressure of her breasts against his chest.

"So we're leaving for the night. We'll see ourselves out. Be good, kids," Austin said.

Neither of them stopped to acknowledge Austin, but Cooper did make the effort to give his brother the finger. The sound of his snicker and then the closing of the door told him they were gone. "I don't want to go home," Cooper said against her mouth.

"I don't want you to go home," she said, pulling back slightly. He looked down at her face, at her swollen lips, and knew this wasn't just lust. It was more…because *she* was more. She ran her hands over his shoulders and made a little sound that sent blood roaring through his veins.

"What time does Morgan get back?"

Her eyes widened. "I almost forgot. You'd think I'd get the hang of this after a week. Her friend is driving her home, and she'll be back any minute."

"Will she be okay if we go out? Can you come to my place?"

She bit her lower lip. He wanted her to come to his house, to share that part of his life. "I don't know," she said. "I mean, she doesn't need a babysitter or anything, but I don't know about leaving her on her own. She seems so fragile, and I'd hate for her to be in this big house all by herself. What if her dad comes over?"

"I know, you're right," he said, bracing his hands on the counter beside her.

"So, um, exactly what were your plans?" she said in a voice that was slightly husky, the corners of her luscious mouth curled up slightly. God, she was going to kill him.

He ran his hands up her denim-clad thighs. "Lots of plans. Plans I may have been fantasizing about since I met you."

"Really?"

He nodded. "When you hobbled into the coffee shop."

She poked his shoulder. "What? I didn't hobble. I had pulled myself together by then."

"Sure you did," he said, stifling his smile as she frowned at him.

"I want to talk to you about something now that no one is here," she said, keeping her hands on his waist.

"Sure."

"I drove out to the women's shelter in Binbrook today. Did you know they operate at full capacity year-round? This entire region is completely underserviced. They don't have enough funding to expand the home or hire more help."

He nodded slowly. "I don't know that much about them, but that's not good. What made you go out there?"

She shrugged. "This whole thing with Morgan really got me thinking about what it must be like to be trapped in a dangerous home without anywhere to go or any options. What about a mother with kids? Like, what does she do? Where does she go?"

He ran his hand over his jaw. "Yeah. This is stuff we don't really think about day to day."

"I know, and it's so private. Do you know how many women stay with these men because they are afraid they'll be killed if they leave, or that they'll be on the streets with their kids because they won't be able to support them? It's heartbreaking."

"I'm sensing you're going somewhere with this," he said, smoothing her hair from her face.

She took a deep breath. "Would it sound completely crazy if I turned this place into a women's shelter instead of an inn?"

He paused for a long moment, floored at the abrupt change in her plans. "No. Not crazy. Unexpected, for sure. I don't want to sound like I'm patronizing you, but that's a helluva huge switch, from top-of-the-line boutique inn to women's shelter. Everything you've done in here is high-end and luxury. Have you researched how you'd actually start one? I mean, is it a charity? What about funding?"

"I know. It's a totally different direction. It would be run as a charitable organization. And I know the finishes and everything in here are luxury…but maybe that's what these women need for a bit, you know? After everything they've been through, this would be like a small way of bringing them a little pampering at a time when they need it most. But I'm getting way ahead of myself, and I need to start exploring this in detail. It could be completely insane and a non-starter, but I want to at least research this idea before I dismiss it."

He didn't say anything for a moment because he didn't want to say the wrong thing. But as he stared into her green eyes, seeing the sincerity, the enthusiasm, the hope, he fell in love with Emily just a little bit more.

He'd assumed things. She was this rich woman from the city, dumping a ton of cash into this old house, and yet she didn't have an ounce of snobbery about her—he'd figured that out very early on. But this. The idea of turning such a grand home into a women's shelter, to use her wealth for something completely charitable, was unbelievably selfless.

He had no idea how she'd pull that off, or even if she would be able to, but that wasn't it. It was the fact that she was willing to try, she was willing to go down a road that would not mean a huge salary or a life of entitlement. She'd be entering a life of service. "I think you're incredible," he said, the only words that really summed up what he was thinking. He leaned forward and kissed her softly. "How about we pick up takeout and stay here tonight?"

"I'm a boring date, aren't I?"

"Hell no. I get it. We're not leaving Morgan here by herself at night. How about, since tomorrow is Saturday, we go out during the day? Have you even had a proper tour of this town?"

She smiled and shook her head.

"Okay, so I'll get some food, and you wait for Morgan to get back from school. Tomorrow I'm your tour guide and then we hang out here again at night. I was thinking maybe we can invite Morgan to my parents' place for Sunday night dinner—if she wants to, of course. If she's not ready for that, we stay home." He was like a kid again. He never made plans, and here he was trying to book up all her time because he didn't want to be away from her.

Her eyes sparkled. "That sounds like the best weekend I've ever had," she said, wrapping her arms around his neck.

He kissed Emily, ignoring the warning bells going off in his head. He'd made promises to himself after Catherine died; he'd promised himself he'd never fall in love again. He'd never let anyone close. And now, here he was, falling for a woman who made him want to believe in forever again.

• • •

Emily settled on the front porch steps, tugging her long cardigan sweater a little closer as the brisk morning wind made her shiver. She picked up her mug of freshly brewed coffee and wrapped her hands around it, letting the warmth seep through. The river sparkled as the strong morning sun shone down. The air was fresh, and the sounds of birds and trees swaying in the wind made her think this was possibly the most beautiful place she'd ever known. She wondered if her grandmother had sat out here, admiring the view. Or her father. Had he run around these grounds, had he gone fishing in the river? How she wished she knew more about this house and the people who'd occupied it.

She probably should seek out more information and lurk on that Facebook page Cooper had suggested. The first time she'd met him—well, second time—seemed like a lifetime ago. Now she saw him every day, and today was all theirs.

She turned at the sound of footsteps approaching from the house.

Morgan stepped out onto the porch with a mug of the coffee Emily had left for her. She was wearing one of the new hoodies they'd bought on their shopping trip to the mall in the larger town. She sat down beside Emily. "Morning."

"Good morning," Emily said with a smile. "Did you sleep well?"

Morgan nodded. "You're funny. You always say things like that."

Emily tilted her head, studying the girl. "What's so funny about that?"

Morgan shrugged and took a sip of coffee. Her long blond hair swayed gently with the wind, and her fine features were relaxed…she seemed peaceful.

"So I'm going to be out for the day. There's plenty of food

in the fridge. Cooper and I will be back for dinner, though."

"You guys don't need to babysit me, you know," Morgan said, looking straight ahead.

"I know that. We want to stay here. I didn't do all this work to be out all the time and never enjoy this house," she said, trying to make light of the situation.

"I'm not going to kill myself or anything," Morgan said with a bitter laugh.

"Hey, I'm not saying that at all. I just like being around. I like you," she said, careful not to push too hard or say things that would make the girl uncomfortable.

Morgan looked down at her cup, and Emily could have sworn she saw her chin tremble for a second. "Do you know how long I can stay here? I was thinking I should start making plans about where to go next. My friend said I could probably crash at her mom's for a week."

Emily's heart squeezed, and she tried not to get choked up. "Don't worry about that now. Just know that this is your place now, okay? I have no intention of kicking you out. We're getting along just fine."

Morgan still didn't make eye contact with her, but she pulled her hood down a little farther. "Thanks," she said softly. "I was thinking I should get a part-time job, though. I think it would be smart if I saved some money, you know?"

Emily nodded. "I think that's a great idea. Maybe when this place is up and running you could work here?"

"Really?" she whispered.

Emily nodded. "Of course! It's perfect. We'll find something you like. But that's a few weeks away, at least, so why don't you use this time to rest and concentrate on school."

Morgan looked down. "Thanks."

Emily placed her empty mug down beside her. "So, um, I don't want to pry, but is your mom around at all?"

Morgan made a sound. "She left when I was five.

Apparently I sucked."

"No," Emily said forcefully. "That's not true."

She didn't lift her head. "You don't know, you weren't there."

"If she left, she had her own reasons that had nothing to do with you. Please don't blame yourself. The stuff that happens between parents has to do with parents, not the kids. Sometimes adults make really bad choices, and sometimes they make the only choice they can. But it's never the child's fault," she said, trying to sound convincing. She didn't think Morgan would just believe her, though, after a lifetime of believing that her mother hadn't loved her enough.

Morgan shrugged. "I went to live with Dad's parents for a couple years, but then my grandma died. Then my grandpa got Alzheimer's and had to go to a home until he died. So I went back to my dad's," she said. Her voice had an edge, and the pain in it made Emily want to reach out and hold onto this girl, tell her that she was special and brave and wonderful, and she'd deserved better than that.

"I'm sorry. You're doing great, though," she said.

Morgan slouched even further. "Yeah, real great. I have no home, no money, and I'm living with a stranger."

"Hey." Emily pretended to be offended, wanting to lighten the mood. "I'm not a stranger anymore. Once people have seen each other in their pajamas in the morning, they can no longer be called strangers."

Morgan snorted.

"I was thinking, though. I have this friend, and she works with teens and women who have family situations like yours. She's a person you can talk to, and it's confidential. She can help you with goals and what you want to do after high school and other stuff, too."

Morgan stared straight ahead, and Emily held her breath, hoping she wasn't going to scare her off. Finally she gave a stiff nod. "That might be cool. I don't want to be a loser when I grow up, you know? Like, I want to have a real job and be able to live in a nice house."

Emily reached out and put her arm around Morgan, despite being wary that the girl might not like the affection. But Morgan didn't make an attempt to move away. She had never really imagined a life outside her father's company, and when she'd been callously tossed aside, her mission had been to start her own chain of inns, to seek revenge and prove she didn't need anyone. It had been a solid plan. It still was. But something was happening. Something was changing. She sat beside Morgan and stared out at the river, thinking all of this was happening for a reason, and she was exactly where she should be.

Chapter Fifteen

"Nothing beats small-town downtown," Emily said as she and Cooper strolled Main Street in Maple Hill. He held her hand as they went in and out of stores like a tourist couple.

"Yeah, it's pretty good. Have you been into the cheese shop?" he asked.

She shook her head. "I've been dying to go in but haven't had a chance."

"Okay, let's go," he said, holding the door open for her.

They walked into the packed store, and she admired the vintage black-and-white checked floor and high, exposed ceilings. The walls were lined with rustic wood shelves filled with all sorts of entertaining needs from cheese boards to different spreads and jams. The back wall had refrigerated display cases, and there was a long line of folks waiting to place their orders. "This is so cute," Emily said.

"I hoped you'd like it," Cooper said, walking over to the line.

She peered into the refrigerated display cases, admiring the different local and imported cheeses. She was impressed.

"So this is where you shop?"

"Me? Nah. Who has time for this? I pick up everything I need all at once when I go to the grocery store. I just thought this would be a place *you'd* like."

She laughed. "Because I'm fancy?"

"Very fancy."

She squeezed his hand and peered into the display cases.

"Hello, Cooper, nice to see you," a middle-aged man in front of them said.

"You, too, Bob. Mary," he said to the woman standing beside them. She looked back and forth between Emily and Cooper, beaming.

"You seem familiar," the woman said, smiling at Emily.

"Oh, I'm sorry. Bob and Mary, this is Emily Birmingham, she moved to town a couple of months ago," he said.

Emily reached out to shake their hands. "Nice to meet you."

"The inn, right?"

Emily winced. "Well, I don't know about that. Still waiting to hear what we're going to do next."

The conversation paused as the couple placed their order, followed by Emily and Cooper.

"Well, we support your idea. Sometimes this town needs to shake things up a bit," Bob said. "You just keep on trying. Don't give up."

"It was nice meeting you, Emily. Good luck to you. It's nice to see you doing so well, Cooper," Mary said, placing her hand on his arm and giving him a sympathetic smile. The couple left, and once Cooper and Emily had paid and were back outside, Emily asked him who they were.

Cooper stared straight ahead. He held the paper bag in one hand and her with the other. "They, uh, were my old neighbors."

Emily glanced at him and squeezed his hand gently. "Oh,

like in the house you and Catherine had?"

He gave a quick nod.

"They seem like nice people," she said.

"They were. They are." She started to pull her hand from his, but he held on and then pointed to a charming little brick house. "Do you like Mexican food?"

They had stopped in front of the large town clock surrounded by giant baskets of orange mums. She stared up at Cooper, memorizing what he looked like, what this moment was like with him. He'd dressed up today, his jeans emphasizing his lean hips and height, his navy sweater hugging his broad shoulders. The navy brought out the deeper shades of blue in his eyes. He was a man she would have watched walk by while she sat in a coffee shop. She might have had a daydream about him. He was someone she would probably never have been comfortable going out with. But that was the old her, the one mired in insecurities and doubt.

"Uh, *of course* I like Mexican food," she said, smiling and following him.

She told herself that nothing had changed between them, but it seemed every time they went out on a date, they were bombarded by Cooper's past. She knew he was trying not to make an issue of it, but it was there. It hung between them, silently reminding them of a tragic past that would never really go away, a wound that would always keep reopening.

They spent the day out in the town and then stopped for coffee at Callie's. "We have a bit of time before tonight. Do you want to come back to my place?" Cooper said, once they'd placed their coffees in the cup holders in his truck.

She didn't want to look desperately excited, but yeah, of course she wanted to see his house. "That sounds great," she said with a smile.

He drove a few blocks away from downtown and then pulled into a modest, one-story ranch house. There was a large oak tree, and the lawn was nicely kept, but it was very nondescript, not an ounce of Cooper's personality. He held the door open for her, and she walked inside. The space was an open concept with a fairly modern kitchen. Dark cabinets and stainless-steel appliances. A large island with chairs instead of a kitchen table, which overlooked a great room with a fireplace and giant flat-screen television. There were two leather couches and an ottoman in the middle. It was a bachelor's home.

He placed their bag of cheese in the fridge and then came back to the entrance. "So, what do you think?"

"This is great. You're very neat and tidy," she said with a smile.

He laughed. "I'm not sure whether I should take it as a compliment that you seem surprised by that."

"A compliment," she said, smiling as he grabbed her hand and led her into the family room. "I thought you would have had an old home, since you like them so much."

His jaw clenched for a moment. "We did. Catherine and I. I'd do some renovation and restoration on the weekends. But when she got sick, there was no time. After…I lost interest in the place. I didn't want to live there anymore."

She frowned, searching for the right words, but they stood in a kind of silence that seemed to swarm them with Cooper's past, making it impossible to know what to say. She happened to glance away for a moment, and her gaze rested on the picture on the fireplace mantel. It was Cooper and Catherine on their wedding day. It was as though the air had been sucked out of her. She tried to blink away the moisture in her eyes, but he made eye contact and knew.

He swore softly under his breath. "I'm sorry."

"For what? You have nothing to be sorry about," she said.

"It's like every time we go out, you get hit with my past, and it's not fair to you."

She shrugged and forced a smile, knowing none of this was fair to either of them. But it wasn't his fault. "You can't hide who you were or that you were married to someone before."

He took a step closer to her and took her hand in his. "I know. But it's not that I was married and divorced and she isn't in my life because we aren't in love anymore. I get that. I don't know what you must feel. I don't know how I would feel, honestly."

Her gaze went from his eyes back to the beautiful picture on the mantel. "I don't know, really. I've never been in a situation like this. Cooper, I'm so in over my head right now I don't know anything about anything. I don't even know *what* we are."

He put down his cup of coffee and reached out to frame her face. Everything inside her lit up as he touched her, his strong, work-roughened hands touching her face with a tenderness she dreamt about at night. His blue eyes had darkened, his face taut.

"I don't know what we are, either," he said, his voice deep and thick and sending goose bumps up her arms. "I don't know what we are, but I know that I can't stop thinking about you. I want to be with you constantly. Hell, I just walked through every store downtown because I wanted to spend the day with you and do something I thought you'd like. I love the sound of your laugh, the sound of your voice. I wake up every day, for the first time in five years, and look forward to my day because I know you're going to be in it.

"But I don't want you thinking I'm looking for someone similar to Catherine or trying to replace her. I don't want you comparing yourself to her, or whatever. You are the first woman I've wanted in five years, and not because I haven't looked at another woman, but because I didn't want anyone else. You," he said, his voice dipping lower, scraping deliciously against her insides. "You, Emily, I want all damn day and night."

She leaned against him just as he kissed her. She ran her hands up his hard chest, and everything changed. He kissed her with a hunger she'd never experienced before, that she'd never even imagined could be like this. This feeling, this ache low in her abdomen wasn't something she could have imagined. His mouth was hard and demanding, and she kissed him back with the same desperation. She'd never felt so wanted, so out of her element yet safe.

He picked her up, and she wrapped her legs around his waist like she was a heroine in a movie. Emily Birmingham didn't do this kind of thing. Emily would have first fought him picking her up, thinking there was no way he'd be able to lift her. Then as his hands went to cup her bottom, she would have been insecure and worried he thought she was too big. But this Emily? This Emily just responded to his touch, to being touched by him. This Emily felt desire pool in her belly, felt the desire in him and trusted it.

With one hand still under her butt and the other at the back of her head, he kissed her as he walked. She loved scrunching her fingers in the thick hair at his nape as she clung to him, loved the rich scraping of his stubble against her smooth skin, the sensation of his mouth on hers. She paused as they entered his room, and she knew this was inevitable. He was how old? Thirty, maybe? This was way past the point in relationships where people slept together, right? Maybe. She clung to him, hoping her rapid-fire internal questions would slow down and she could get back to being in the moment with him.

But reality had a funny way of slapping her around, because as the sun shone through the window, it highlighted two gold bands on Cooper's dresser. She was in Cooper's bedroom, the king-size bed a glaring symbol of what they were about to do, yet there were two bands symbolizing his love and commitment to another woman. Had he moved on, really? Was she someone he was attracted to because he hadn't been with someone in five years? Had she been easy for him…this shy woman from the city with no history or ties to anyone in Maple Hill? She didn't think he was that callous, but maybe he wasn't even aware of it.

He set her down in front of the bed, and she put her hands on his chest.

"No pressure," he said.

She tore her gaze from his, from his, and tried to voice her concerns in a way that wouldn't be insulting. "I know this is going to be disappointing, especially if you haven't had sex in five years—"

"What? Hell. I don't need you doing me any favors," he said, taking a step back, his face like stone. So much for not being insulting.

"Oh my gosh, I didn't mean it like that," she said, covering her face for a second, frantically trying to explain. "I just meant…I don't do this. I…I've never had a boyfriend before. Like, never. I've never gone on a date, I've never talked on the phone with a guy, nothing."

The anger drained from his expression, and he went white. "What?"

She shrugged, increasingly embarrassed as the seconds went by. "I told you about my past and the…issues. I was just never comfortable enough with myself to trust a guy. You saw the contract. You know I have issues. I would clam up every time I talked to a guy, I would stand there and hear all the words that had been spoken to me growing up, and I would transpose them onto the guy, thinking that was what he was thinking. It's insane, I know, and I'm embarrassed to even tell you."

He ran his hands through his hair and let out a breath.

"You mean, like, what I think you mean?"

She threw her hands up. For a girl that didn't like a lot of attention or embarrassment, this situation was going sideways fast. "Yes, I mean I've never had sex. I haven't even worn a bathing suit after the age of twelve. I've never been naked in front of a guy."

That pathetic admission hung in the air, and she told herself that she wouldn't cry, because that would be even more humiliating. She told herself there was a reason she was confiding in him, that her gut had decided he was a man who could be trusted. She told herself, even as he stood there not saying a thing, that he would come through for her.

He shook his head. "I don't know what— Hell. This isn't what I expected. To be honest, that pisses me off."

She swallowed hard and folded her hands across her chest. "What?"

"I mean, it pisses me off to think of you going through life with such little self-esteem. Like, you turn heads, and you don't even realize it. I know that it shouldn't be about that, but it's like you've grown up thinking you're some kind of monster, when the truth is that you're incredibly attractive. Beautiful. On the inside and out."

She stood across from him, from the most kind, handsome man she'd ever known, in his bedroom, and they were worlds apart. He'd experienced a full life. He'd experienced love and death. She'd experienced nothing compared to him. She was only just now finding out who she really was, who she wanted to be, what she wanted to do with the rest of her life. She was years behind him.

He took a step closer and wrapped his arms around her. She slid her arms around his waist and rested her face on his chest, listening to the strong beat of his heart. Was this what it was like to be in love with someone? To have them know everything about you and have them defend you and see the best in you? He kissed the top of her head and whispered something. She leaned back and looked up at him.

"We should probably stop this here," he said.

She tried not to appear disappointed. It was the right thing to do. She knew she was falling for him; she was in love with him. And as much as he might like her, or be fond of her, or attracted to her, she didn't think forever was in the cards for him anymore. And if she slept with him, she would get herself into trouble, because she knew she'd fall for him completely. But the saddest part was that he knew it, too, and was doing the right thing by not getting that close to her.

As they left the room, her eyes went to the rings again, and she came to terms with the fact that everything they symbolized would prevent her from ever having Cooper's heart.

Chapter Sixteen

"I'm so happy you and Cooper are together," Callie said after Emily ordered. The coffee shop was bustling, and Emily knew her friend didn't have time to stand and chat—which was perfect because, after her time with Cooper last weekend, she didn't really know what to say.

Something had changed. Their easy banter had slowed, and she found herself avoiding him and suspected he was doing the same. But it had been easy to justify because they were both busy. He and his brothers were finishing up the major parts of the renovation, and she was busy with her new plan, which was the other reason she was at Callie's shop today.

She didn't want things to get awkward between her and Callie, because she'd grown so close to her and she loved their friendship. But she couldn't confide in her about Cooper.

She forced a bright smile on her face. "Thanks. Me, too. Is your friend here yet?"

Callie shook her head. "Noel texted to say she's running a few minutes late, but the window seat is empty. How about you go over and snag that spot, and I'll bring you guys coffees when she gets here?"

She nodded. "That's perfect. You're the best, Callie." Emily made her way through the tables, and once she reached her favorite spot, she pulled her laptop and notepad out of her bag. She settled in, telling herself to concentrate on the appointment she had with Noel, who was moving to Maple Hill and could potentially help her pull together her idea for the women's shelter.

If she and Noel clicked, then she'd have the support and expertise to move forward with her plan. She hadn't told anyone yet, but if she could make this happen, then at the next town council meeting, she'd be presenting an entirely different idea.

The distinct impression that someone was watching made her turn her head to the line, and her stomach dropped as she saw Cooper's former mother-in-law staring at her. Emily gave a wobbly smile and turned back to her screen.

Had Bernice heard what Callie had said? Obviously she must know that she and Cooper were dating, since she'd seen them together, and it's not like she'd expect Cooper to live the rest of his life by himself. She tried to shake off the guilt, but it wasn't easy, especially with Cooper's distance. She had believed for a while that she was starting to belong in Maple Hill, but this past week kept reminding her that she was still an outsider. All these people shared a history she wasn't part of. Maybe she'd never fit in here.

She glanced back at the line, somewhat relieved to see Bernice wasn't there anymore. Her pain was palpable, and she couldn't imagine what that would be like…to see the man who was supposed to be by your daughter's side for the rest of their lives now living a new life, a life that included a new woman, a new path.

She tried to shake off her sadness as she settled into her

spot and reviewed her notes. This time she would be more prepared for the opposition. She started making a list of the most likely concerns neighbors would bring forward, and then after her list was done, she was going to come up with at least three counterpoints for each. She pulled out a notepad and pen, ready to jot down ideas so she didn't forget anything.

"Emily, right?"

She glanced up to see Catherine's mother standing in front of her. Her heart pounded, and she forced a casual smile. "Hi, Bernice, nice to see you again."

She smiled back her, but it was a tight smile, and Emily's heart squeezed. She couldn't even begin to imagine what this woman had lived through, what her day-to-day life was like without her daughter, how many dreams she'd been robbed of. "Yes, it's nice to see you again, too. We were very happy to see Cooper out again with women," she said, her voice thin, not sounding happy at all, but her message registering that maybe Cooper was seeing other people, too.

Emily wasn't going to take any of this personally, and she knew full well that Cooper wasn't seeing other people. "Would you like to sit down?" she asked, gesturing to the empty seat across from her. She hoped she wouldn't, though, because she didn't really sense any friendliness from the woman.

She gave her a small nod and sat down with her cup of tea. "Are you liking Maple Hill?"

Emily tried not to let her trepidation show and nodded, pushing her notepad and laptop aside. "I am. I wasn't sure at first, since I've always lived in the city, but I really think this is becoming home."

Bernice toyed with her tea bag, her thin hand trembling slightly. "So you'll be staying here, then?"

Emily wished Callie would come soon with her coffee refill. She would serve as a great distraction, too. "Yes, I think so. I have plans for my grandmother's old house," she said softly.

Bernice gave her a nod, her gaze darting from Emily to her cup of tea. "The Merrick family is wonderful. I see you've also gotten to know Callie. She and Catherine were also very close. Like sisters, really," she said, her voice a thin whisper, as though the words were barely able to come forward.

"Yes, they have all welcomed me and become dear to me," Emily said, aching for the woman across from her, for how tortured she was, while at the same time uncomfortable. It was obvious this was all still very painful for her.

Bernice pursed her lips. "That's nice. Do you have a family of your own?"

Emily opened her mouth and shut it, not knowing how to answer that question without hurting her. She didn't want to feel guilty, like she and Cooper were doing anything wrong. But even worse was the possibility that Cooper felt the same way. The image of the wedding rings on his dresser was vivid and stabbed her with insecurity. She cleared her throat and shifted in her chair. "I have a brother in Toronto. My parents passed away almost a year ago."

She frowned slightly. "I'm sorry to hear that. But you and Cooper seem very happy."

"We…are. But it's…we're not serious or anything like that," she said, her voice trailing off.

She pulled the edges of her sweater coat closer over her thin frame and gazed into the distance, almost like she wasn't even talking to Emily anymore. The chatter from the crowded coffee shop receded, and Emily clung to her words, even though she knew they were meant to hurt her, but she clung to them because they offered her a glimpse of the man Cooper was before she knew him.

"He was wonderful to my Catherine. He was like a knight in shining armor, always there for her when she needed him.

I knew right from the beginning, when he rang our doorbell and respectfully came to meet us and take Catherine out on their first date, that he was a good man. Of course, he was very young then, but he grew into a wonderful man. They were so lovely together, so vibrant, so happy. Best friends. Soul mates."

Emily took a shallow breath, because all of it, hearing about Cooper and Catherine and this woman who was stuck in the past, was so heartbreaking. "He speaks of Catherine that way, with that love you are describing."

She folded her hands and stared at Emily. "They were supposed to have children. They were supposed to have the world. They wanted them so badly, and Cooper would have made a wonderful father. They were robbed of that. I've never seen such a doting husband. Even when she…when she got her diagnosis, he never gave up hope, he never stopped looking at her like she was the most important, beautiful woman in the world."

Emily forced a smile, despite the ache in her heart. "She was so beautiful. I saw her picture. They made a lovely couple," she said, hoping that she might at least ease her pain slightly.

"It wasn't fair," Bernice whispered. "I…I have to go," she said, gathering her purse, about to stand.

Emily reached across the table and held Bernice's hand, compelled to do something. "I'm sorry. I know Catherine was special. I'm so sorry she is gone, I'm so sorry for what you all had to endure."

Bernice stood abruptly, pulling her cold hand from Emily's. "Thank you. Sorry to have interrupted your work," she mumbled.

Before Emily could say that she hadn't bothered her at all, she was gone.

As soon as she walked out the door, Emily put her hands

over her face and rested her elbows on the table, the load of that conversation weighing her down as Bernice's words ran through her mind. *Cooper would have made a wonderful father. Soul mates.* Would any of them ever be able to get on with their lives without Catherine? She had no idea. She had no idea if she was setting herself up for a hard fall. Never mind—she was beyond setting herself up, she was already all-in. She was already in love with Cooper, and no matter what happened, she couldn't undo that.

Her stomach churned painfully, and she felt like she was going to be sick. She stared at her closed laptop, wondering how she was going to focus.

"Hey."

Emily looked up to see Callie standing there with a sympathetic smile and two mugs of coffee. "Hi," Emily said, trying not to sound upset.

"Sorry I couldn't get over here sooner. That conversation didn't seem very fun," she said, softly, sitting down across from her.

Emily pulled the mug of coffee closer to her, wrapping her hands around it and taking a sip, trying to collect her thoughts. She couldn't be honest with Callie… Catherine had been her best friend; she'd been Cooper's wife. They were all part of that life she knew nothing of. "She seems like a nice lady," she said, forcing a smile.

Callie frowned and opened her mouth, but a young woman walked up to them. "Callie!"

Callie stood up and smiled, hugging her. "It's so good to see you!" she said. Emily stood, too, as Callie introduced her to Noel.

"I'm going to grab you a coffee, Noel, and give you two a chance to get started. I know Emily has big plans. I'll be back," Callie said with a smile, walking to the counter.

Emily was relieved because now she'd be forced to get

Cooper and Bernice off her mind. She turned her attention to Noel, who was unpacking her bag. She was very pretty, with long, wavy blond hair and big brown eyes. "Thank you so much for meeting with me," Emily said.

Noel smiled at her, leaning forward. "I should be saying that to you. Based on our emails, I think you're onto something important and special, and I'd be really proud to be a part of this."

Emily let out a deep breath and relaxed her shoulders. At least something was turning out according to plan.

• • •

"This is what I want to do. For sure," Emily said.

"What?" Cooper asked, trying not to notice how gorgeous Emily looked today, trying to keep his emotional and physical distance. He'd barely slept a wink this week because he couldn't get Emily off his mind, or the fact that he was falling for her, harder than he thought possible. When he wasn't with her, she was all he thought about, and it had been good to feel, to want, until the other thoughts shoved their way through. He didn't know what to do with those—the ones that told him to back the hell away before something bad happened, before he got his heart ripped out again. He was mad at himself for thinking like that and for having no solution other than to pull back for both their sakes.

She spread her arms wide. "This. These girls. Morgan. I don't want an inn. I don't want to build my new life around my old ways. I don't want revenge. I don't need to prove to my family that I can make my own company and my own set of inns to compete. I don't want any of it. I want out of the game, and I want to do something meaningful. For the first time in my life, I believe I can do something meaningful, I can impact someone's life, I can maybe change the course of someone's life. I have been given this amazing opportunity through the circumstances of birth, and I can either use it to continue to stick it to my brother, or I can change a few lives at a time."

God, he loved all that about her. He fought the urge to kiss her and tore his gaze from hers before his control was shot. "So you've decided, then. You're positive?"

"I want to run a home for girls, teenage girls. Or maybe women and children. I don't know! I need advice and research, but all I know is that I want to use this big old house for women who need a safe place to live. Is that crazy? Am I crazy?"

He shook his head. "No."

Cooper listened intently as Emily read her bulleted list for the town council meeting. He'd never met someone with such drive and enthusiasm. They were sitting outside, enjoying what would probably be one of the last warm days of fall.

"What do you think?" she said, looking up from her laptop screen.

"I think you're incredible. I think you're the most ambitious person I've ever met."

She smiled—a beaming, proud smile like his opinion of her was that important. "Really?"

He nodded, and a wave of uneasiness gripped him by surprise. "You took this from one project to another without blinking an eye. From a business to a charity. Hell, you're amazing."

Her eyes shone, and she glowed. Instead of kissing her, he felt something tighten and was almost...repulsed...at himself. What was he doing? What was he saying to her? He was speaking to her like he was that significant in her life.

It hit him, then, all this worry for her, this wanting to be around her constantly, the thinking about her constantly, that he was most himself when he was with her.

He knew what all of this meant because he'd been down this road before. He knew what it was to love, and to love deeply. He knew the pain that went alongside that love, too, and he'd vowed to never go there again. And here he was, in love.

"So, by next year, I could have funding in place, zoning approved, and this house could be full. You and I can build this together, and we wouldn't even have to live here in the future and..." She stopped talking, her face turning red. Hell. He should say something to reassure her. But she was making plans...for a future. He didn't do that. Making plans meant nothing because then life happened and screwed up those plans.

He'd be worrying about her. He'd be worried that some enraged ex would come charging in here and go after one of the women and Emily would get hurt. What if she got sick? He didn't want that. He didn't want to worry about anyone ever again.

"Sorry, that was stupid," she said, tucking a strand of hair behind her ear. He saw the flash of embarrassment and the wobble of her smile—he'd caused that. He caused that to a woman who had worked so hard to get to a place where she was completely comfortable with a man...him. And now he was going to destroy everything she'd built, because he was a coward.

"I think we should slow down. Maybe step back from whatever it is we are," he said, doing his best to sound firm but not like an ass. He knew this was coming out of left field, but he had to stop everything. It was too much. Too fast.

Her face drained of color. "What?"

He ran a hand over his jaw and maintained eye contact with her, even though it was painful. "I didn't intend for us... to be anything. We started as friends, and I enjoyed my time with you, but I'm not interested in more than that."

Her mouth dropped open for a half second, and then she crossed her arms. "Right. That's perfect. I wasn't interested in anything more than a friend, either. I think I was the one who said that originally, right? That's why we have the contract. Great. So. Phew. Dodged a bullet there." She was speaking a mile a minute and backed up a few steps, her laptop almost falling as she tucked it under her arms. Her heroic attempt at saving face was killing him.

He shook his head. "No, not at all. I realize I'm not looking for commitment again, and it's not fair to drag this out."

She was nodding a little too quickly for it to be good.

"Me too. This is great timing, anyway. I have friends here now. And Morgan. And the women I'll be helping. Who has time to date their contractor?"

He swallowed hard, knowing this was all bullshit, knowing that he was hurting her just as much as he was hurting himself. He didn't want to be like the other men in her life who'd let her down.

"Emily…"

She gave him a sad smile, like a pitiful smile. "I know you've been incredibly, unbearably hurt. I know you were married to the best woman out there. I know you guys had all the same hobbies and interests, and she was brave and strong, and I probably would have loved her just as much as everyone else did. Still does. I know you miss her, and I know there is a part of you that will always, always love her. I was fine with that. I don't think you can love someone deeply and then just shut out that part of your life when someone else comes along. I may never have been in love before…but I understand that. So, you can go, guilt-free. Goodbye."

He wanted to take that offer and run, but he knew it wasn't that simple. He knew she was trying to hold onto what was left of her pride, and he hated himself for it. She was so incredibly wrong about him. She believed this was because of Catherine, that he was still in love with her, but that wasn't it at all.

The last thing he wanted was to hurt her, but if he laid it all out there, if he told her everything, there would be no going back. He'd be all-in. He swore he'd never be all-in again.

Her phone rang, and the Darth Vader ringtone filled the silence with cruel irony. She shot him a smile. "See? I have lots going on."

He clenched his fists, hating that she was still dealing with that jerk, and now she'd be doing it all on her own again. "You don't have to answer it."

She stared at him as the music continued. He'd lost the right to give her advice, to be protective. "Don't worry about me. I'll be fine. I'm always fine," she said.

He turned from her because it was killing him to know he was the cause of the pain and vulnerability on her face.

"No, wait," she called out.

He reluctantly stopped.

"Just in case you get it in your head that I'm not going to be okay without you—I'm going to be just fine. I came to Maple Hill because the men in my life screwed me over. I vowed to get revenge, but I did even better than that because I'm helping other women. But don't for a second think I can't move forward with this plan without you. I'll go to that council meeting without you, and I'll convince the town that approving this is the right thing to do. I'll build this place into something amazing for other women, and I'll do it without a man. So, thanks for our time together. You're a great guy, and I'm so glad you ended this now."

Well, hell. He'd never considered himself one of the bad guys until now. The fact that she lumped him in with her father and brother was insulting, but he knew from her perspective, it was pretty damn accurate. He'd failed her. She'd given him her honesty and her secrets, and he was turning his back on her. He cleared his throat past the lump in it and stared into her defiant eyes, admiring her strength. "I know you will."

He left, walking away from the woman who'd managed to enter his heart when he'd closed it off. She was the woman who made him laugh, who got under his skin, who listened to him, who trusted him. She was the woman that turned him on and made him feel alive again for the first time in five years. And he was a coward. He was a coward who was afraid of loving her unabashedly in case he lost her. He knew there would never be another chance if something happened to her. He knew he would never recover again. He was fine living alone. He was fine not having kids.

He was fine with all of it until Emily came along. She made him wish for things

But he wasn't fine with how he broke her heart along with his own. He wasn't fine with how he let her believe he wasn't able to love her because of Catherine, or that she couldn't come first over a woman who was no longer here. He wouldn't forgive himself for that. Because Emily was a woman who deserved to come first.

Chapter Seventeen

"Cooper?"

He looked up to see Catherine's mother standing in the doorway of Emily's home, her lips pinched and a deep worry line in her forehead. "Hi, Bernice, are you okay?"

She gave a small smile and nodded, walking in, turning her head, taking in the restored entrance, her gaze lingering on the freshly painted and stained staircase. "This is beautiful. You boys have done a wonderful job."

He nodded. "Well, it's all Emily's direction, her vision," he said gently. He had actually just been admiring the place, and the fact that Emily had decided to change her plans from making this a profitable five-star inn to opening a shelter for women and children. That kind of selflessness was inspiring… it was who she was…and he'd broken her heart.

He had believed that by breaking up with her, he was protecting himself. The only problem was, he was in too deep. Because not being with her every day was no kind of life, either. He just didn't know what the hell he was going to do about it. He had been thinking far too much lately. He was second-guessing things. He was letting fear control his life.

Bernice's eyes filled with tears. "Oh, Cooper, I'm so sorry."

He walked over to her, placing his hands on her arms. "You don't have to apologize to me. What's happened?

"I was horrible to her. I was a jealous, petty woman, and I'm so sorry. I came here to apologize to Emily," she said.

He swallowed hard as dread filled him. He'd hurt Emily, he didn't need to hear that she was now being hurt by other people, too, because of him. "She's not here."

"Can you call her for me?"

He let his head fall back, dropping his arms. "We're not in a very good spot right now, but I can leave her a message that you stopped by."

She covered her mouth with her hand. "Oh, please don't let it be anything I've said."

His stomach dropped. "Why? What did you say?" he asked, trying to keep his voice calm.

"I…I saw her at the coffee shop, and she was sitting there, beautiful and alive and…I was overcome with rage and jealousy. It should have been my Catherine sitting there, happy that she has you in her life, but she's gone. I sat there and talked about how you and Catherine were soul mates and how much you both wanted to be parents. Oh, Cooper, I'm sorry. I made it sound like there would never be anyone as good for you as Catherine. I think I broke her heart," she said, covering her face and sobbing. He pulled her into his arms, and she clutched his sides.

"It's okay. I'll talk to her," he managed to say through the ache in his throat. Emily didn't deserve any of their baggage, and she'd been saddled with all of it. All she'd heard about was Catherine. He had seen the sadness in their faces, and he didn't even know how to introduce Emily. It felt stupid to say she was his girlfriend, because she hadn't been, and he didn't want to hurt them.

He wasn't doing anything wrong, and he wasn't guilty of anything. He knew they would never want him to remain single for the rest of his life. But he cared deeply for them. They were good people, and while he could go on with his life, they couldn't. They couldn't go back and have more children. They would never have grandchildren. Their lives were set in stone now, and it was just the two of them living out the rest of their days without the daughter they adored.

Bernice pulled back and sniffled. "She should have been angry with me. She should have yelled at me and told me to leave. Do you know what she did?"

His teeth were clenched, and he shook his head.

She wiped her eyes. "She reached across the table and held my hand, Cooper. She knew I was in pain, and she showed me so much compassion. I didn't deserve her compassion. She's a lovely person, inside and out."

He nodded, the emotion in his chest making it impossible to speak. God, he loved Emily.

"I will never get over my daughter not being here, I will never get over all my old dreams of holding grandbabies one day, but that doesn't mean you shouldn't. You're a young, wonderful man, and you deserve all of that. You were the best son-in-law we could have ever asked for. You made us so proud. Please, please don't ruin the rest of your life by living on memories or living in fear of loving again. In my heart, as I was sitting across from Emily, I knew she was special. Live your life, Cooper. Fall in love again, have babies, have dreams to grow old."

He reached out for his former mother-in-law's hand, staring into the eyes of the woman he'd held when she was overcome with grief, when she'd whispered goodbye to Catherine. "You will always be like a second mother to me. You will always be family. I will never forget Catherine," he said hoarsely.

She nodded, reaching out to hug him again. "You stay in touch, Cooper. But only if it means you can still move on. Don't come and visit us if it drags you down."

"You've never dragged me down."

She pulled back. "I should go and apologize. Do you know when she's coming home?"

He shook his head. He needed to see Emily; he needed to make things right. "I don't, but I do know she'll be at the council meeting this week, trying to get this place approved for housing a shelter for women and children."

"That's lovely," she whispered. "I'll go to the meeting. Frank will, too. We'll say something in support of her."

He tried to smile. "I think Emily would really appreciate that. I don't know what kind of a response to expect. You know how much people hate change around here."

She patted his arm. "We'll show our support. We'll see you there, Cooper."

He nodded. "Okay."

He watched his former mother-in-law leave, knowing he had to make this up to Emily.

• • •

"What the hell did you do, Cooper?"

The banging on Cooper's door, followed by his sister's yelling, made him haul his ass off the couch. He should have known one of his family members would find out. Maybe he needed to see Callie, though. Maybe she would be able to tell him how Emily was doing.

He put down his beer, lining it up with the others on the coffee table, and walked to the front door. He supposed Callie was the best choice of his family members if he had to talk to someone. His brothers would have been much more irritating. After his talk with Bernice, he'd come home and drowned himself in beer and self-loathing. At least if he was forced to speak about his feelings, the alcohol had numbed things a little.

He opened the door to find all three of his siblings standing there.

He swore as Austin bulldozed his way through. "That's no way to greet family. And yes, we were quiet on purpose because we knew Callie had the best shot at you opening the door."

He moved aside as his siblings invaded his home and his personal space. Austin had already gone to the fridge, presumably to get beer for everyone, while Callie started straightening up the living room. Brody flopped down on the armchair and turned on the television, probably to irritate their sister. He watched with mild amusement as Callie snatched the remote out of his hand, shut off the television, and put the remote in her back pocket.

Austin entered the room a moment later and handed out beers. "Care to join us?" he asked.

Cooper leaned against the doorway. "Not particularly, no."

Callie grabbed a beer and then glared at him as she sat down. "Cooper, you better tell me why you broke my best friend's heart."

He looked down at the ground and clenched his teeth. He had no good answer for her.

"Because he's an idiot. One too many baseballs to the head," Brody said. "No one with half a brain would walk away from Emily."

Cooper shot him a look.

"That's not helping," Callie snapped at Brody. "If you have nothing nice to say, then keep it zipped."

"I thought you signed a contract that prevented you from

acting like a douche?" Austin said, propping his feet up on the coffee table.

Callie shook her head. "I've heard enough from the both of you. Leave the talking to me. Cooper, can you please sit beside me on the couch so we can talk?"

He almost smiled at the tone of his sister's voice, but instead he opted to scowl at his brothers as he sat on the couch. "I didn't mean to break her heart," he said.

"Well, you did."

He cleared his throat and made eye contact with her. "Did you talk to her?"

"She avoided me. *Avoided me.* Her best friend. Because of you. When you guys started dating, we acknowledged it might be weird, and we both agreed not to share sordid details and that whatever happened between the two of you wouldn't come between us. But it's easier said than done when you actually destroyed my best friend. And the worst part," she said, taking a huge gulp of air and then a long swig of beer—which was probably for dramatic effect, knowing her history, "the worst part is that she didn't even trash-talk you. I would have. Hell, I tried. But she didn't. She just said something sad, like you would never be able to get over Catherine, and that was okay, and she was fine with her life."

He opened his mouth, trying to come up with something to say, but couldn't because he felt sick. He knew it had nothing to do with the mass consumption of beer. Callie swatted him with a pillow. "You're ruining your life, Coop. You're ruining your life and hers, and you know what?"

He shook his head. "No, what?"

"She's wrong, isn't she? It's not because of Catherine at all. It's because you're afraid. You're afraid of loving her so much that it hurts," she whispered, pausing to blow her nose. He caught the sad expressions on his brothers' faces. He hated pity. He hated being the object of their worry, but they were right. They knew him better than himself, and if Emily had known her own self-worth she would have known he'd been lying to her.

He leaned forward and braced his forearms on his thighs. "You're right. I was an asshole because I thought I was protecting myself. I don't just want to...screw around with Em. I want her forever. I'm in love with her."

Silence clung to the air, and he felt somewhat better having that out there now.

"Well, then fix this," Brody said.

"That's my problem. How the hell do I fix this?"

"She'll talk to you," Callie said softly.

He hung his head and forced himself to speak to them and be open, when he hated being open. "It's not that. How do I convince myself to take a chance again?"

"Do you have a choice?" Brody said, putting down his beer and leaning forward, giving him that serious big brother stare that he'd mastered early on in his role as the oldest sibling.

"What do you mean?"

"What's the plan? Can you forget about Emily? Can you just walk away and live your life happily? What happens when you see her? When you see her with some other guy, are you going to want to rip his head off? Are you going to sit around like some loser wondering what your life could have been like with Emily if you weren't so damn scared?"

Cooper stared into Brody's eyes a little longer than was comfortable, mostly because he had already thought of this but was still incapable of getting off the couch and acting on it. "I know. I know you're saying the truth, but none of you really get it. You can sit there and tell me the logical thing to do, but none of you have had to watch your spouse die."

"You have to get that line of thinking out of your head," Brody said harshly.

Cooper stood up, adrenaline and anger kicking in. "You don't know what the hell you're talking about. Any of you. You just perpetually date whoever the fuck looks good to you on any given weekend, and it never goes anywhere. So until you have to watch someone die, then shut the fuck up. You know what I saw when Emily was telling me about her plans for that women's shelter she wants to build? I saw her as my wife. Pregnant. And then I imagined her dying. Like, who the hell have I become? I picture people dying? This is who I am now?

"I don't even know what I am, what I want. All I know is that I never want to do that again. I never want to lose someone again." His voice broke, and he wanted to kick something or someone. The silence in the room told him what he already knew—he had deep issues. Maybe they'd never go away.

"You lost your faith, Cooper," Callie said softly.

He turned away from all of them, bracing his hands on the fireplace mantel and purposely not looking at the picture of Catherine. "I don't want it, Cal. It got me nowhere. It means nothing. Faith means nothing when everything gets taken away from you."

Callie walked over and put her arms around him. "We know, Coop. We know. Which is why we want you to live your happily ever after. No one deserves it more than you."

Hell. Maybe it was that moment, his little sister's tear-filled plea about no one deserving a happy ending more than him, that got his head out of his ass, because there *was* someone who deserved a happy ending. An incredibly beautiful woman who'd trusted him, a woman who deserved the love of a man who'd make her first in his life, who'd show her with words and actions how amazing she was.

He'd been selfish, thinking just about how he couldn't go through grief again, how he was so scared of losing Emily. But what about Emily? She told him she didn't need a man—

that she'd gotten to where she was without one and that she'd get to where she needed to be without one. Maybe he needed to prove his worth to her, because he knew the power of two.

He kissed the top of Callie's head and said a sort of thanks. "Okay, I'm good. Get out."

Austin was the first to stand. "I see our work here is done."

Callie nodded, standing as well. "At least we can tell Mom and Dad not to worry about him anymore."

"Getting really sick of that conversation," Brody added.

"Yeah, you owe us one. They were going to come here tonight, and Mom had highlighted passages from the Bible she was going to read you," Austin said, slapping him on the back a little too hard to be friendly.

Cooper folded his arms across his chest and glared at them. "Fine. I owe you guys."

"Don't worry," Austin said as they left the house. "We'll be sure to collect."

Chapter Eighteen

Cooper stood by Pine Lake, the exact spot where he and Catherine's parents had spread her ashes. He'd come here a lot after she died. He'd sit on the dock and talk to her as though she were still alive. It had never felt stupid to him. She'd been a part of his life for so long, his best friend, that when she died, he'd longed to keep talking to her. But time had passed, and he'd slowly learned that in order to really move on, he'd have to let go a little. It wasn't that he'd forgotten her, but it was that he needed to start living again.

He'd thought he'd started to. He thought he'd re-entered the real world, but he hadn't. He knew that now, because of Emily. He hadn't been living until Emily came along. He'd been living a half life, a one-foot-in-the-lake kind of life. That half-assed approach was now going to cost him his relationship with Emily. Because when push came to shove, when he'd been faced with his greatest fears, he'd chickened out. He'd let Emily walk out of his life. He made a woman who'd never believed she was good enough trust him with her heart, only for him to basically confirm that she wasn't enough for him, either. He was an asshole. If he could have gone back and done things differently, he would have.

He would have protected her from his past. He would have talked to Catherine's parents before he was serious about Emily, so that he could protect her from them. But Emily hadn't signed up for any of their baggage. She could have any man she wanted, someone who didn't have issues with faith and trust, someone who could have given her the best of themselves. He didn't know what he had left of himself, and it clearly wasn't good enough for someone like Emily. She'd trusted him with her heart, with her secrets, her insecurities, and he'd walked away.

He pressed the heels of his palms into his eye sockets and swore out loud toward the empty lake. He was so damn sorry for hurting her and losing her. No, he was afraid of loving her more and more and then losing her. He didn't know how to explain that. He had never started out wanting to fall in love again. With Catherine it had just been natural. They were so young neither of them really had any idea what they were doing. They had no idea how shitty life could be, how cruel. They just went in blind—and they'd gotten burned.

Now that he was older, he knew what it meant to love someone with everything you were and to make dreams for a future that would never happen, and he was afraid. Emily made him alive again. She gave him purpose. She made him laugh. He was humbled by her faith and trust in him, which was why he hated himself for letting her down.

He sat on the edge of the dock. He needed to get this over with and make things right.

"Hi, Cath," he said, letting out a deep, weighted sigh. He still came here now and again, but he didn't have that need to speak aloud anymore. Sometimes he'd stand here waiting, searching for the guy he used to be, searching for the life he used to have. He didn't need that today. Today he needed closure; he needed to move forward.

"I was thinking back to that night we talked about me moving on." He could remember like it was yesterday. The doctors had told them hope was gone, that there was nothing left to try. They had stayed in bed, and he'd just held her. They had clung to each other as though there might be some way they could stay like that forever. If he'd been a kid, he'd have wished he might be enough, that his holding her in the real world would be enough to keep her there. They had talked the entire night, and he'd been so grateful for that because it was the last night she'd really talked. They had talked and cried and kissed, and he'd told her there would never be anyone else for him.

And yet now, here he was, in a place where there was someone.

Five years ago, he never could have imagined himself with another woman, let alone another woman he loved more than anything. He ran his hands through his hair. "You told me you didn't want me to spend the rest of my life alone. You told me you wanted me to get married again and have kids, and we argued until I finally agreed, because I didn't want you to be upset. But I lied. I lied to you to give you peace. You know how much I missed you; you know how much we all missed you. You were my best friend and lover and wife, and I never thought I would want that again. Losing you almost killed me. It changed me. I'm not the same person I was. I've realized I was half-living because I was afraid of full-living and loving.

"I met someone. Emily. She's new here and, uh, as weird as it sounds, I think you'd have liked her. She's different from you; she's different from anyone I've met before. I've fallen for her. I see myself with her forever. And I just want you to know that my loving her doesn't ever change the love I had for you. And I'll still watch out for your parents. They will always be a part of my family."

He wiped his palms down the front of his jeans and took a deep breath, the heaviness in his chest easing as he stood. He pulled out the two wedding bands that had been on his dresser for the last five years, clutching them for one last moment before dropping them into the water. They belonged with Catherine, with whatever part of him she took with her when she died. They belonged with his old life. This part of his life wasn't erased, but it was over. He was ready to move forward, fully.

He wasn't afraid of the depth of the love he had for Emily. Now, he just needed to make things right for her. He needed to prove she was the only woman on his mind.

• • •

Emily finished applying a coat of neutral lip gloss and then assessed herself in the front hall mirror. She needed to appear professional, but not too dressed up or no one would identify with her at the town hall meeting. She needed to seem approachable. She also needed to look good and not like she was dying of a broken heart, because she knew Cooper and his family would be there tonight. Or maybe just his family. Regardless, they'd tell him if she was thriving or if she looked like a zombie. This wasn't about her and her drama; this was about convincing the town that a women's shelter was the right thing for it.

She double-checked that her notes were in the bag. She had prepared as much as she could, and at least this time she knew what to expect. She was ready to fight for her shelter, with or without Cooper's help.

The doorbell rang, and Emily's heart leaped. She foolishly hoped it was Cooper coming to tell her he'd made a horrible mistake. What she hadn't realized when she started falling for him was how much it would hurt to be rejected by him. She'd been able to save face that night because she'd had years of practice, years of being hurt and not letting it show. She had put herself out there for the first time in her life, and she'd been shot down. The old her might have picked apart all her worst qualities and then said that was the reason. But she knew it wasn't her fault.

She was barely making it through the days. She kept busy by avoiding Cooper and getting to know Morgan more and more. She and Morgan had developed an understanding, and she was so happy to see that the girl seemed to be coming out of her shell. She'd even been able to see her laugh, and some nights they'd watch TV together and order pizza. She had never imagined that helping someone like this would help heal her own wounds. Callie's friend Noel had been the biggest blessing, helping her with the new plan to turn the house into a women's shelter. She knew the exact people to reach out to for approval and to get funding and nonprofit status. If all went well tonight, she would be able to make this a reality and help countless women and children.

She walked to the door, refusing to hope for something she knew wasn't going to happen, but still having a tiny glimmer of hope that Cooper was standing on the other side. She opened it, and dread pooled in her stomach as she found her brother standing on the porch.

It was cruel—of all the people in the world to show up, and right before she had to get to the town hall. She clutched the door, trying to summon strength for the blow she hadn't seen coming. She'd thought it was Cooper. How pathetic could she get?

"Hi," her brother said, for a second looking as though everything was fine. She knew it was all an act. This was the calmness and pleasantness before she said *no*. When you said no to him, that's when all hell broke loose.

She tilted up her chin, clutching the door tightly. "Hi. What are you doing here?"

He straightened the lapels of his suit. "You need to face your responsibilities and come back home."

She stepped out onto the porch, shutting the door behind her because she didn't want Morgan hearing what she knew would soon be an argument. "I am home. *This* is my home. I've made it very clear I'm not coming back. Also, I think the last time we talked you were pretty insulting. Maybe you should be starting this conversation with an apology."

He smirked and held up his hands in a patronizing motion. "Easy there. Don't go getting all angry. Calm down."

She clenched her teeth and forced herself to play the game and not lose her composure. "I'm speaking in a calm voice. All I said was that you owe me an apology."

"I heard you didn't get zoning approval for your stupid inn. What, did you actually think you were going to be able to compete with our inns?"

She focused on the trees in the distance, on the sounds of the rushing river, the rolling thunder in the distance, and not on the past. She needed to stay confident, to remember she was here for a reason. Everything that had happened in the last year was for a greater purpose. She knew who she was now, she knew the kind of woman she was supposed to be, with or without Cooper. "I'm starting something else, and I'm actually late for a meeting, so I've got to go."

"You can't just leave. I'm here to talk about the business."

"It's not my business. If you wanted to have a serious discussion about this you should have called or texted first. I have a life. I can't cancel my plans just because you decided you need to speak with me right this very second."

"Oh, right, the big important CEO whom I need to schedule an appointment with. I don't know who you think you are, but you're just my little sister. Show some respect," he said, his lips twisting into an ugly snarl.

"Why do you even want me around? I would think this is a dream come true for you. You have the business and you can do whatever you want with it."

"It's not about that. It's about family legacy and loyalty."

She fought the urge to scream. "No, it's about control. You want control over me. You want to lord it over me that it's your company and I'm just an employee like everyone else. You have no one in your life. Mom is gone and she was the only person who did whatever you wanted her to do. So now you're here, not because you think I'm particularly great in the hotel business, not because you even like me. You're here because you need a minion. Well, it's not me."

He ignored what she said completely. "I think you've had enough playing house out here, and it's time to come back home and start over. You sure packed on the pounds. Your face has gotten fat."

Five years ago, insecurity would have held her prisoner, wondering if he was right, rushing to a mirror when she was in private. Ten years ago, she would have crumpled like a paper bag, unable to deal with wounds inflicted by a person of authority. But she wasn't that same girl. She didn't fall for these games anymore. "I'm not five, you can't just tell me to come back home, and if I want to pack on pounds, that's my choice," she snapped, starting to lose her cool.

His face twisted, and she knew he was close to losing his temper, too. She couldn't ever say no to him. "I'm your brother, and I'm in charge of the company. You're a very selfish person, going so far from home and abandoning the family business."

"There is no family anymore. If you wanted me as part of your family, then you should have treated me better. And this display isn't exactly endearing you to me."

"You're just jealous Dad didn't leave you the company.

Stop your whining."

"I'm not. But I have a right to build my own life, and I'm doing it here. I can make that choice because I'm an adult and don't need to follow orders."

He rolled his eyes. "You were always into this feminist crap."

She closed her eyes for a second because there was too much to process too fast. She counted backward from ten and then opened her eyes. Unfortunately he was still there. "So, let me explain something to you about how the real world works—there are women who own businesses. It's not part of some secret underground feminist agenda. It's that women, *like men*, can also enjoy running corporations and having careers."

He must not have liked her carefully enunciated words or primary-school tone, because he moved closer to her. The old Emily would have shrunk back, would have backed down. But she'd left that girl in Toronto. This Emily took a step forward. She took a step forward for all those girls and women who would one day fill her house.

He grabbed her wrist and got way too close to her for comfort. Her heart beat painfully against her chest, but she refused to cower or break eye contact with him, even when she saw the rage spewing from his eyes.

"I'm not going with you. I think you need me because you don't know how to run that business, and no one likes you because you treat people like crap."

He twisted her wrist, and she writhed trying to free herself. "Bitch," he snarled.

He shoved her hand away, and she fell. She landed with a painful *thud* on the lawn and cried out as her elbow hit the ground with a painful snap. Searing pain stole her breath, and she was only vaguely aware of her brother leaving, the sound of his car pulling out of the driveway. Closing her eyes, she lay back on the ground, trying to catch her breath and find a way to make the pain in her elbow stop. She was not going to overthink this. She was fine. Everything was going to be fine.

"Who the hell was that douche?"

Emily opened her eyes to see Morgan running down the steps and crouch beside her.

"My brother," she managed to rasp, cradling her elbow with her other hand and then shooting Morgan a smile, as if none of this was a big deal.

"I should have come out here when I saw him grab you," Morgan said, her voice suddenly changing and her eyes filling with tears. It was a rare display of emotion.

Emily tried to smile for her sake, despite her pain. "What are you talking about? I'm fine. You didn't need to come out here, Morgan. I'm an adult, and I can take care of myself."

Morgan gave her a pointed stare, and she forced herself to sit up, ignoring the blinding pain that ran through her back and arm as she moved.

"I kept telling myself to just open the door and tell him I was going to call the cops, but I was so scared," Morgan said, tears spilling from her eyes. "I had my phone, though. If he did something bad, I was going to call the cops."

Emily squeezed her hand. "You did the right thing. He… It's over. He left. I'm okay."

Morgan brushed aside her tears angrily. "You didn't tell me you had a loser in your family, too."

Emily forced a smile. "Everyone's got one, right? I never thought he'd show up here. But, um, listen, I'm going to have to go get this checked out," she said casually, like she was planning on picking up a pizza. She didn't want Morgan to freak out or be worried for her, but she knew there was something wrong. She was pretty sure she'd broken her wrist or elbow. Or both.

Her eyes grew wide. "Like at the hospital? Do you want

me to come with you?"

Emily stood slowly, holding her arm in place. "I'm okay. You've got homework. I'll be fine. It's really not a big deal. I'm probably being overly cautious, but I might as well get it checked out."

"I think you should call Cooper," Morgan said, following her up the steps as she went to get her purse. *Cooper.* Poor Morgan had no idea, and she wasn't about to ruin her perception of Cooper, who had treated Morgan so kindly. She needed to know there were good men out there. She wouldn't say anything about him. So much for the council meeting and getting her life under control. Maybe she could call Noel, and she could stand in for her.

She grabbed her purse with her good arm and started walking toward the driveway, Morgan following her step by step. "Uh, that's okay. I don't want to bother him."

"Why not? He bothers us all the time," she said.

Emily forced a laugh, even though she wanted to cry. "He's busy."

"He's always around here; he can't be that busy. Call him. How are you even going to drive to the hospital? That's, like, over half an hour away."

She waved her good hand as casually as possible and not like she felt her entire arm might fall off. "I'll be fine. I don't need Cooper. Are you afraid of mice?"

Morgan shook her head. "No."

She patted the girl on her shoulder. "Good, then we really don't need Cooper. I'm fine. We'll be fine. It's my left elbow anyway, and there's, like, no one on those back roads. I'll be lucky if I spot a deer."

Morgan was eyeing her suspiciously as she opened her car door for her. "Did you guys break up?"

"Morgan, I have to go. Remember the rules—lock the door, and don't answer it to strangers."

"You mean strangers or my dad or your brother."

Emily forced a smile. "We're going to be okay, kid. I'll text you later."

"I still think you should let someone drive you," Morgan called out as Emily sat in the driver's seat. The pain stole her breath away, and she tried not to scream. She shut her eyes as a wave of nausea hit her. She slowly adjusted her arm into a position that wouldn't hurt if she kept it perfectly still.

"I'll be fine! See?" she said again, attempting a flippant and light tone. Really, what was there to be sad about? The one man in the world she wanted and loved desperately couldn't let go of his past or his deceased wife, her monster brother had returned and manhandled her, breaking her arm or something, she was missing the town council meeting and would probably not get her zoning amendment because everyone in this town hated change—and her—and now she had to drive with one arm while the other throbbed painfully. It was all fine.

Or she was going to cry all the way to the damn hospital.

• • •

Cooper peeled out of the town hall parking lot and drove to Emily's house as fast as he could. When he pulled into her driveway, his instincts told him something was very wrong. Her car wasn't there, and he knew there was no way in hell she'd deliberately miss the meeting tonight. It meant too much to her—the women she was going to help, Morgan. There was no way she'd blow this off just because of him or how much she hated him.

He parked and exited his truck, running up the front walkway, only to find Morgan sitting on one of the wicker chairs. "Well, it's about time. Some boyfriend you are."

He stilled, and panic—which was very rare for him—took

over. "What happened?"

She crossed her arms and glared at him. "Em's loser brother came here, and they got in a fight, and he was really mean," she said, her voice going from anger to vulnerability.

He walked over to her slowly, trying to keep his cool, trying not to scare her. "What happened?" he asked again, crouching in front of her.

Her face crumpled up, and she started crying. Holy shit. "Morgan, what happened?" he repeated, keeping his voice calm and soothing when he wanted to yell.

"He grabbed her and pushed her, and she fell off the porch. He just left, but she was lying there funny. When I came out she pretended like it was no big deal and that she was fine, but she couldn't move her arm."

He stood abruptly and shoved his hands in his pockets, and rage and self-loathing washed over him. He wanted to find her brother and hurt him and tell him to stay the hell away from Emily. But the self-loathing...because if he hadn't been such an ass, none of this would have happened. He would have been here today, picking her up to go to the meeting. He would have been here when her brother showed up. He could have kept her safe. He wouldn't have let him close to her, let alone lay a hand on her. "Where is she now?" he asked, still trying to appear calm.

"She insisted on driving herself to the hospital."

Shit. He started walking away.

"I told her to call you, and she said we didn't need you," Morgan said, the accusation in her voice making him cringe. He paused and looked over his shoulder at her, at this girl that had entered their lives. Emily had taken her in without question, had given her the best of everything without blinking an eye. She deserved so much more than this.

"I'll fix this," he said, hoping to hell he could.

He was halfway down the walkway when she called out

to him. He turned around.

Morgan stood at the end of the porch, her arms tightly wrapped around her waist, looking young and afraid. "She asked if I was scared of mice. Of course, I'm not, but I didn't want to make fun of her, you know, because she's been so nice to me."

He clenched his teeth and managed a nod. He didn't think he'd ever felt like such an asshole before in his life.

"Then she said that was fine, because we didn't need you."

He paused, hating himself a little more before turning to leave.

"Cooper?"

It dawned on him that this was the first time Morgan had called him by name. She stood there, small and thin, that chip on her shoulder fading and the vulnerability shining through. He hated that he was contributing to her anxiety in any way or to her perception of what men were really like. He had to make it right. "She said she didn't need you, but I think she does. Even though the guys I've known haven't been the best…you seem okay."

He cleared his throat past the lump of emotion. "Thanks. The real truth is that I need Emily just as much. Maybe more."

"You're going to find her, right?"

"Yeah. Of course. She'll be fine. This will all be okay. Why don't you go inside and lock the doors? Noel and my sister, Callie, will come over and keep you company, okay?"

He waited for her to argue that she wasn't a baby, but instead she nodded, walking into the house. She paused at the door. "Emily is the nicest person I ever met. She's the only adult who ever cared about me. Make sure she's okay."

He nodded and started running toward his truck.

Chapter Nineteen

Emily squeezed her eyes shut as a wave of pain swept over her when she pulled her SUV into a parking space outside the emergency room of the hospital. She'd driven for half an hour with her arm lying limp in front of her, each jostle and bump making her cry out or curse.

She'd had bad days, she'd been hurt in life, but nothing had prepared her for the onslaught of bad luck and misery over the last few days. First Cooper and his admission that he couldn't ever give her what she needed, and what she suspected was his love for Catherine that he couldn't let go of. Then the chat with his former mother-in-law, followed by her demented, misogynistic brother's sudden appearance and assault. Oh, and of course, the fact that she missed the meeting and the town was probably busy turning down the outsider's plans.

It was laughable. A part of her wondered if she could just sell the house and leave. She'd take Morgan with her if she wanted to come, because what was left for her here? The only problem was all the money she'd invested in the house—she'd never get that much back even if she sold.

Emily parked her car and slowly got out, somewhat distracted from her pain as she walked toward the hospital. It was tiny. Like a cute shoebox. She'd never seen such a small hospital. She walked toward the red EMERGENCY sign, noting how old but well-maintained the building was. If she hadn't been in so much pain and if the reason for being here weren't so pathetic, she would have lingered to admire how adorable this was.

The automatic glass doors whooshed open, and she walked into a lobby that was even smaller than her house's foyer.

A nurse behind a desk enclosed by a plastic barrier smiled at her. "Hi there, honey. Come on forward."

Emily looked around and saw no one else. This would be fantastic. Maybe the wait time would even be under an hour. Emily pulled out her wallet, wincing with pain as her wrist moved.

"Oh, honey, can I help you with that?"

"I've got it," Emily managed, pulling out her card and handing it to the nurse.

She asked her address and phone number and a few other things before pointing her to a triage room across the small hallway. Emily thanked her and made her way over, sitting down with a tired sigh. A moment later, the same nurse came in. "Okay, so tell me what happened."

Emily stared into the woman's eyes and contemplated telling her the truth, that she'd been on the receiving end of a violent outburst and had moved away to protect herself and had fallen. But who cared? Really, none of it mattered anymore. She had brushed herself off and driven herself here. This woman didn't care about her problems, and Lord knew she'd seen much worse. "Uh, well, I fell off a porch step and landed on my elbow. I think I heard a snap."

The nurse winced and made a *tsking* noise, and she touched Emily's arm and elbow in a few different places. Emily tried not to make a sound as she pressed on the sensitive area. After asking a few more questions and taking her vitals, she gave her a kind smile, her weathered features calming and soothing to Emily. "Well, you'll need X-rays, and then the doctor will see you. I'm going to get you ice and ibuprofen while you wait. I'll be right back."

Emily sat in the small bland room and blinked a few times as tiredness set in. This was a different kind of exhaustion, though. This was the exhaustion of defeat, of finally waving the white flag of surrender. She didn't want to think about everything that had happened, but she couldn't stop. She hated a pity party, but this was a new low, the kind that Cheetos and wine couldn't cure. Her notes for the council meeting were poking out of her bag, a cruel reminder of everything she lost tonight.

She closed her eyes and tried not to relive the week's events, but they played across her mind like a dramatic movie trailer.

What was she doing here? Was this really her life?

She was so incredibly alone. She belonged nowhere. She didn't belong in Toronto anymore, but she didn't belong here, either. These people didn't want her; they didn't think she'd ever be part of their world. Maybe they were right. Maybe she didn't understand how things worked here. Maybe there was no way she'd have received her shelter approval tonight at the council meeting, anyway.

So, maybe she should just get a real estate appraisal and cut her losses. She'd put her grandmother's house up for sale and leave town. She had no other choice. She couldn't live in Maple Hill with all the Merricks around. She would run into them regularly, then she'd run into Catherine's mother, and then what would happen to her relationship with Callie?

Callie ran the only coffee shop in town.

"Okay, my dear. Ibuprofen," the nurse said, walking through the door. She held out a tiny paper cup with an Advil in it and another paper cup with water.

"Thank you," Emily said, taking the pill then the water.

The nurse tossed the cups in the garbage when she'd finished and then wrapped an ice pack and towel around Emily's elbow. "Now you go sit in the waiting area and someone will come and get you for X-rays, okay?"

Emily forced a smile and stood, careful not to jostle her arm. "Thank you."

She walked toward the little waiting room, mildly impressed to see a television broadcasting HGTV. She sat down opposite the TV and tried to focus, but then grew irritated as she saw the couple renovating a house together. They were married and laughing and joking—the last thing she needed to see right now.

She leaned her head back against the wall and shut her eyes, hoping the Advil would kick in soon to alleviate the throbbing in her arm. She wasn't sure if she'd dozed, but the sound of a baby crying had her glancing in the direction of the admitting area. A young woman around her age was standing there with a baby in her arms and a toddler clinging to her leg, pulling on her leggings. The woman hobbled over to the triage station, dragging the leg with the clingy toddler.

Emily closed her eyes again, exhaustion and depression making her just want to sleep the time away. She hoped that since she was the first one admitted that meant she'd be seen soon. She was dreaming of going home, having a hot bath and then putting on her favorite pajamas and crawling into bed.

"Mommy, I want to go home!"

Emily opened her eyes again and spotted the clingy toddler now climbing over the waiting room chairs. The poor mother was flushed and rocking the whimpering baby in her arms. "Luke, Mommy told you, we have to wait for the doctor to see you and Maddy. Then we can go home."

"It's boring here. I'm hungry. Is it dinner yet?"

Emily offered the woman a sympathetic smile, not really expecting her to say anything. But she gave a laugh. "Sometimes I don't even know if I'm going to make it through the day," she said to Emily.

Emily winced. "Well, hopefully you won't have to wait long. There doesn't seem to be anyone else here," she said.

The woman rolled her eyes. "Don't let this waiting room fool you. There's only one ER doctor at this hospital, and I bet there are at least six other patients in the exam rooms."

Dread pooled in Emily's stomach. "Are you serious? Here I thought I'd hit the jackpot."

"Sorry to burst your bubble, but I've never been out of this place in under three hours."

"Is that a long time, Mommy?" the toddler said, crashing into his mother.

"Sort of," she said. "Come on, let's go sit down. Mommy's getting tired."

"Can I get you something?" Emily asked gently. At least she didn't have to worry about kids. She just had herself to take care of. This young woman was all on her own with two little ones.

"Oh, no, that's okay. Thank you, though," she said, sitting and adjusting the baby, who had finally fallen asleep.

"Seriously. I'm sure there's a place to get coffee. I don't mind at all. I'll get one for myself, too."

She could tell the woman was caving, and for a second, her lip wobbled, like she was touched that Emily had asked her. She gave a small nod and reached for her purse. "Thank you," she whispered.

"It's on me," Emily said firmly. "Can I get your little guy something?" she whispered, glancing at the toddler who was momentarily entertained by the small children's play table.

The woman shook her head. "Don't worry. He's fine."

Emily tilted her head. "I'm getting him something. Just tell me what *not* to get."

The woman smiled up at her. "Okay, he'll eat anything, really. He has no allergies, so it's up to you."

Emily winced as she stood up and swung her purse over her shoulder while trying to keep the ice pack wrapped around her elbow. "I'll be right back."

"I wish I could help you, but if I put this one down she'll wake up, and she hasn't slept all night," the woman said.

"Don't worry about it. I'm fine. Okay, point me toward the coffee shop," Emily said.

The woman gestured to a corridor opposite them. "Don't expect much, but if they're closed, there are a few vending machines beside the shop."

"Great," Emily said, walking slowly in the direction of the coffee shop. The small hospital was dated but was very clean and very quiet. She saw a sign indicating that the "Cozy Corner Cafeteria" was straight ahead. She smiled at the name. She walked inside the empty place, worried that it was closed. There was a young man behind the single cashier desk. "Food service is closed for the night," he said before she could even ask.

Her heart sank, thinking about that poor woman. "How about coffee?"

He nodded. "We have coffee and tea until eight o'clock. It's self-serve," he said, pointing to a small coffee station.

"Great," Emily said, walking over. She desperately needed a cup to combat her exhaustion and the night ahead. She awkwardly filled two cups and snapped the lids on after adding cream to both and securing them in a cardboard tray. Once she paid, she stopped by the vending machines to find snacks for all of them. She gasped out loud as her ice pack fell and her elbow moved unnaturally. Pain seared through her body and tears stung her eyes. She took a few deep breaths and put the coffee down on the bench then started the gruelling, tedious task of putting change in the vending machine with her one working arm.

She stared at the bag of Cheetos like it was a mirror to her life. She had broken her addiction, but for what reason? She was going to eat the Cheetos. Three chocolate bars, three bags of Cheetos, and three bags of assorted candies later, she made her way back to the waiting room. She was surprised to see an elderly couple also in the waiting room now, as well as a man at the admitting booth. She walked over to her new friend, who now had the toddler on her lap and the baby on her side.

"I've got treats," Emily whispered.

The little boy jumped off his mother's lap. "For me?"

Emily nodded, smiling at the cute, blond-haired little boy. "As long as your mom says it's okay, you can pick anything from this pile," she said, placing her purse with the treats stuffed inside on the chair. She handed the woman her coffee and then took a sip from her own. She tucked her bag of Cheetos into her purse.

"Thank you so much," the woman whispered. "I didn't even think to bring snacks, I just rushed out of the house, and it's almost dinner. I wasn't thinking at all," she said, her voice breaking. That's when Emily noticed the woman didn't look good at all, and it was more than just exhaustion. The dark circles under her eyes had to have been from just one night of no sleep. Her pale skin and wan appearance made Emily think she was struggling.

"Well, don't worry about it. A vending machine dinner is fun," Emily said, winking at the little boy who had chosen a caramel bar and a bag of Cheetos.

"What do you say to the nice lady, Luke?" his mother

asked.

The little boy grinned up at her. "Thank you."

Emily smiled back. "You're welcome, honey. Why don't you sit down, and I can help you open your treats, okay?" He nodded and did as she suggested.

Once Emily had opened his food and he was eating contentedly, she sat beside the young woman. "I'm Emily, by the way."

The woman smiled. "Tracy."

They sipped their coffees, the both of them quiet. That's when Emily overheard the conversation at the admitting station. "I don't have any papers, though. I have nothing. I don't even have my health card. I was just released from the federal penitentiary today."

Federal penitentiary? And here she assumed this was a quiet, boring little hospital. Emily tried to inconspicuously turn around so she could see what the man looked like. She didn't want to panic, but really it was slightly disconcerting to know there was a man who'd just gotten out of a maximum-security prison in the hospital with them.

From the corner of her eye she could see he was massive—bigger than Moose and heavily muscled and tattooed. His long hair was pulled back in a ponytail, and he had a jagged scar from his ear down to where it disappeared under his shirt. He glanced in her direction, and she quickly turned away, not wanting to draw any attention to herself or make it look like she was eavesdropping or judging…which was exactly what she was doing.

"This coffee is just what I needed," Tracy said, leaning her head back slightly, but being careful not to wake the baby.

"Me, too. I'd offer to help you with your baby, but I can't move my arm," Emily said, thinking that the woman must be exhausted.

"Oh don't worry. I'm okay. The fact that you managed to

keep Luke happy and quiet is the kindest thing. Luke, how's your head, honey?" she asked as the little boy touched his head and winced.

"Okay, Mama," he said, looking into his chip bag.

Tracy blinked away tears.

"Oh, poor little guy, did he hurt his head?" Emily whispered.

She lifted her guilt-filled eyes to her and shook her head. "An accident. My husband—"

"Emily Birmingham?"

A nurse was standing in the waiting room doorway. Emily stood, hating the timing and that the young woman couldn't finish her story. "I'll be back soon. We can talk. Hang in there, okay?"

Tracy nodded and gave her a small smile.

"I'm going to take you to X-ray," the nurse said, offering a friendly smile. Emily followed her down the hall and into a room with X-ray equipment. The woman was efficient and chipper, and the few X-rays were completed quickly.

"Do you know when the doctor will get the results?" she asked after the nurse said she was all finished.

"He'll get them right away, but Dr. Morrow is super busy tonight, and honestly, since you're not critical, it might be a few more hours until he gets to you."

Emily tried not to let her frustration show as she thanked her and made her way back to the waiting room. If she weren't in so much pain, she'd just leave and go to a hospital in the city tomorrow, where there was more than one doctor. But that would also require driving, and there was no way she'd be able to handle a two-hour drive. She needed to get back to Tracy, because that situation and what she was about to tell her didn't sound good at all.

On her way back, she spotted the elderly couple from the waiting room standing in front of the vending machine and repeatedly pressing the change button.

"That machine giving you trouble?" Emily asked, approaching.

"Oh my dear, it seems to have swallowed our money and didn't give us our chocolate bar," the white-haired lady said.

"Hmm, do you mind if I take a peek?" Emily asked.

"Be our guest," the man said, a kind smile on his weathered face.

Emily pressed the button to clear their order and then reached down to retrieve the dropped coins and placed the order for them again, asking which bar they wanted. The bar dropped and they were adorably sweet as they oohed and aahed at her ability to work the machine. She smiled at them. "It's no problem at all. Can't sit in a hospital waiting room for hours and not have a snack!" Emily said.

They agreed and the three of them made their way down the empty corridor.

Emily walked over to the young mother, who was pacing, rocking her crying baby while her toddler cried that he needed the bathroom. "I can hold her," Emily said, holding out her good arm, determined to help. "How about you place her in the crook of my right arm," she said, positioning herself to hold the baby.

"Are you sure?" Tracy said, bouncing the baby while Luke danced frantically around her yelling he needed to pee.

"Go. We'll be right here," she said as Tracy placed the baby in her arms.

"Okay, we'll be right back," the woman said, and she chased her son to the bathroom.

Emily tried walking with the baby cradled in her one arm as the baby cried. She tried bouncing her, but it was painfully hard not to move her other arm in the process. She was pleased that after a few walks around the waiting room the baby seemed to quiet to a whimper.

"Looks like you're doing a good job," the giant man said in a gruff voice.

Emily glanced up at him, startled. She smiled tentatively, her heart squeezing as she saw the kindness and insecurity in his eyes. She'd judged him. She'd expected him to be mean and rough, and he was smiling at the baby as though she were a little angel. "For now," she said with a soft laugh.

He smiled back at her, his eyes crinkling in the corners, a sparkle in them. The elderly woman came over and cooed at the baby. When Emily worried her arm wouldn't hold out anymore, Tracy came back with her much calmer toddler.

"I'm so sorry," she whispered, taking the baby.

"No problem, she calmed down."

Tracy's gaze went over Emily's shoulder. "I need to find a spot to warm up her bottle."

"You know I think the cafeteria had a microwave. Let me go," Emily said.

"Oh my goodness, you are like an angel," Tracy said, her eyes flooding with tears as she reached into the diaper bag and pulled out a bottle. Emily tried not to stare as the woman's sleeve rose, revealing a deep-purple bruise in the shape of a hand.

"Ha. No, I'm not. But I don't mind helping at all. There's not much else to do in this place anyway," she said, taking the bottle, trying to sound normal, trying not to jump to conclusions. She'd had lots of strange bruises before. But added to what Tracy had already hinted at about her husband, her suspicions might not be completely unfounded.

She gave her instructions on how to warm the bottle, and Emily went back in search of the Cozy Corner Cafeteria. It was empty, and she finished heating the milk quickly. As she left, she noticed the ex-con at the vending machine.

She slowed her steps when she noticed nothing was coming out of the machine, and he was still standing there.

"That machine has been giving everyone trouble tonight," she said, forcing a little laugh.

He straightened his shoulders and a faint tinge of red struck his cheeks. She remembered him saying to the admitting nurse that he didn't have any papers. Maybe he didn't have any money, either.

Emily pointed to the machine with the bottle. "Why don't I try to see if it works?"

He took a step back. "Uh, sure. Yeah, you go ahead," he said, putting his hands in the pockets of his jeans.

She put in enough money for a bottle of water, chips, and a chocolate bar. All the items came tumbling out. "Why don't I grab those for you?" he said, pointing to her bad arm.

"That'd be great," she said.

He held them out for her. "Here you go."

She tilted her head. "You know, I'm actually kind of full. Why don't you have them?"

He opened his mouth, and she could tell he was ready to protest. Instead he gave her a nod, his eyes watering for a second before he blinked. "Thank you," he said, and they walked back to the waiting room.

Emily walked over to the young mother, noticing now how pale her skin was, how deep the circles were beneath her eyes. "Here's the bottle," she said, forcing herself to sound chipper, even though she was now very worried for her, and her own arm was throbbing uncontrollably. She needed to sit and keep her arm motionless.

"Thank you," Tracy whispered, taking the bottle and feeding the baby. The little boy curled up beside his mother on the other seat, his eyes droopy, on the verge of a nap.

Emily sat down on her other side. "No problem. Your kids are so cute," she said softly, now that they both seemed settled and calm.

The woman gave her a faint smile and leaned her head

back against the wall. "Thank you," she whispered.

Emily toyed with a loose thread at the bottom of her shirt and tried to sound nonchalant. "Will anyone be coming here to meet you guys?"

"Uh, no. I, um, don't know where my husband is right now. We had a fight and…I just left."

She nodded slowly, noticing the slight tremble in the young woman's chin. She was going to ask her if she was safe and then let her know about her house, but she heard her name being called. She looked toward the voice and saw a handsome young doctor with a clipboard. "Emily Birmingham?" he repeated.

She nodded and stood slowly, holding her arm in an awkward position in an effort to keep the pain at bay. "That's me," she said, walking toward him. She turned back to Tracy. "I'll talk to you when I'm finished, okay? I can help you," she whispered.

Tracy nodded, her face pale and her eyes shining. Emily quickly turned away from the woman's obvious pain. She walked over to the doctor. He gave her a quick smile and then motioned to a corridor opposite of the one she'd been going down for snacks.

Emily followed him into a small exam room. "Okay, so it says here you injured your elbow. And I can see from your X-rays, you do have a small break. Nothing to be worried about, it's a clean, simple break that will fully heal, but we'll have to put it in a cast," he said.

Emily groaned. "I was hoping I'd escape that," she said.

He gave a small laugh as he started taking supplies down from the shelves. "Sorry about that. It won't be too bad. Six weeks and it'll be off. Here, have a seat on the bed while I do this. What color would you like?" he asked.

Emily sighed. "Pink, I guess." There was no denying who she was.

"So how'd you manage to do this?" he asked as he held her arm and began wrapping white cottony material around it.

"Long story, but I ended up falling off the porch step and landing on it," she said.

"Ouch," he said, working efficiently and quickly. "Do you have anyone driving you home?"

She shook her head and suddenly the urge to cry was overwhelming. "Nope. I drove here on my own, and I can make it back okay."

She was fine. She could do it all on her own. Who needed men, who needed Cooper?

She did.

She really wished he were here, not out of duty, but because he loved her enough to fight for them. She didn't think she'd ever get over Cooper. She had believed she'd found her soul mate, only to discover he'd found his before and didn't want another one. A part of her had held out hope that he'd stop her when she gave him her speech, when she told him to leave. A part of her had naively hoped he would say he loved her, too, that there was room for both Catherine's memory and for Emily. But he hadn't.

Chapter Twenty

Cooper slammed his truck door shut and ran to the emergency room, his heart in his throat, hating himself. He scanned the waiting room, not seeing any sign of Emily, and then ran to the admitting desk, but no one was there. He walked back to the waiting room and went up to a young mother who was staring at him. "Was there a young woman here with brown hair and a hurt arm?"

She nodded. "The doctor called her in a little while ago. They went that way," she said, pointing to one of the hallways off the waiting room.

He mumbled a thank you and ran down the hallway, stopping when he heard Emily's soft laugh coming from one of the rooms. It almost made him smile, and it also reminded him that he was the biggest ass in the world. He followed the sound and stood in the doorway, watching Will Morrow, his old friend from high school, hold Emily's arm and regale her with a funny story about his day.

He cleared his throat and walked in. "I came as soon as I heard," he said.

Emily looked up at him, and heaviness settled in his chest, one that he knew wouldn't leave quickly, couldn't leave until she was okay. For a second, her face crumpled, the vulnerability and exhaustion so clear and painful for him to see, making him wish he hadn't failed her, that she'd called him. He hadn't been there for her, and he'd regret that for the rest of his life.

"Whoa, careful there, Emily, I don't want you moving," Will said, holding onto her upper arm.

"No worries. I'm in good hands," she said with a wan smile, without meeting his eyes.

"She'll be okay," Will said with a nod. Clearly he had no idea what their dynamic was, or that Emily was important to him. Very important. Of course he wouldn't know that, because Cooper hadn't brought her here. She was by herself. Cooper rubbed that spot in his chest that ached as he watched Will finish Emily's cast.

"I'm all done here," Will said, attaching the final piece of pink webbing to Emily's cast. How had things gone this wrong? He could barely even stand to see her like this. This never should have happened. It was his fault. He waffled between rage and concern and wanted nothing more than to spend the night explaining to her what an idiot he'd been and then making it up to her.

Will helped her down from the examination bed, and she winced, and he noticed again how pale she was. "Is Cooper your ride home?" Will said to Emily, not addressing him at all.

"No," she said at the same time he said, "Yes."

He looked back and forth between them. "Okay, how about I let you two figure that out. I've got a full waiting room."

"Thanks, doctor," Emily said, shooting him a beautiful smile. He wanted to tell her he was just Will who was an idiot in high school, but he didn't think she'd appreciate that.

Will patted him on the shoulder. "Good to see you, Coop. How's, uh…Callie?"

Cooper frowned at him. "Fine. Why?"

He averted his gaze. "Just being friendly," he said before leaving.

The room was empty, and Emily tried to bypass him, but he didn't move. "Sweetheart, I need to talk to you."

"Maybe tomorrow. I'm so wiped. I just want to go home," she said in a voice devoid of the emotion that usually filled it.

"I can drive you."

"No thanks. Please move away from the door."

Before he could even move, a large hand clamped down on his shoulder. He turned around to see a giant beast of a man glaring down at him.

"I think Emily asked you to move away," he said in a threatening voice.

What. The. Hell.

"I'm okay," Emily said, shooting the giant man a smile. "He's just a harmless, confused friend."

Cooper shoved his hands in his pockets and forced himself to keep his mouth shut.

The man narrowed his dark eyes on Cooper. "Are you sure? Is this the guy who put you in that cast?"

Cooper stood straighter, heat searing through him at the comment. "Of course not," he snapped.

Emily tugged on the back of his shirt. "No, it wasn't him. He's a *friend.* Time for us to go." She patted her new friend on the arm. "Good luck to you."

The man's features softened when he looked down at Emily. Cooper was speechless and intrigued all at the same time. The man moved aside and continued to glare at Cooper as they left the room.

"Thank you," he heard the man whisper to Emily.

"Bye, lady!" a little boy yelled as they made their way through the waiting room.

"Thank you so much, Emily," the boy's mother said.

"Oh, I need to talk to her," Emily said, and left his side, crouching next to the woman. He couldn't hear what she was saying, but the young lady was nodding and wiping tears from her eyes. Emily opened her purse, her movements awkward and jerky with only the one arm in use. He kept his hands in his pockets because he wanted to help and knew she wouldn't welcome it. She finally pulled out a notepad and pen, and when a bag of Cheetos dropped to the ground, he walked over to pick it up for her. His chest squeezed uncomfortably tight as she remembered the first time he met her, the first time he'd touched her orange, Cheetos-stained hands. He'd fought her appeal for so long, and then he'd fought his own love for her even longer, until he'd shut her down. He took a shallow breath as he waited for Emily to finish, very aware of how this entire waiting room was somehow connected to her. *He* was the outsider.

Emily reached out and squeezed the woman's hand before standing. She smiled up at her as though Emily had just handed her a million dollars. He had no idea what the hell was happening here or how Emily knew an entire waiting room full of people.

"You got yourself a special lady there, boy. Better treat her right," an elderly man, who could barely stand, yelled from the other side of the waiting room, poking his cane in the air.

Cooper gave him an awkward nod.

"Bye, Edna, bye, Sawyer!" Emily said, waving at them with her good arm.

He kept his hand on the small of her back and tried to keep them moving toward the exit. Somehow, Emily had endeared herself to a bunch of strangers. He shouldn't be surprised; she was special. If he managed to convince her to speak to him tonight, he'd tell her about the other crowd she'd managed to win over as well.

When they reached the parking lot, she stopped walking suddenly and looked up at him. "While it was very thoughtful that you, a *friend*, or rather, a *contracted tradesman*, would drive all the way out here to help a *customer*, it is not needed. I'm more than capable of driving myself home, and if I were really desperate I would have asked one of my newfound friends to drive me."

He stared at the pride stamped so clearly on her beautiful features and wanted to call bullshit on all of it but realized he'd lost the right. He'd failed her. He cleared his throat.

"You must be exhausted and in pain and in no condition to drive. Let me take you," he said gently, taking a step closer to her.

She gave him a tight smile. "I don't need your pity drive. I don't know how you found out I was here, but I don't need help. It's not personal. I just don't need help from anyone."

He clenched his teeth. He knew this was going to be hard. He knew she was going to be mad at him, but he hadn't counted on how much it would hurt him to be one of the bad guys. He reached for her hand, but she backed up a step, holding her chin high. Even though it was dark, he could see how tired she was. "I don't pity you. I'm here because I love you, and I screwed up badly, sweetheart."

Her chin wobbled, but then she crossed her arms—or tried to cross her arms but gave up because of the cast. "You can't just come and stalk me and tell me…things."

"I love you, that's why I'm here. I want to make things right. I want to make you understand why I did what I did. But before anything else, you need to know that I walked away because of how much I love you."

"Cooper, I'm tired, I'm hungry, and I'm cold. I don't

know what to think anymore, and I don't even *want* to think anymore. I've had one of the crappiest weeks of my life, and I want to go home."

Her voice was small and defeated, and it ripped right through him, making him want to take back everything he'd said to her that day. He wanted to give her the love she deserved to have, the life she deserved to have. "Let me take you home," he said, reaching her good hand.

She looked up at him and didn't remove her hand from his. "Am I an idiot for letting you?"

"I promise, you won't regret it," he said, taking a step closer to her, desperate to hold her but not wanting her to shut down on him completely.

She closed her eyes. "I'm so tired, Cooper," she whispered.

"I know," he said, wrapping his arms around her and kissing the top of her head. She rested her head against his check but left her arms by her side, and it killed him because a few days ago, she would have called him, a few days ago he would have felt her hands around his waist, a few days ago, she would have smiled up at him. "Come on. Let me take you home. I'll get your car for you tomorrow."

Cooper opened the passenger side of his truck and supported her as she climbed in before he walked around to his side. He started the car and pulled out of the parking lot without saying a word. He glanced at Emily, but she was hunched over as far from him as possible, her head resting on the back of the seat, her face toward her window. "Are you cold?" he asked.

"Sort of."

He turned on the heat and drove in silence, not wanting to talk about everything now because he needed to give her his full attention. He wanted to watch her. He wanted to reach out and hold her hand or put his hand on her thigh, but this wasn't about what he wanted.

His gut churned and his mind raced as he tried to piece together what had happened today. "Are you warmer now?" he asked as they approached the outskirts of Maple Hill.

When she didn't say anything he turned to look at her, only to find her soundly sleeping. When he looked at Emily, he knew in his gut that it was beyond her beauty, beyond the wild attraction to her, he knew it was her heart that made him want to be by her side forever.

He took the turnoff to her place and soon he was pulling into her circular driveway. Once he parked, he looked over, hoping Emily had woken, but he could still hear her deep, even breathing, and her eyelids didn't even flicker.

He got out of the truck quietly and then opened her side. Without thinking twice, he leaned in and scooped her up. She let out a sad whimper when her injured arm came in contact with his chest, and she opened her eyes. He was halfway up the walkway.

"What are you doing? Put me down, Cooper. I can walk. I broke my arm, I didn't break my leg."

"You're exhausted."

"You don't have to be nice to me because you feel guilty. I have friends, you know. I just decided to go to the hospital on my own."

He clenched his teeth and put her down once they reached the door. She thought this was all out of guilt. "I don't feel guilty. Well, actually, I do, but that's not what this is about." He unlocked the door and held it open. She passed through, but not before giving him a glare as scary as the beast in the hospital waiting room…which reminded him, if she was still speaking to him later tonight, he would question her about that. He couldn't question her about anything right now, though, because Morgan and his sister came barrelling down the hallway.

"He broke your arm!" Morgan raged, running over

to Emily, and shocked the hell out of him by throwing her arms around Emily's neck. Emily stumbled back a step but held onto the girl. He had seen a whole other side to Morgan today, and even if the girl didn't realize it, even if Emily didn't realize it, Emily had become an important and trusted person in her life. His sister nudged him with wide eyes, and he knew then that she was just as shocked as he was about Emily's brother.

As soon as Morgan let go of Emily, his sister bulldozed her. Callie's eyes were filled with questions and concern as she held his stare over Emily's shoulder. He glanced away because he felt helpless and without answers, and more than anything he wanted to make this right for Em. "Are you okay, sweetie?" Callie asked, holding Emily's good arm when she finally pulled back.

Emily nodded, and to her credit even managed a smile. "I'm fine, I promise. I just need an Advil and a good night's sleep."

"Okay, done. Morgan, you get the Advil and a glass of water. I'll help Emily upstairs and get her settled," Callie said, taking charge.

He stood there like the odd man out. They were women comforting Emily and supporting her, and he was grateful that she had them. It also made him realize he wasn't what Emily needed right now. He'd had his chance with her, and he'd blown it. It was going to take more than some one-sided conversation in the car that was too little too late.

Chapter Twenty-One

Emily walked through the open doors to the council chamber with Morgan and Callie by her side. She held her head up high and plastered the fake smile she'd rehearsed for so many years in Toronto as she walked to the front.

"There's tons of people here," Morgan whispered.

"It's all good. I'm getting good vibes," Callie said as they kept walking.

"It'll be fine," Emily answered, not really sure it was going to be fine at all. She needed to get through this council meeting and then she could go back home and sleep for days. By herself.

Callie and Morgan sat beside her in the front row. Her stomach was tied so tightly that the snug cast on her arm felt loose by comparison. There were way more people than she'd hoped. Judging by the ever-escalating voices, more people kept pouring in. How big was this small town, anyway? How much of a fight did she have left in her? They were going to get her when she was down.

"There's my family," Callie whispered. "Everyone except

Cooper, but I know he'll be here. He wouldn't miss this. He was the one who got the mayor to agree to having this meeting tonight because of your...emergency situation."

Emily didn't want to burst Callie's bubble about her brother. She had already spotted the family—and the fact that Cooper wasn't with them. That ache in her heart seemed to double and intensify. She hadn't seen him since he'd dropped her off at home last night. She had hoped that he'd be by in the morning, but there'd been no sign of him. Maybe rushing out to the hospital had just been a heroic display, but ultimately he knew they could never be more. Emily forced herself to glance in the direction of the Merrick family and gave a little wave before returning her attention to the front of the chamber, where the mayor began speaking.

After about five minutes of trying not to fidget in her seat, her name and property proposal were announced. "Good luck. You got this," Callie whispered.

"Whoever doesn't agree with you is a loser," Morgan added.

Emily almost laughed, except when she saw the size of the line forming at the second microphone, she forgot how to breathe. This town didn't give up; they didn't want her here. Lifting her head high, she stood. "You got this, Em," Callie whispered.

Emily made her way to the podium, carefully avoiding eye contact with anyone. With her good arm, she awkwardly laid out her notes while inwardly chanting that she could do this. She cleared her throat and adjusted the microphone a little lower and waited for her cue. The noise from the crowd died down as her heart rate increased.

Within ten minutes she'd made her pitch succinctly and confidently, despite the panic that rose as more and more people lined up at the other stand while she spoke—including Bernice, Catherine's mother. Emily clutched the side of the wood podium with one hand as dread pooled in her stomach faster than the night she caught Buttons with her first mouse victim.

She glanced at Callie and Morgan. Callie gave her a thumbs-up, even though Emily could see the panic in her eyes. Morgan was glaring at the people in line.

Bernice spoke first. "I am wholeheartedly in support of Ms. Birmingham's shelter. I think her generosity and kindness are a wonderful addition to this town. I would personally love to volunteer at a charity such as this."

Emily's mouth dropped open, and her throat tightened as she continued to listen to Bernice—and then everyone else echoing Bernice's statement.

"If we are ready to take a vote on the proposal to amend the zoning?" the mayor asked, pausing as the council members agreed. "All those in favor?"

"Wait! I have something to add."

She knew that voice. Emily sucked in a breath as though she'd been punched.

Cooper strode down the aisle, holding something in his hand, holding her gaze. He stood in front of the microphone, still staring at her, ignoring Austin's remark about it being about damn time, and cleared his throat. "I would also like to show the council the additional plans I've made," he said, shooting her a quick glance before unraveling a set of blueprints. She walked forward hesitantly as he spread the rolled-up sheets on the table.

"I'm proposing that the town approves the building of five two-bedroom cottages on the property in the future."

"For what, Cooper?" one of his brothers yelled out.

Cooper cleared his throat and turned to her. Her breath caught in her throat and her mouth went dry at the vulnerability stamped across his handsome features. "I was thinking that in the future, it would be nice for mothers with children to have a small place of their own."

"That's a great idea," she whispered, waiting, praying, for more.

"Because families need more room…and maybe, one day, one of those could be ours."

Her pulse raced, and he took a few steps toward her. The room was silent, and she was almost certain her heartbeat was loud enough that everyone could hear. "Us?" she whispered.

He gave a nod.

"I thought—" She paused as her vision blurred with tears. "I thought there was no us."

He took a step toward her. "That's my fault. There is an us as long as you want there to be. I love you. I was wrong. I'm sorry. I'm so damn sorry I was too afraid to tell you the truth. I love you. That's what I should have told you that day. I was attracted to you the first time I saw you. I fell in love with you the day you threw that ball at my head."

She sniffled and almost laughed. "I was aiming for your chest."

"I know. You didn't deserve my baggage, and I'm sorry you got caught up in it. I thought I was doing the right thing. I told myself I was ready to fall in love again."

"It's okay, you don't have to try to explain."

"He has to, we want to hear!" Brody called out.

"I do, because it keeps sounding like I'm saying I can't fall in love because of Catherine. That's not it at all."

"I have issues and you have issues. Together maybe we have too many issues," she whispered.

He placed his hands around her waist, and her heart skipped a few beats. "I'm working through my issues, namely needing to have faith that I will never lose you. Your issues… like baseball, I can help you with."

She frowned as he pulled a red jersey out of his back pocket. He held it up and turned it around. Her last name was stitched across the back. "We need a new first baseman."

She fought her smile. "I may have to get a better coach."

"You'll never find a better one."

"False. Pretty sure we can!" Austin interjected.

Emily tried not to laugh at his brother's antics. "You did miss that ball I threw."

He laughed, and her toes curled.

His gaze went from her eyes to her mouth, and he took a step closer, his voice dropping. "It might take a few days of one-on-one coaching. With no one else around."

She almost smiled as a shiver stole through her, but she remembered the rest before she went in headfirst again. "I'm not going to do this without getting everything off my chest. I am who I am, and you need to know that. I'm not going to ever pretend to be who I think you need me to be. I've spent my whole life doing that. I will never be Catherine.

"I will never be your small-town, country girl. I like my spreadsheets, I like starting companies, I can't throw a ball, and I hate mice. If I ever have a mouse in my house again, I will buy a hazmat suit. I like designer handbags, and Kate Spade ships internationally for a ten-dollar flat rate that I take advantage of on a regular basis. I like my imported SUV, and I'm never trading it in for a truck."

• • •

Cooper smiled, but he didn't want to offend her, he didn't want her to think her fears were amusing, because she was laying it all out there. He'd made her think she would never be as good as Catherine, that he would never be able to love her as much. He'd rather never touch her again than have her think she wasn't enough.

He walked closer, and she held up her hand, her gorgeous eyes filled with pain and heartache—that he'd caused. "I'm also…" Her voice cracked and tears spilled from her eyes and ripped through his heart. "I'm also a good person. I try to be a good person. I'm loyal. And I'm loving, and I will always try to take care of the people I love—"

"Stop it," he choked. He didn't need her standing there telling him she had good qualities, as though she had to advertise what he'd known all along. The crowd receded, and he stood close enough to Emily that no one could hear them anymore.

Everyone had scars. People were all the same in that they all carried war wounds. No one could get through life without them, especially not if you'd ever loved. He thought he'd be able to escape the pain that came with love if he just got out of the game, but he knew it wasn't possible, and that wasn't the kind of life he wanted to live. He wanted to live fully, completely in the game. He wanted to be all in…with Emily. He had realized he was strong enough to bear whatever the world had coming for him. Whatever their future, he wanted to face it with Emily.

Because maybe, when illness or death came knocking, there needed to be more than skin-deep beauty and lust. To the outside world, to strangers, his wife may have lost her beauty at the end. She may have just been a shell of the woman she once was, but to him she had been beautiful. When he'd looked at her, on her hardest days, on her sickest days, he'd seen the girl he'd fallen in love with. Beneath her tired, dark-circled eyes, he still saw the vibrant, sparkling ones. He still saw the carefree smile, he still heard the unencumbered laugh, when it was too damn painful for her to even fake a laugh anymore. He was a man who knew that all that superficial shit people spent time worrying about meant nothing in the face of death. It was love and kindness; that was all that mattered in the end.

He took that last step to Emily and framed her gorgeous

face with his hands, desperately grasping for that faith he'd abandoned five years ago, because he knew he'd do anything to keep this woman in his life. "You have nothing to prove to me, but I have everything to prove to you. I knew the second you walked into Callie's coffee shop, looking out of your element but incredibly beautiful, that there was something about you.

"I avoided all those feelings for as long as I could, but hell, there was no way I could deny that I was falling hard for you, Emily. You blew me away—your plans, your drive, but most of all, it was your incredible heart. You give and you give, and I want to be the man who stands by your side and gives to you. I want you to know every damn day how much I appreciate the person you are. You are more than good enough. You will always be more than I deserve, and this was never about Catherine in the way you think.

"When she died, I didn't know what hit me. While she was sick I was just going day by day, being the husband she needed me to be, to be strong for her when she had no strength, to be her voice with the doctors when she didn't have a voice anymore. It scared the shit out of me, and when she died it ripped me in two. It destroyed me. I swore, never again.

"So then you come along with your big dreams and big heart, and you had me questioning everything. You had me wanting to take that chance again, and I got scared because I pictured you…gone." He squeezed his eyes shut against the sting of tears and looked at the ground. "I couldn't," he choked out, trying to keep it together to get the rest out and reach her. "I couldn't."

She took his face in her hands. "It's okay. Besides, we have a contract, remember?"

He blinked and cleared his throat, reaching into his back pocket and pulling out his notepad.

"How much more do you have in those jeans of yours?"

"I saved the best for last, but it's not appropriate to share in public."

She leaned her head forward until it was on his shoulder and laughed. He kissed the top of her head. "Well, maybe one day you can show me. Maybe you can add that to the contract."

"Gladly."

"We should also add in something about any rodent situations."

"Naturally," he said, still smiling.

"Do you have anything else to add?"

His smile dipped. "How about that you promise to trust me? With everything. When you're scared, or tired, or lonely. You let me be your rock. You let me walk beside you and hold you up when you need it."

She nodded emphatically. "That goes for you, too."

"Done."

"It's about time!" Austin yelled as everyone erupted into applause and cheers. He leaned down to whisper the rest, because he wasn't done and had to be sure she understood.

"You have to know…for me, this is it. You are it. I love you. I love you like I didn't know I could love, and I swear to God, I want so badly to believe, to have that hope you're filled with. But if I dared to believe in all of it, then I'd wish for a lifetime with you, Emily. I'd wish for babies, and I'd wish for all the crazy that goes with it. I will gladly deal with any rodent issues we ever have, for as long as I live."

He leaned down to finally kiss her, to finally promise what was in his heart.

She pulled back slightly, only to smile up at him. "I love you," she whispered.

Epilogue

Emily stood on the porch of The Maple Hill House for Women and Children and closed her eyes, the warm spring air filling her lungs and her soul with peace. She let the screen door bounce lightly against the frame, letting the excited chatter of women—her friends—slowly recede into the background. She took a sip of her cold peach Perrier and savored this moment. She knew Morgan, Noel, and Callie were busy getting ready for the wedding. The house wasn't officially open yet, but it was already making a difference. Tracy, the sweet young woman she'd met that night in the ER, had moved in along with her kids, and Noel was helping her reclaim her life. Noel had become an invaluable asset and friend and had moved in as a full-time counselor. Morgan was doing well and graduating soon.

The sound of footsteps along the walkway made her turn, her heart in her throat, tension filling her body, not wanting anything to ruin this day for her.

She closed the silk edges of her robe with her fingers as a man approached. "Emily Birmingham?" he asked as he stepped onto the porch.

She nodded. “Yes?”

“Registered mail for you. Please sign here.” Emily took the pen from the man’s outstretched hand and quickly signed the form. She accepted the large envelope and mumbled a “thank you” as he walked away.

She flipped the envelope over, and her stomach twisted as she recognized the name and address of her family’s attorney. What could they want? Was this something she really needed to deal with on her wedding day? Or maybe she did, so she didn’t think about it today. She wanted to walk down the aisle free of her past, free of anger, not with the contents of this letter tucked away in the corner of her mind. If only Cooper were here.

She walked to the steps and sat down, placing her water beside her. Staring out at the river in the distance, she opened the envelope. *Just get it over with*. She reached inside, only to find another envelope. It was in her father’s handwriting.

She squeezed her eyes shut. Not today. This entire year had been about letting go, about finding a way to love her father’s memory despite his betrayal. Why, of all days, would this letter arrive today?

Emily stared at the envelope, at her father’s handwriting, but didn’t make a move to open it; she couldn’t. Her hands trembled, and she didn’t know if she was prepared to open her heart to him again. This year she had been on a path to finding out the truth about herself and her role in her family. She had gone down a road that she never imagined herself on. She had decided to let go of entitlement and bitterness. She didn’t ever want to go back to her old self. She didn’t want the contents of this letter to take her back there. She would never understand how her father did what he did, but she was trying to accept that and move on.

She took a deep breath and looked out onto the ravine

filled with trees, their vibrant shades of green and the dense leaves almost plush enough that she wanted to grab a handful and hold onto a season that had served her so well up until now.

If she could have named a season, she would have named it the season of Cooper. He treated her like she was the most important, most special person in the world. He'd helped her find who she really was, and in turn, she'd helped him live again.

She took a deep breath and pulled out the two papers inside. Somehow, maybe it was easier to receive this letter now that she had Cooper, now that they had their whole lives together ahead. She knew that whatever the contents, Cooper would be there for her.

She forced her gaze to the paper, tears immediately blurring her vision at the sight of her father's handwriting. It was dated the day before his heart attack. The writing was shaky, but it was undeniably his.

My sweet Emily,

I'm writing this to you from my hospital bed, and I pray to God that I make it out of here, but in case I don't, there are things I need to tell you. Feelings that I was never able to voice because I didn't know how.

I know you are probably very angry with me right now. I know you think that I've betrayed you, but you are wrong. You worked beside me day in and day out. You were my little companion, my little angel, and you brightened up every one of my days with your sweet smiles.

I know what life was like at home, and I did my best to change things, but because life is complicated and marriage is hard, I didn't do enough to protect you.

I didn't give you the company because I wanted more for you. I wanted you to leave. I wanted you to go to Maple Hill and find a new way of life and meet new people and hopefully fall in love with a man worthy of you. I didn't want you living here, spending the rest of your life competing with your brother, trying to gain everyone's approval, and wasting the best years of your life on bitterness. You are capable of so much more.

I didn't make the stipulation about the financial inheritance upon marriage to belittle you. I did it because you are far too special to spend the rest of your life alone. You need a soul mate, Emily. You need more than business, more than approval from your family.

I hope this letter finds you well on your way to living the life you so deserve.

One of my biggest regrets was not making up with your grandmother. I wanted you to have her house because you are so much like her. Grandma Julia was a force to be reckoned with. She was smart and stubborn and powerful. Very much like you. I hope her house serves you well and brings you good fortune. To secure your future, enclosed you will find a cheque that you deserve for your loyalty and your hard work. I know that you will use it wisely for whatever business venture you embark upon.

And I hope you understand, now, that I didn't think less of you because you were a girl. How far from the truth. You were more than I could have ever hoped for. I love you dearly.

Go and live,
Daddy

By the time she was done reading, she openly wept with the relief of knowing she hadn't been wrong about her father for her entire life. He *had* valued her. He had just wanted more for her. He knew what she needed, and he was right. But she wept with the intense sense of loss. It was as though she was grieving his death all over again, except with guilt, because the first time, she'd thought he'd betrayed her. Now, it was like agony, knowing she had been angry with him for so long. What a gift to receive this today of all days.

She squeezed her eyes shut and saw her father. Not all the things he hadn't done, or all the ways he hadn't been perfect, but she saw him for the man he was—the man who'd loved his daughter in the best way he could. And that was enough. What she wouldn't give right this moment to have him stand in front of her. She would have shown him the house. She would have explained her plans, the future she was building here. And she would have introduced him to Cooper, and he would have loved him.

She looked at the cheque and let out a long breath. The future of this house would be secure. These women and children and all the other ones that would one day fill the place would have the funding they needed to start a new life.

"You okay, sweetheart?"

Emily gasped and quickly wiped the tears from her eyes as Cooper sat beside her. She was going to yell at him for seeing her before the wedding, but one look at the concern on his handsome face, and she threw herself at him. He caught her better than he caught any baseball and held on tight. "I got this letter," she managed to whisper, handing it to him, but holding onto the cheque.

He frowned, taking it from her and reading. After a minute he looked up, his own blue eyes filled with moisture. He took her hand and kissed her palm. "I'm happy for you. So damn happy for you. I always thought you deserved more."

He leaned forward and kissed her, and soon his hands were tangling in her hair, but then she remembered what day this was and pulled back. "You're not supposed to be here," she whispered against his mouth.

"I know, but I'm not much for superstition, and I needed to see you."

Who could argue with that logic? "Everything okay?"

He nodded. "I just wanted to make sure you knew… before you walk down that aisle, how much I love you. That this, what we have is special and unique, and you are the most important person in the world to me."

She squeezed his hand. "I know. I know this must be hard—"

He cut her off. "It's not. It's not hard for me. Starting a life with you, loving you, that is not hard. I just want you to know that. You were meant to come here, to Maple Hill. We were meant to be together. You pulled me out of my hiding place, and you made me strong again, and I will be strong for you, I will be here to pick you up, to be your shoulder, to be whatever you need me to be. You made me take risks again. I'd do it all, I'd risk it all, for however long we have together. You are worth it."

She threw her arms around his neck again and held onto the man that had given her everything.

He pulled back slightly and reached for something in his back pocket. She stared with puzzlement at the folded-up notepaper. "I thought I owed it to you to put it in writing."

"What are you talking about?" she said as he handed her the paper.

"Open it," he said, his eyes sparkling.

Emily tore her gaze from his to read:

The Husband Contract:

1) Cooper Merrick promises to forever deal with all rodent and pest control issues.

2) Cooper Merrick promises to love Emily Birmingham for the rest of their lives together.

3) Cooper Merrick promises to go in the basement and let Emily continue to pretend it doesn't exist.

4) Cooper Merrick promises to continue baseball coaching until Emily hits a home run.

5) Cooper Merrick promises to always be there for Emily, to be her shoulder, her rock, and the man she can trust for the rest of her life.

The rest was blank. "Cooper," she said softly, torn between kissing him and laughing.

"Is there anything you want to add?" he asked, taking her hand in his.

Emotion clogged her throat. "You're catching me at a very emotional and sentimental moment. I'm racking my brain to add something to this list…but you…there is nothing more that I could ever want from you. You've given me everything," she said, leaning forward and meeting him halfway when he kissed her.

"There is one more thing you need to know, though," he said, pulling back, the worry in his voice making her nervous.

"What?" she whispered.

"I want you to have all your dreams. I think you're amazing, and what you're doing here for these women and kids is amazing, and I want to help in every way I can. I make good money, I can do repairs and whatever is needed to keep this place running, but I'm worried that you might think I have more than I actually do, and that I can offer a lot of financial help to keep this place running."

Her mouth dropped open. "I think I have the answer to that."

His jaw clenched, and he didn't say anything. She handed him the cheque. The color drained from his normally tanned face. "You're kidding me."

She shook her head slowly.

"You're about to change so many lives," he said, his voice gruff and tender.

"We are. You are as much a part of this place as I am. I mean, now we know who to call for pest control, and the contract did stipulate for the rest of your life."

He was grinning when he reached for her again. "The rest of our lives."

About the Author

Victoria James is a romance writer living near Toronto. She is a mother to two young children, one very disorderly feline, and wife to her very own hero.

Victoria attended Queen's University and graduated with a degree in English Literature. She then earned a degree in Interior Design. After the birth of her first child she began pursuing her life-long passion of writing.

Her dream of being a published romance author was realized by Entangled in 2012. Victoria is living her dream—staying home with her children and conjuring up happy endings for her characters.

Victoria would love to hear from her readers! You can visit her at www.victoriajames.ca or Twitter @vicjames101 or send her an email at Victoria@victoriajames.ca.

Also by Victoria James...

THE TROUBLE WITH COWBOYS

CHRISTMAS WITH THE SHERIFF

THE BABY BOMBSHELL

THE DOCTOR'S REDEMPTION

BABY ON THE BAD BOY'S DOORSTEP

THE FIREFIGHTER'S PRETEND FIANCE

THE RANCHER'S SECOND CHANCE

THE BEST MAN'S BABY

A RISK WORTH TAKING

THE DOCTOR'S FAKE FIANCÉE

RESCUED BY THE RANCHER

FALLING FOR THE P.I.

FALLING FOR HER ENEMY

THE REBEL'S RETURN

THE BILLIONAIRE'S CHRISTMAS BABY

THE BILLIONAIRE'S CHRISTMAS PROPOSAL

Discover more Amara titles...

Pushing His Luck

a *Winning the Billionaire* novel by Kira Archer

Today is the biggest day of my professional career. I've got one shot to prove I can play with the big boys, and the Lachlan account is my ticket. I've never been more prepared for anything in my life. So of course my morning goes up in flames. Had I known before walking into my business meeting that the sweaty Thor look-alike I fought with at the grocery store was none other than Christopher Lachlan, the new client my entire career hangs on, I'd have definitely skipped my morning stop. Curse my dumb friggin' luck.

No Heartbreaker Required

a *Biggest Little Love* story by JoAnn Sky

When an avalanche crushes her world, Olympic hopeful Starr loses her job, her boyfriend, and worst of all, her confidence. She's working on getting her life back together and moving forward, and it certainly won't be with Spencer, the far-too-attractive playboy lawyer she's forced to play nice with at their friends' wedding. Unfortunately, Spencer's trip to Reno gets extended unexpectedly, and Starr suddenly finds herself way too close for comfort with the man she's quickly realizing is more than he appears.

Story of Us

a novel by Jody Holford

Declan James has been Brockton Point's most ineligible bachelor, but now that his closest friends have found their happily-ever-afters, he can't help but wonder what that might be like. And then Sophia Strombi shows up on his doorstep. Sophia's life is a mess. Since she's working hard to get her life back on track, she's desperately trying to ignore the fact her boss makes her heart pound in a good way. Besides, she has a huge secret she's keeping from everyone––one that's a life-changer.

Just One of the Groomsmen

a *Getting Hitched in Dixie* novel by Cindi Madsen

Addison Murphy is the girl you grab a beer with—and now that one of her best guy friends is getting married, she'll add "groomsman" to that list, too. When Tucker Crawford returns to his small hometown, he doesn't expect to see the nice pair of bare legs sticking out from under the hood of a broken-down car. Certainly doesn't expect to feel his heart beat faster when he realizes they belong to one of his best friends. Hiding the way he feels from the guys through bachelor parties, cake tastings, and rehearsals is one thing. But he's going to need to do a lot of compromising if he's going to convince her to take a shot at forever with him—on her terms this time.

Printed in Great Britain
by Amazon